A CHANGE OF HEART

THE ISLES OF SCILLY SERIES: BOOK 2

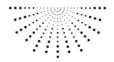

HANNAH ELLIS

Published by Hannah Ellis
www.authorhannahellis.com
Postfach 900309, 81503 München
Germany

Cover design by Mario Ellis

A CHANGE OF HEART

CHAPTER ONE

The tanned and toned gardener was making it difficult for Seren to concentrate. If he'd turn around she could figure out if he was as attractive from the front as he was from the back. Even from a distance she could make out his undulating muscles with every stroke of the shears.

The patio at the Trenearys' place had always been a favourite spot for Seren. Growing up, the house had been a second home to her, and hanging out with her mum's best friend always made her feel close to her mum, who'd died before she was old enough to form any memories of her.

Mirren had been chatting away since Seren had arrived five minutes ago, so there hadn't been a chance to ask about the hunky gardener. With five sons, Mirren didn't usually have a problem finding someone to do jobs around the place, but on the Isles of Scilly there were always people looking for work, and Mirren would help someone out if she could.

As a warm wind whipped strands of hair from her ponytail, Seren turned to look over the garden at the front of the house. It was wilder at that side, where the land dropped at a gentle slope to the lichen-covered rocks which provided a barrier to the swell of the Atlantic. The rocky headland gave way to a long crescent of vanilla-coloured sand, and a strip of turquoise water hugged the shore. Out in the bay, a collection of small boats and buoys swayed gently to the tranquil rhythm of the waves.

"The view's great in all directions today," Seren said, breaking into a grin as her gaze returned to the back of the house. Talking about boys with Mirren wasn't anything new, so she was surprised by the way her eyebrows shot up at the cheeky comment.

"My baby boy's really growing up, isn't he?" Mirren's eyes were fixed on the guy cutting the bush into a neat, round shape as though he'd done it a hundred times before.

As Mirren's words sank in, Seren stopped with her glass of iced tea hovering before her lips. Her heart rate went wild and her breath caught in her throat. Calmly, she set her glass back down.

"I meant the garden," she said weakly. "Obviously I meant the garden."

"I thought you were checking out Kit."

Seren shook her head in jerky movements and attempted a small laugh. "Of course not." There's no way she'd be checking out Kit. He was six years younger than her and practically still a kid. At twenty-two, he was definitely an adult, but in Seren's eyes he was a kid. Obviously she wouldn't be perving on *Kit*. Especially not in front of his mother. Except for the fact that she quite blatantly had been.

How the hell hadn't she realised it was him? She'd known him his whole life – remembered clearly the day he was born and her excitement at having a real-life baby to play with. And now she was checking him out in front of his mum, who was like a surrogate mum to her. What was wrong with her? And when had Kit morphed into some hottie who she barely recognised? She saw him most days for goodness' sake. Maybe she was dehydrated. It could be heatstroke. Reaching for the glass again, she gulped at the sweet liquid.

"He's filled out," Mirren said. "It's all the time he spends helping at the lifesaving club. He's been doing a lot of football training too. And there's the rowing."

"Mirren! I wasn't looking at Kit." Seren did her best to sound indignant. "I meant the garden. It's so colourful now. What are those pink flowers?"

"Sea thrift," she said flatly. "But I'm fairly sure you were commenting on the way Kit's bloomed, not the flowers. You were looking right at him."

"I was looking at the garden. And Kit's *in* the garden. That's all."

"Talking about me?" Kit said, appearing beside them and making Seren's cheeks flush.

Mirren flashed Seren a knowing look. "Just saying how healthy you look. All the swimming and football is obviously good for you."

He dropped into the chair beside Seren. "I'm already missing football. It's a shame we only play in the winter."

"You could always meet up with the other lads and play for fun," Mirren suggested.

"I don't have time now that tourist season is picking up. Which is why football season only runs over the winter." He gave Seren's leg a nudge. "Did you ever congratulate me for my team winning the league?"

She rolled her eyes. "There are two teams in the league, so you had a fifty-fifty chance."

"Would it kill you to say 'well done, Kit'?"

"It probably wouldn't *kill* me, but it would be extremely painful."

His features flashed with mischief as he reached for her drink. After gulping it down he sighed happily.

"You could have got your own!"

"I could have, but that wouldn't have annoyed you, so it would have been less satisfying." He set the glass down again. "I reckon this summer is going to be a scorcher. It's not usually this warm in June, is it?"

"It's not that unusual," Mirren said.

Kit ran his hands through his thick blonde hair, which curled slightly around his ears.

"You've just sprayed me in sweat," Seren said, shuffling her chair away. "You're gross."

In reply he leaned closer to her, shaking his head so the damp strands whipped around him.

"Kit!" Seren shrieked. "Grow up, will you?"

"I'm trying very hard not to." A dimple puckered in his cheek. "You make it look incredibly dull."

She gave him a playful punch on his bicep as she told him to shut up.

"What time are the happy couple arriving?" he asked his mum, putting an end to the teasing.

Mirren checked her watch. "The flight should be in the air by now. They'll land in half an hour or so. I'm pleased things have worked out so well for Noah."

"Me too," Seren agreed.

"I thought you'd be heartbroken at losing your best friend," Kit said, stretching his legs out in front of him.

"I haven't lost my best friend. What are you talking about?"

"His girlfriend is moving here," Kit pointed out. "Which means he's not going to be allowed to hang out with you any more."

She tilted her head, loathe to acknowledge that he probably had a point. "When you grow up, you'll learn that men and women can just be friends."

"And that women don't have a problem with their boyfriends spending loads of time with another woman?" He was goading her and she should completely ignore him … which was all she could do since she didn't have a decent comeback.

"Keira and I get on well," she said with as much confidence as she could muster. "So I'm actually gaining a friend."

"Are you both meeting them at the airport?" Mirren asked.

"*I* am." Seren had offered to give them a lift home. She checked her watch, realising she'd need to leave soon.

"I wasn't planning on it," Kit replied. "Noah said they only have a couple of suitcases."

"At least be around when they arrive," Mirren told him. "Make Keira feel welcome. I'll cook them a meal for this evening so they don't have to worry about that. Shall we all have dinner together, or shall we do a family dinner another night and let Keira get settled this evening?"

"I'm working tonight," Seren reminded her. Her shifts at the bar hampered her social life somewhat, but she enjoyed the buzz of the place.

"I'll come for dinner if you're cooking," Kit said to his mum, then glanced at his watch. "I've got a train trip in between though." It still amazed Seren how successful Kit was with his sightseeing trips around the island. His electric train was a huge hit with tourists on the island, and his online reviews were absolutely glowing.

"Are you going to have time to mow the grass before then?" Mirren asked, looking pointedly over the lawn.

"Yep." He shot out of his chair like a hunky Energiser Bunny.

Seren spent the next twenty minutes trying to concentrate on her conversation with Mirren and avoiding letting her gaze stray to her best friend's baby brother.

CHAPTER TWO

By the time he'd finished pushing the lawnmower back and forth over the grass, Kit's T-shirt was stuck firmly to his back. He cupped his hands under the outside tap and splashed water on his face and neck before shouting through the back door to let his mum know he was leaving.

The gentle whisper of a breeze that swept off the sheltered bay did little to cool him as he wandered away from his childhood home. Walking through the garden gate brought him to the narrow lane and the row of four cottages. Two were owned by his brothers and two by his mum, who rented them out to holidaymakers.

Kit needed to go home and shower before work but stopped at Noah's cottage to say a quick hello. After a quick rap at the door, he tried the handle and let himself in. His brother was nowhere to be seen, but Keira and Seren were on the couch, chatting away.

"Don't hug me," he said, when Keira jumped up from the couch. "I'm on my way to shower but thought I'd call in and say welcome back."

"Thank you." She beamed. "I'm a bit giddy. I can't believe I'm actually moving here."

"You're going to love it."

"I think I am," she agreed, perching on the arm of the couch.

Seren hooked a lock of her striking red hair behind her ear as she turned to look over the back of the couch at him. "Is that sweat? Your T-shirt's soaked."

"Yeah." He took a decisive step back. "Sorry. I shouldn't get too close. The amount of pheromones I'm giving off will probably drive you both crazy."

Keira snorted a laugh while Seren rolled her eyes.

"You're gross," she said. "I can smell you from here."

"Try and control yourself." He waggled his eyebrows suggestively, causing her to roll her eyes even more.

"I need to go," Seren said, standing. "The stench is overwhelming."

Kit looked to Keira. "She's making out like she can't stand to be around me, but in reality she just needs to get away quick before she tries to jump my bones in your living room."

With an exaggerated sigh, Seren walked to the door. "In your dreams."

"It's kind of spooky, our connection," Kit said dryly. "You even know what I dream about."

"Don't be gross." She reached for the door handle and looked back at Keira. "I'll talk to you tomorrow."

Keira thanked her for picking them up from the airport and Seren called goodbye as she walked out. Kit watched the door close behind her.

"Where's Noah?" he asked Keira, forcing himself to focus.

She gave him an odd look. "Upstairs. Making space in his wardrobe so I can unpack. Apparently he didn't think to do that before I arrived."

"Sounds about right."

"Do you want a drink?"

"Water would be great." He followed her to the kitchen and hopped onto a stool at the island. "I promise I'm not staying long," he said, when she set a glass of water in front of him.

"You can stay as long as you want."

He smiled widely. "You're giving me a funny look. I do realise I stink. And you should know that we're the sort of family who just tell each other that they smell and should go home and shower. It's not the sort of thing we get offended by."

"I wasn't thinking that …" Her forehead creased and she turned away from him to fill the kettle.

"What's with the odd looks then?"

"I wasn't …" She trailed off, keeping her attention on the kettle until she'd flicked it on. "Maybe I was," she said when she looked at him again. "I was just thinking …" She shook her head as though trying to get her thoughts in order.

"What is it?"

"I'm probably way off … but is there something going on between you and Seren?"

"No." He gulped at the water. "There's definitely nothing going on between us."

"Sorry." She stood across the island from him, her hip pressing into the edge of the counter. "I kind of thought there was some sexual tension between you."

"Well, yeah, there's that. But I don't think you can count that as something going on between us. Especially as it's very much one-sided."

"So you like her?"

He was surprised she hadn't already heard about his feelings for Seren from Noah. Briefly, he wondered whether letting her in on his secret was a good idea, but only briefly. "Yeah, I like her." Though *like* was entirely the wrong word.

"How long have you liked her for?"

Kit had just opened his mouth to speak when the creak of the stairs made him turn.

"Hi." Noah tipped his chin at Kit before turning his attention to Keira. "There's loads of space for your stuff."

"Thanks," she replied.

Noah looked from her to Kit. "Did I interrupt something?"

"Keira was asking how long I've been in love with Seren for."

"Oh." Noah grimaced. "I didn't tell her."

Keira's eyes widened. "You're *in love* with her?"

"Unfortunately, yeah."

"How long have you been in love with her for?"

Noah tapped on the countertop. "It's gotta be a couple of years now, right?"

"It's more than two years since Dad's funeral, so yeah, just over two years."

"Since your dad's funeral?" Keira asked loudly, over the noise of the kettle.

"Yes." Kit leaned forward, dropping his elbows onto the counter. "Totally inappropriate, I know, but she was wearing this cute little black dress and she looked all sad and beautiful. After the service, she came over to me and squeezed my hand and it was like – bam! I was totally in love with her from that moment."

"Oh my god!" Keira dropped her elbows to the counter, mirroring his stance.

He smiled at the shock in her features. "For a while I thought it was some sort of coping mechanism … you know, giving me something else to think about other than Dad …"

"But you're still in love with her two years later?"

"Yeah."

Keira craned her neck to look up at Noah. "You knew about this and didn't tell me?"

"I can't tell you my brother's secrets."

She instructed him to make tea before turning her attention back to Kit. "Does Seren know?"

"No! The only people who know are Noah and Trystan. And now you. Seren can't find out."

"Why not?"

"It would make things awkward."

"But what if she feels the same?"

"She doesn't," Kit and Noah said at once.

Keira's eyes bounced between them. "You can't know that for sure."

"It's pretty obvious if you spend any time with the two of us. She speaks to me as though I'm about twelve and tends to ruffle my hair as though I'm a puppy."

"Maybe that's her way of flirting."

Noah snorted a laugh. "It's definitely not flirting."

"Well, maybe she's trying to hide her feelings because she's worried about things being awkward."

Kit sighed heavily. "While I wish that were true, it isn't."

"I can't believe you've been in love with her for all this time and not done anything about it," Keira said.

"There's the age gap," he said. "Which I think would be an issue for her."

"There's not much of an age difference is there?" Keira asked.

"I'm twenty-two, she's twenty-eight. It's not huge, but I'm fairly sure she sees me as a kid. Anyway, that's not the only reason I haven't done anything about it." He thought back over the last two years and how the timing had never felt right to say anything. "To start with, I thought it was just a fleeting crush. And she was seeing someone at the time."

Noah groaned. "Ritchie Scaddan. What an idiot."

"When she broke up with him, I considered telling her how I felt," Kit went on. "But I kept chickening out and then she started dating this other guy."

"Wayne Guillimot." Noah set steaming mugs of tea on the counter. "Also an idiot. Seren has really bad taste in men."

"She does," Kit agreed.

"She's single now," Keira pointed out. "You should tell her how you feel. Isn't it killing you to not say anything?"

"Yes," he admitted. "It's killing me. But it's *Seren*. She's pretty much family. If I tell her how I feel, all I'll do is freak her out and make her uncomfortable around me. Which will be unpleasant given how much we see each other. I suspect she'd start avoiding me, and that would be way worse than the current situation."

Keira blew on her tea and seemed to mull the situation over. "I think maybe she likes you too …"

"No," Noah said firmly. "She doesn't see him that way."

Keira shook her head. "I swear when you were joking about her jumping your bones, she looked super uncomfortable."

"Yes," Kit agreed. "Because the thought of it disgusts her."

"No! Because you were too close to the truth."

"That's really not what was happening," Kit said sadly. "I'm almost sure she's never had any thoughts about me that were in any way sexual or romantic."

"Don't you want to find out for definite?"

"No. I already told you it would only make things awkward."

"Maybe Seren needs a little nudge in your direction," Keira said coyly. "Perhaps someone making a few comments about what a catch you are …"

Kit's shoulders shook as he laughed. "If you're thinking of matchmaking, don't."

"Please," she said with a pout. "I took two weeks holiday from work to give me time to settle in. So I've got two weeks with nothing to do. Even when I do start working again, I'll only be sitting in front of the laptop for a few hours a day. I need some purpose in my life. Matchmaking could be just the thing."

"Or maybe you could focus on finding a job on the island," Kit said. "Didn't you say you wanted to find something part-time?"

"I'd like to find something to get me out of the house and meeting people, but I've got no idea what."

"You'll find something," Kit said. "Around here, it's more a case of speaking to the right person than anything else." He sat up straight and took a sip of his tea. "You could always drive the train a couple of days a week, if you want?" He fully expected her to laugh at the idea, but she stared at him with an expression he couldn't read.

"Are you serious?" she asked.

"Yeah, if you want to."

"Do you actually need someone, or are you asking because you feel sorry for me?"

He dragged a hand through his hair. "I wasn't looking for anyone, but the summer is always busy so I generally work seven days a week. Noah covers for me now and then, and one of the bus drivers will help in a pinch, but mostly it's just me working my arse off. It might be good to have a couple of planned days off a week."

"And you can afford to hire someone?"

He caught Noah's eye and they exchanged a small smile. "The train's a gold mine," he said. He wasn't usually one to brag about how successful his business had turned out to be, but he didn't see harm in mentioning it to Keira. "I could employ someone to drive it full-time while I sit around doing nothing, but I enjoy it. Besides, it's my baby – I'm a bit protective of it."

"But you'd let me do it?"

"Yeah. We'd have to do some trial runs, and you'd have to swat up on the area and be okay giving the guided tour as you drive … but I have a script for that so you could theoretically just learn it by heart."

"Are you really serious?" Keira asked, hands on her hips. "You're offering me a job?"

He shrugged. "Yeah. Why not?"

She bit down on her lip, looking a little teary-eyed as she came around and hugged him, not caring about his sweat-soaked T-shirt. "Thank you," she whispered.

"Do you seriously want to drive the train?" Noah asked her, the corners of his mouth twitching in amusement.

"Yes!" She remained with an arm slung around Kit's shoulders. "It sounds brilliant. Working outside, chatting to holidaymakers and telling them about this lovely island while taking in the wonderful views."

"It's not many hours," Kit said. "Mostly I do three trips a day in the summer. Maybe four in August when the island's busiest. A trip around the island only takes an hour."

"That's perfect," Keira said. "It'll fit around my other work."

"It would be a good way for you to meet people," Kit agreed. "You can come along with me sometime and see what you think. Being a tour guide isn't for everyone."

"I really think I'd enjoy it," Keira said enthusiastically.

The conversation was interrupted by Noah's phone vibrating on the counter. "It's Trystan," he said as he scanned the message. "He's not going to make it over for the next few weeks. Work's busy, apparently."

Kit frowned. "More like he's hiding away and licking his wounds over Jenny. I still can't believe they've split up. I thought they'd work things out."

"Have you spoken to him much recently?" Noah asked.

"No," Kit replied. Even though their older brother lived in London, he usually visited a lot and was very good at keeping in touch by phone, but he'd been quiet recently. "He seems to be throwing himself into work. Never has time to chat when I call."

"Same with me," Noah said.

"I was thinking of heading over to London one weekend to see how he's doing. Any chance you can take care of the train if I go next weekend?"

"Sure," Noah agreed. "I just need to check I can rearrange my shifts at the pub, but it shouldn't be a problem."

"Or maybe *you* can drive the train," Kit said to Keira with a cheeky grin.

"Next weekend?" she asked, wide-eyed. "I don't know. I might need a bit longer to learn the ropes ..."

"We can do it together," Noah said. "It'll be a laugh."

"That sounds better," Keira said with relief.

"It'll be nice to get away for a weekend," Kit said, thinking of a weekend in London with his brother. "If Trystan's not too heartbroken over Jenny anyway."

"You should invite Seren," Keira said, eyes sparkling.

"What?"

"You should ask Seren to go to London with you. If you spend the whole weekend together it might give her a chance to see you in a different light."

"Seren knows me as well as anyone does." Kit rolled his shoulders and stretched his neck. "If she needs to see me in a different light to realise she likes me then we have a problem."

"But sometimes you get so used to having someone around that you take them for granted … spending quality time together might make her open her eyes to what she's missing."

"I'm fairly sure I just offered you a job to distract you from matchmaking," Kit said dryly. "That didn't last long."

"You could at least *ask* her to go with you," she said, with a gentle roll of her eyes. "What harm can that do?"

He blew out a breath. "Fine. I'll ask her. If only to prove a point."

"What point?" Keira asked.

"That she's not interested. If there was even the tiniest part of her that was interested in me, she'd be keen for a weekend away with me, wouldn't she?"

"Yeah, I'd say so."

"Good. So, I'll invite her and when she says no you can drop your matching notions. Deal?"

Keira pouted. "I think she'll say yes."

"We'll find out," he said, already feeling the hurt of her turning him down. Which she inevitably would. There was no doubt in his mind.

CHAPTER THREE

Seren smiled at the cute young guy walking up to the bar shortly after she'd opened on Monday morning.

"Hello!" he said cheerfully.

Inwardly she winced as she registered it was Kit but tried to keep her facial expression fixed. "You look different," she said, thinking she might need an eye test. How on earth had she managed to not recognise him again?

"Just got a haircut," he told her.

"Looks good." Casually, she straightened the drip tray under the beer tap. "Bit early for a drink, isn't it?"

"Yep." The way he looked her right in the eyes made her self-conscious. "I'll have a coffee, please."

She turned and put a cup on the coffee machine, then pressed the button for a cappuccino.

"I wanted to ask you something," Kit said, making her glance back at him. "I'm going to visit Trystan next weekend. Any chance you fancy coming with me?"

She put his drink in front of him and tilted her head as though she hadn't heard the question.

"Everyone's worried about how he's dealing with the break-up with Jenny," Kit went on. "He's not talking about it much, so

I thought I'd go and hang out with him for a weekend." He paused and sipped his coffee. "I thought you might fancy a weekend away …"

"You want me to go with you?" she asked slowly. "To London?"

"Yeah."

She puffed out her cheeks and tried to ignore the way her heart was pounding. The new haircut seemed to change the whole shape of Kit's face. It felt as though she was standing opposite a stranger. A hot stranger. One who was asking her to go to London with him.

"I'm not sure I'd be able to get out of work," she finally said.

"That's what I thought, but I wanted to check just in case."

"Thanks. I mean it does sound like fun. I haven't been to London since I was a kid. And I've been worried about Trystan too."

"I'm sure he'd like to see you," Kit said. "And you'd be better at talking to him about Jenny. I'm not great at emotional stuff."

"And *I* am?" Her eyebrows shot up. "Because I'm a woman?"

"Yeah." His tone was deadly serious but his mouth twitched to a smile as he lifted his coffee to his lips again.

"Idiot!" she said lightly.

"So do you want to try and get out of work and come with me? We can do some sightseeing and stuff. It'll be a laugh."

Seren tapped the polished wood of the bar as a battle raged within her. It was slightly disturbing how much she wanted to say yes. It wasn't very often that she went away anywhere, so that was probably part of the attraction. Unfortunately, she knew it was only a tiny part of why she was desperate to say yes.

The idea of spending a whole weekend with Kit was very appealing. Which was also the reason she couldn't possibly agree to go with him. Kit was her best friend's little brother. She was six years older than him. Her sudden feelings for him were inappropriate on so many levels.

"I'm scheduled to work all next weekend," she said, racking her brain for a further excuse, since Kit knew the pub was over-staffed and it would be easy to get someone to cover for her. The fact that her boss was also her uncle made it easy for her to get time off too. "My car needs some work doing on it so I specifi-cally asked Charlie for more shifts. I need the money." She smiled, hoping that sounded more believable to Kit than it did to her. Was it obvious she was making excuses?

"That's fine," Kit said, sliding off his stool. "I presumed you wouldn't be able to. Maybe another time."

"Yeah," she said feebly. "You and Trystan will have more fun without me around anyway. Boys' weekend!"

"True." He turned on the way to the door and gave her a heartbreaking smile. "Definitely more fun without you."

The way his eyes sparkled when he teased her brought a slow smile to her face. How long had he had sparkly eyes for? That must be a new thing too.

"Have a good day!" he called before the door swung closed behind him.

Slouching against the bar, Seren sighed heavily and ignored the voice in her head telling her to chase after him and say she'd changed her mind. There was no real harm in spending a weekend with one of her oldest friends.

Standing up straighter she gave herself a mental shake. Of course she couldn't go to London with Kit. Not given how jumbled her feelings were. If anything, it was just a crush. And the thing about crushes was they didn't last long. She'd ignore it until it passed. All she needed to do was make sure no one found out about it.

If Kit knew he'd be unbearable. He'd no doubt tease her mercilessly … and probably end up with a massively inflated ego. Either that or he'd be completely weirded out by it.

The pub was busy all day, which meant time went fast. But it wasn't enough to fully distract Seren from the thought of wandering along the Thames, laughing in the sunshine with Kit.

"You're miles away today," Charlie said when he caught her staring into space at the end of her shift.

"I'm tired," she said vaguely.

"You work too hard. Why don't you take some time off? Have a holiday or something."

She laughed lightly. Was the universe ganging up on her or what?

"It's the wrong time of year to be taking a holiday. Things are getting busy around here. I need to take advantage of it and earn some money."

"A few days off wouldn't hurt."

She sighed loudly. "I don't need time off. I just need an early night. I'm going home, unless you need me to stick around?"

"No. You get off. I thought you were having dinner with Mirren, though?"

"Crap! I forgot." Seren checked the clock on the wall, then made a dash for the door, calling goodbye to Charlie as she went.

∾

"Perfect timing," Mirren said when Seren wandered into the homely kitchen, inhaling the soothing aroma of home-cooked food as she went.

"That smells amazing." After kicking her trainers off, Seren kissed Mirren's cheek and peered into the dish on the counter. "Please tell me that's chicken and mushroom pie?"

"It is." Mirren nudged her aside and cut into the flaky pastry. "How was your day?"

"Fine." Her mouth watered as she took her plate to the table. "The pub was so busy I barely had time to eat. I wolfed down a few mouthfuls of club sandwich at lunchtime but didn't even manage to finish it." She took a mouthful of creamy chicken with deliciously buttery pastry and rolled her eyes in delight. "This is so good."

"I invited Noah and Keira but they've been over to Bryher to visit Lowen today and aren't back yet. They said to save them dinner but not to wait for them to eat."

"There's no way I could've waited," Seren said through a mouthful of pie.

Mirren told her about the new guests who'd arrived earlier that day for a week-long stay in Kensa Cottage. A family of four who'd been thrilled with the cottage and its phenomenal view.

"It's always lovely to have returning customers," Mirren said. "But I'll never get tired of seeing people's reactions when they arrive for the first time."

"I bet they'll wish they were staying for longer than a week." With her initial hunger satisfied, Seren slowed down, savouring every mouthful of the delicious meal.

"Nobody ever likes to leave. Not when the weather's like this." Mirren glanced out of the kitchen window at the dazzling blue sky over the calm sea.

"The next time I have a day off I'm going to spend it lying on the beach. I sometimes forget to take advantage of living in the perfect holiday spot."

"You should take a proper holiday. Get away somewhere."

"Don't you start. Everyone seems to be on my case about that today. First Kit, then Charlie, now you."

"What was Kit saying?"

Chewing slowly on the last mouthful of her dinner, Seren set her knife and fork neatly on the plate. "He asked me to go to London with him to visit Trystan."

"That's a good idea. When?"

"Next weekend. But I'm working."

"Take the time off. It'd be good for you to get away."

"I need the money. And London's hectic. That's not the sort of holiday I need."

"Trystan would love to see you." Mirren looked at her with

raised eyebrows. "And I won't have to worry about Kit if you're traveling with him. You know what he's like – he'll just about get lost en route."

"I'm sure he'll manage," Seren said, trying to ignore her instinct to say she'd go.

Mirren finished her dinner in silence, then reached over and put a hand on Seren's arm. "Please will you go to London? I'd like to know how Trystan's doing and I'm not going to get anything out of Kit. You go and report back for me. I'll pay for your flights if you're strapped for cash."

"Maybe *you* should go," Seren said, feeling as though she was being sucked into a trap.

"I'm too busy with guests. You go … keep an eye on Kit and see how Trystan's doing. Please!"

"Stop looking at me like that!" Keira laughed as she brushed Mirren's hand away from her arm. "How can I say no when you look at me like that?"

"You can't. That's why I'll keep looking at you like this until you crack."

"Okay. I'll speak to Charlie tomorrow and see if I can get the time off."

"You're the best." Mirren gave Seren's shoulder a tap before taking their plates to the dishwasher.

Seren was left wondering what she was getting herself into, and trying her best to pay no attention to the tingle of anticipation deep in her stomach.

26

CHAPTER FOUR

When Kit's train had first gone into operation, alterations had been made to the promenade at Porthcressa Beach. At the far end of the concrete walkway there was now a turning space and dedicated parking spot. A noticeboard gave the timetable, price list and other information. Kit left the train there during the day and drove it back to the garage near his studio flat at the end of the day.

On Tuesday, Keira came with him on his first train trip of the day. Initially she'd seemed excited about the ride-along and had been at ease with helping him welcome passengers, but once they'd set off, she'd gone suspiciously quiet. Of course there wasn't much time to chat while he was giving the tour, but even afterwards she was withdrawn and smiled benignly while he made balloon animals for the lingering kids. It was his little party trick that the children always went mad for.

"They're biodegradable," he told Keira after the crowd had dispersed.

She looked at him in confusion. "What?"

"The balloons." He stretched one out before shoving it into his pocket. "If you're worried about me destroying the environment and polluting the sea … they're biodegradable ones from a sustainable source."

"That's good. But I wasn't judging you for your balloons."

"You look very serious. Didn't you enjoy the train trip?"

"It was great," she said. "I loved it."

He wasn't convinced she was telling the truth but decided not to press her on the matter out in public. He'd promised to buy her lunch so they set off at a slow walk along the promenade. The long stretch of sand beside them was dotted with holidaymakers enjoying the warm weather. Several small children played nearby, building sandcastles and splashing in the shallow water – their laughter mingled with the gentle rush of the waves and the piercing cries of gulls overhead.

"Do you want a tour of the town?" he asked, realising it was a little early for lunch. "Or has Noah already showed you around?"

"I'll take your tour," she said. "You'll definitely be a better guide than Noah."

He chatted away as they walked, pointing out places and answering her questions about life on St Mary's. They'd just passed the tourist information when a voice called out to him. It took him a moment to remember the name of the woman with loose blonde curls. Holly had been in the same year as him at school but they'd never really been friends. She had a rather bland personality as far as he remembered.

"Hi, Holly." He took a couple of steps towards her, surprised she was seeking him out.

"I've been meaning to speak to you," she said, with a bright smile. "I saw you through the window and thought I'd grab the opportunity but if you don't have time …" Her gaze shifted to Keira.

"This is my brother's girlfriend," he said, then introduced them both. "Keira just moved to St Mary's at the weekend."

"That's great." Holly lifted her shoulders as she smiled. "I hope you settle in quickly. If you have any questions about the island, feel free to come in and ask." She tipped her chin towards the building behind her.

"You work in the tourist office?" Kit asked. "Since when?"

"About a month."

"Weren't you working at the hotel?"

"Yes." A blush coloured her cheeks. "I needed a change. Anyway, my new job is the reason I wanted to speak to you. Every day we have people asking if they can buy tickets for the train from us …"

"And you wanted to know if you could sell them for me and take a cut of the ticket price?"

Her neck turned as red as her cheeks. "I wondered if we could come to some sort of arrangement. I feel as though I'm constantly answering questions about the train."

"You have flyers with the information, just give people that."

"Yes, we do. Sorry, I only wanted to check that you didn't *want* us to sell tickets. It might make things easier for you."

"Thank you," he said softly. "It's not something I'm interested in."

"You already spoke to Audrey and Wyatt about this, didn't you?"

He smiled lightly. The owners of the tourist office had been on at him about it ever since the train went into operation. "Several times."

"Sorry." She put a hand to her chest. "I shouldn't have accosted you in the street."

"Don't worry about it."

"I should get back." She aimed a thumb at the door, then smiled at Keira. "Honestly, just come in if you need anything."

They waited until Holly had disappeared inside before ambling along again.

"I don't think I ever manage to walk through town without someone stopping to ask me something about the train," Kit said.

"Do they all flutter their eyelashes at you like Holly did?"

He raised his eyebrows. "I don't think she was."

"She definitely was. I'm surprised she came out on the street to ask you about the train tickets. I'd have thought she'd have suggested chatting about it over a meal."

He bumped his shoulder against hers. "Get lost!"

"I'm telling you, she totally fancies you."

"She has a boyfriend, I think."

"I feel sorry for him, if she's looking at other guys the way she looks at you."

"You're very good at seeing stuff that isn't there. Anyone ever told you that before?"

"No," she said, the corners of her lips pulling upwards. "Aren't you tempted to check her relationship status? Maybe she's single and you could ask her out."

"You're really getting into this matchmaking thing, aren't you?"

"I can't seem to help myself."

"Are you hungry?" he asked when they looped back to the promenade by the beach.

She nodded. "How about the Pottery Cafe? I love looking at Lowen's creations."

The cafe which sold his older brother's ceramics wasn't overly busy and they found a table easily. Once they had food in front of them, Kit broached the subject of Keira driving the train again. The more he thought about it, the more he liked the idea of having someone to help him on a regular basis. If Keira wasn't up for it, he might look into finding someone else.

"How are you feeling about driving the train?" he asked bluntly. "If you've decided it's not your thing you can say so. Driving a tourist train isn't for everyone." He took a bite of his sandwich, then wiped a blob of mayo from the corner of his mouth. "I promise I won't be offended."

"It wasn't quite how I expected," she admitted with a bashful smile.

"That's fine. You don't need to feel bad. It's not the sort of thing you should do if you don't enjoy it. The customers would pick up on it."

"It's not that I don't *want* to." Keira set her sandwich down and looked at him intently. "I don't think I *can* do it."

He gave a quick shake of the head. "The lanes seem narrower than they are. There are plenty of places to pass any cars you meet. You can take a turn driving while I'm with you and you'll see it's actually pretty easy."

"It's not that. It's *you.*"

"What do you mean?"

"I mean I can't do what you do. People love the train because of you. You're so knowledgeable … and you're funny too. You had everyone hanging off your every word. Kids and adults alike. How do you engage everyone and make it seem effortless?"

"It's just practice. Once you've memorised all the information it won't feel so daunting."

She shook her head. "I love that you think anyone can do what you do, but I'm telling you they can't. I'm fairly sure I can't."

"You can," he insisted. "You're good with people. You were great with the kids today."

"I can't make balloon animals," she said with a crooked smile.

"Neither can Noah. You don't need to. And you don't need to do the trips exactly like I do. You can add your personality. I honestly wouldn't have suggested you doing it if I thought you wouldn't be a hit with the customers."

She took a tentative bite of her sandwich, then put a hand in front of her mouth, talking as she chewed. "I also feel a bit of a fraud playing tour guide when I'm not from the island. That's what makes your tour special."

"So long as you love the place it doesn't matter."

"What about when people ask me questions and I don't know the answer?"

He smiled widely. "Tell 'em to Google it."

"I'm serious."

"So am I. It's what I do … then I get them to share the answer. Everyone learns something. If you're genuine it doesn't matter if you don't know absolutely everything." He chuckled. "You'll never know everything anyway. People come up with weird questions sometimes."

"Maybe if I do a few more ride-alongs I'll feel more comfortable, but I won't be ready to go it alone by the weekend, if ever. I'm thinking a career in matchmaking might be a better idea after all."

He grinned. "No way. I'm not interested in Holly, and Seren turned me down for the trip to London. You agreed you'd leave the subject alone when she did. You have to back off now."

"It just seems wrong." Keira pushed her bottom lip out. "You'd make a lovely couple."

Kit finished his sandwich and wiped his hands on the paper napkin. "I don't mean to sound harsh, but …" He paused and cleared his throat. "Could you please pretend you don't know how I feel about Seren? I seem to spend my life trying not to think about her. Noah and Trystan mostly do me the courtesy of not mentioning it. Generally, I'd rather not talk about it. If you don't mind."

"Shit. I'm sorry. I must sound insensitive. I didn't mean to make light of the situation."

He smiled gently. "It's fine. I'd just rather not talk about it."

"Okay. But if you ever do want to talk about it, you can."

"Thanks." He checked his watch. "Are you coming on my two o'clock ride?"

"Yes. If that's okay."

"Of course. I'll pay for lunch and we should get going." While he paid, Keira wandered over to the display of ceramics. It looked impressive arranged on the rustic wooden shelving.

"Lowen's pretty talented, isn't he?" Kit asked when he joined her.

"I can't believe he can make all this. I watched him at work yesterday and he makes it look so easy."

"Did he let you have a go on the pottery wheel?"

"Yes. Which proved to me that it's not easy. I managed a slightly wonky bowl."

"It's fun, though."

"So much fun," she agreed as they made their way to the door.

The sun had emerged when they stepped outside, and Kit pulled his sunglasses down from his head. "How do you feel about having a go at driving the train on this trip?"

"I'd love to," Keira replied, then asked him a bunch of questions as they wandered along the concrete promenade.

They were nearing the train when Kit's phone rang. He was about to send it to voicemail but paused when he saw who was calling. His heart rate increased as he answered.

"Hi, Seren."

"Hi." There was a pause and he wondered if they'd lost the connection. Meanwhile, Keira was pretending not to be interested in the phone call. "I was just thinking," Seren went on hesitantly. "About London. If it's still okay, I think I'll come after all."

He stopped dead, putting a hand on Keira's arm to draw her attention. "You want to come to London with me?" he asked down the phone, while conveying his absolute panic to Keira with a wide-eyed look.

"Yeah. I was thinking about it, and maybe it would be good for Trystan to have both of us there ..." A short silence followed. "Is that all right with you?"

He swallowed hard. "I guess so. I was going to book the flight this evening."

"Great. Then book me on too. Message me the details later and how much I owe you."

"Um ... yeah ... sure."

"I need to get back to work. I'll talk to you later."

Keira squeezed his arm as he slipped his phone into his pocket. "Has she changed her mind?" she asked excitedly. "She wants to go away with you for the weekend?"

"Yes." He felt slightly shell-shocked.

"That's so amazing!"

"Calm down." Kit wished his heart would do the same. "Don't start making out like it's some romantic getaway. It's a weekend with my brother. The only reason Seren agreed to come is because she's worried about Trystan."

Keira schooled her features into a serious expression. "You're right. It's best if we don't get carried away." She bit down on her lip. "It's kind of exciting though, isn't it?"

"Exciting probably isn't the right word," Kit said on a sigh. "I'm not sure my heart can take an entire weekend with Seren. It might just be torture."

CHAPTER FIVE

After leaving the Mermaid Inn on Thursday, Seren walked along Hugh Street and through the centre of the town. Reaching Porthcressa Beach she caught sight of Kit, busy wiping down the seats of the train while several gulls gathered around his feet, scavenging for crumbs. She always saw him when she worked a day shift, both on her way into work when he'd be driving the train down to the promenade for his first trip of the day, and at the end of her shift when she was walking home. On the days when she worked in the evening, he'd generally come in for a quick drink at the end of the day.

Staring at him, she pondered how long it'd been that she'd seen him every day. It can't have always been that way, but in the past year or two he'd featured heavily in her day-to-day life. The thought popped into her head that he engineered their meetings, but she pushed it hastily away again. Their overlapping work schedules and the fact that they lived on a tiny island were the reason they bumped into each other with such regularity. That was all it was. Surely. Unless …

Her thoughts were disrupted by Kit's gaze meeting hers. His smile made her heart pound roughly against her rib cage.

He raised a hand and shouted a greeting.

"Hi," she said, walking over to him.

"I was going to call you later," he said. "Do you want to meet at the airport tomorrow, or shall we go over there together?"

"I can drive to the airport. I'll pick you up."

"Thanks." He flicked the cloth in his hand, shaking out crumbs and sending the black-headed gulls into a frenzy. "I'm looking forward to it."

"Me too." Eye-contact felt suddenly intense and she studied the screeching gulls before shifting her gaze to the boats bobbing in the bay. "I better go. I'm having dinner with Dad and Naomi."

"Tell them I said hi. I'll see you tomorrow."

Feeling self-conscious with every movement, she walked away, resisting the urge to look back when she reached the corner.

Her dad's house was only a five-minute walk, and she spent the time lost in thought. Her brain churned over random encounters with Kit, trying to figure out if her feelings were one-sided or if he felt something for her too. The other day when he'd joked about her jumping his bones, had it really been a joke or had he just been covering his true feelings with banter?

What if she and Kit had feelings for each other? Could they ever act on them? He was practically a kid, and she'd known him his entire life. It'd be weird and creepy. No doubt she'd be branded a cradle-snatcher. She tried to imagine how Noah would react – and Mirren.

Abruptly, she brought her head up to find she was standing outside her dad's door. Why was she even considering people's reactions? There was no way anything could ever happen between her and Kit.

After ringing the doorbell, she pushed the handle and let herself in. She followed her nose to the kitchen, where her dad was stirring a pot on the stove while her stepmum, Naomi, leaned against the counter beside him. Technically, Naomi wasn't really her stepmother, since she'd never married Dad.

They'd been together for ten years though and living together for eight. Stepmum felt like a better description than 'Dad's girlfriend'.

"How was work?" Naomi asked, stepping forward to kiss Seren's cheek.

"Fine." When she moved to greet her dad with a kiss his grey beard tickled her cheek. "Busy over lunchtime, but the usual lull in the afternoon."

Her dad turned the heat down on the hob. "I heard you're having a weekend off and jetting off to London."

"You heard right." She took a seat at the table which was already set and poured herself a glass of water from the carafe, not surprised that they already knew about her plans.

"I had a pint with Charlie last night. He mentioned it."

"It was a bit of a last-minute thing. Kit's going over to visit Trystan and asked if I wanted to tag along."

Naomi joined her at the table. "It'll be good to do something different for a weekend. Have you got much planned for when you're there?"

"Nothing so far. I guess we'll see what Trystan's in the mood for. It seems as though things are definitely over with Jenny."

"They'd been together a long time," her dad remarked. "It'll be hard for him, I'm sure."

Propping her chin on her hand, Naomi looked intently at Seren. "Will you get a chance to go to the Warner Brothers Studios?"

"I don't think so." Seren felt a flush of affection for Naomi and the fact she knew that the set of the Harry Potter films would be top on Seren's list of places to visit in London. She'd been wanting to go since it first opened. "Apart from anything else, it's not really within my budget." She'd checked during a quiet period at work that afternoon.

"We can pay for you," Naomi offered. "Call it an early birthday present if you want. It seems a shame to be so close and not make the effort to go."

"Thank you," Seren said. "But we're only there for two days and I don't think Kit and Trystan would be overly keen."

Her dad rolled his eyes. "You have every one of those Treneary boys wrapped around your little finger. They'll do whatever you say. Don't pretend you don't know it!"

"I won't deny that," Seren said lightly. "But Mirren's worried about how Trystan's doing after the break-up, so turning up with a load of sightseeing plans might be a little insensitive. I'll wait and see what the mood is when we get there."

"I hope you're hungry," her dad said, bringing his signature beef stroganoff to the table. "I made too much as usual."

"I'm starving," Seren announced as he dished her up a healthy portion.

They ate in silence for a few minutes before her dad spoke again.

"I don't suppose you going away this weekend has anything to do with your wayward cousin's imminent arrival?"

Seren laughed and almost choked on her dinner. "Dad! He's your nephew ... maybe you should be more complimentary about him."

"He might be my nephew, but the lad's an idiot. He gets that from his mother's side, I guess."

"Cadan's all right," Naomi said. "You're too hard on him."

"Because there's always trouble when he's around, and he usually manages to get Seren involved in it."

While Seren had to agree that her cousin could be a bit of an idiot, she also had a soft spot for him. He wasn't a bad guy but had grown up with separated parents, neither of whom were good at setting boundaries. As a kid, he'd spent term time living with his mum in Bournemouth and school holidays with Charlie on St Mary's. Seren had always enjoyed his visits – his rebellious streak had livened up many a dull school holiday.

"Credit *me* with getting myself into trouble," she said to her dad. "I didn't need leading astray."

"Funny how I never got calls from the police station on the

nights you were out with Noah ... only ever when Cadan was around."

Seren exchanged an amused look with Naomi. "You make me sound like a teenage delinquent! You never even got a call from the police station – the friendly officer just escorted me home to make sure I got back safely."

A guffaw erupted from her dad. "So nothing to do with you shooting fireworks into trees?"

"We weren't firing them into trees." She smiled at the memory. "That was Cadan's bad aim. We were just having a bit of fun."

"What about the time Cadan got you involved in drugs?"

She shook her head, amused. "I hardly think smoking a bit of pot at sixteen is the crime of the century."

"I actually think you had it easy with Seren," Naomi put in. "From the stories I've heard, her teenage years were pretty tame."

"It wasn't you who was staying up worrying every weekend."

"You survived, Dad! And to answer your original question – no, I'm not avoiding Cadan. He reckons he's staying for the whole summer, so I'll have plenty of time to get stoned with him and burn down trees." She smiled mischievously, but only Naomi seemed to find the joke funny.

"A whole summer of him?" her dad grumbled. "That's all we need."

"He's not a teenager any more," Seren said, feeling a rush of defensiveness for Cadan. "He's twenty-eight and he outgrew his rebellious streak a long time ago."

"Maybe so," her dad conceded. "I reckon he retained his idiotic streak, though."

Even with the stern set of his features, it was hard to take her dad seriously. Seren and Naomi laughed in unison before changing the subject to Naomi's job at the flower farm.

The evening passed amiably. When Seren arrived back at her

one-bedroom flat above a quaint little craft shop at the edge of Hugh Town, she vaguely contemplated packing for the weekend before deciding to leave the job until the morning. Instead, she flopped in front of the TV, flicking through the Netflix menu without finding anything that caught her interest.

Taking herself off to bed for an early night turned out to be an almighty waste of time. Her brain wouldn't switch off, and the thoughts of Kit that swirled in her mind were entirely inappropriate.

Somehow, she was going to need to put her feelings aside for the weekend in London.

She just wasn't sure how.

CHAPTER SIX

The noise of the plane's engines made it difficult for Seren and Kit to chat. At least, it made it difficult to chat without having their heads practically pressed together, which wasn't helping Seren in her mission to only see Kit as a friend. The smell of his aftershave and the feel of his shoulder pressed against hers was playing havoc with her hormones. Discreetly, she leaned away from him, peering down at the rugged Cornish coastline and taking slow breaths to settle her heart into a steadier rhythm.

Kit nudged her leg to get her attention again and she turned back to him.

"You're not scared of flying, are you?" His breath tickled her ear.

"No. Why?"

"You're quiet."

"It's too loud to talk."

He smiled and moved his face back to her ear. "Is there anything you want to do in London?"

"I haven't really thought about it. I imagined we'd just see what Trystan felt like doing."

"I thought you'd be desperate to go to the Warner Brothers Studios …"

She pulled back, scanning his features. His blue eyes sparkled and his smile was eager. To be fair, anyone who knew her well knew of her obsession with Harry Potter, so she shouldn't read too much into the fact that Kit remembered.

"I booked tickets for tomorrow," he told her. "We'll be able to walk along Diagon Alley, and I can take your photo on Platform Nine and Three Quarters."

A lump formed in her throat and she swallowed hard. "Is Trystan okay with that?"

"Of course." The light went out of his eyes. "I thought you'd be excited."

"I am." She curled her lips to a smile. "It'll be fun."

"Do you remember lending me the books?" he asked in her ear, the scent of him invading her senses once again.

"What?" she asked vaguely.

"You lent me all the Harry Potter books."

She nodded. "It rings a bell."

"You got annoyed with me and took them all back before I'd finished them."

She trawled her memories until it came back to her. "Because you dog-eared the pages!"

"I hadn't read the last three books when you demanded them back. I was so annoyed."

"It was a fitting punishment for your crime. Did you just watch the films in the end?"

"Yes. I didn't have much choice. I asked Mum to get me the books for Christmas, but I guess she forgot."

"So you've never read the last three books?"

He shook his head sadly. "Do you feel bad?"

"A little bit," she admitted.

"Can you lend them to me when we get home?"

"Depends." She raised an eyebrow. "How do you feel about bookmarks these days?"

"I still think you overreacted," he said, chuckling. "What's the big deal about turning down the corners of books?"

"That's something you'll have to figure out before you borrow any of my books again."

"I could probably find a bookmark if it'd make you happy."

The warmth of his arm pressing against hers seeped through her clothes to make her skin tingle. Her sudden desire to kiss the dimple in his cheek made her head spin. It wasn't just the physical attraction that worried her, though. The fact that he was so easy to be around complicated things even more. If it was just a physical thing, it would be much easier to ignore. Giving herself a quick mental shake, she told herself she was being ridiculous. They were having a conversation about Harry Potter for goodness' sake.

"I think I was babysitting you that weekend," she blurted out.

A line appeared between Kit's eyebrows. "What?"

"The time I took the books back. Your parents had gone away for the weekend and they didn't trust Noah and Trystan to look after you, so they asked me to stay at the house with you."

"I'm fairly sure I was old enough to look after myself. You were just always at the house."

She shook her head adamantly. "Your parents paid me." They'd paid her to look after him because they trusted her completely with their son. Which was why Mirren had asked her to go to London. To keep an eye on Kit and make sure Trystan was okay.

As Kit leaned back in his seat, the atmosphere between them turned slightly frosty. Seren told herself that was fine. A slightly uncomfortable atmosphere was preferable to them being *too* comfortable with each other.

Although Seren was probably worrying about nothing when it came to blurring the lines of their friendship. In the same way that she'd previously always seen him as a kid, he probably viewed her as old and boring.

By the time they picked up the rental car at Exeter Airport, Kit had given up on talking to Seren about anything more than traffic and the weather. It seemed as though everything else he said annoyed her, so there didn't seem to be any point in bothering. Inviting her had been a stupid idea, and he cursed himself repeatedly for letting Keira get in his head. The last thing he needed was a spark of hope that something might happen between him and Seren. What he should be doing is putting the whole thing behind him and moving on with his life.

Arriving at Trystan's place was a relief. His brother's presence eased the tension and made conversation easier.

"I thought we could go out for dinner," Trystan said, as they all stood around in the modern open-plan kitchen. "There's a decent Asian place just down the road."

"Sounds good to me," Kit said.

"Me too." Seren took the beer Trystan handed her and drank a long swig.

After pouring himself a glass of water from a filtration jug, Trystan wandered over to the living room where a sofa bed was made up. "I presume you two are fine sharing this thing?" he asked. "I'm a bit short on space."

Kit tried to catch his brother's eye. When he'd previously been over to visit with Noah there'd been an air mattress. Surely it would be better for him to sleep on that? Except he had an inkling that Trystan purposely hadn't suggested that arrangement.

"It'll be fine," Seren said, then looked at Kit. "As long as you don't snore."

"I'll try not to." The thought of sharing a bed with her wasn't quite as thrilling as it should have been. Given that his feelings were entirely one-sided, it would likely feel more like torture than anything. "Did the tickets arrive for tomorrow?" he asked Trystan in a bid to move the conversation on.

"Yes, they're somewhere here." Trystan flipped through a pile of post on the kitchen island. "Though I'm not sure why you didn't just get electronic tickets."

"Because it's not the same as having paper tickets. And they were offering limited edition keepsake tickets – they looked awesome."

"I have a bit of a problem tomorrow," Trystan said, a slight twitch to his left eyebrow. "I have to work, so you two will have to go alone."

"I thought you were taking the weekend off?" Kit said.

"That was the plan. Unfortunately, my demanding clients are insisting on meeting tomorrow."

"Is that just a ploy to get out of going to Warner Brothers Studios?" Seren asked, casting Kit a look of pure boredom.

His plan to surprise her with the day trip hadn't gone the way he'd expected. He'd genuinely thought she'd be over the moon, but clearly he should have mentioned it to her before he'd paid for the tickets. It didn't seem as though she was bothered about going at all.

"I'd actually like to go," Trystan said, finding the envelope with the Warner Brothers crest and sliding it across the counter to Kit. "It would definitely be more fun than sucking up to clients for the day. Plus, it's a cool place."

Seren looked unimpressed. "Isn't it the sort of place where you should have a child with you?"

"Not really," Trystan said. "Harry Potter fans are all ages. I enjoyed it last time I went, and I was never even that into Harry Potter."

"Did you have a child with you?" Seren asked.

"Actually, we did. We took Jenny's niece for a birthday treat." He leaned on the counter and his eyes glazed over as they descended into an uncomfortable silence.

"How are things with Jenny?" Seren asked. "Are you still on speaking terms? It must be hard after you'd been together for so long …"

He sank onto a stool, rubbing the creases at his forehead. "It's all pretty amicable. We still speak sometimes. I've been trying to give her space."

"I thought things were definitely over," Kit said.

"She says so." Trystan took a slug of water. "But she's said that before."

"So, you're still thinking you might sort things out?" Seren asked, looking confused.

"Maybe," he said with a shrug. "Who knows?"

"Mum seemed to think it was over." Kit idly tapped the envelope against his palm. "She spoke to Jenny."

"I know." He shook his head. "It *is* over. But occasionally I wonder if I should have just given her what she wanted."

Seren raised an eyebrow. "Like marriage and kids?"

"Yeah."

"Do you really not want kids?" Kit asked. The whole situation with Trystan and Jenny confused him. They'd seemed happy together, and Kit had assumed getting married and having kids would be the next step for them.

"I'm not completely against the idea of kids. But I'm too busy with work, and Jenny's committed to her career, so I'm not sure how we fit kids into that picture. There's no point having kids if you don't have time for them."

"You could have married her and waited a couple of year to have kids," Kit said. "Surely if you love her and want to be with her long term, you could have figured things out."

Moving over to Trystan, Seren put an arm around his shoulders while surreptitiously glaring at Kit.

"I think you were right not to marry her if you weren't comfortable with the idea," she told Trystan. "It's your life and you shouldn't sacrifice your happiness for someone else. You'd end up miserable in the long run."

"Yeah, but if you love her—"

"Kit!" she snapped, cutting him off. "Shut up!"

Annoyed, he cast his eyes down and opened the envelope in

his hands. The sight of the tickets cheered him immediately. "Look!" he said, holding one up. "That's way better than an e-ticket. It's got gold embossing. That's a keepsake if ever there was one."

Seren rested her head on Trystan's shoulder. "When I said it's the sort of place you should take a child, I'm not sure what I was worrying about. I'll have Kit with me!"

"Whatever," he said, running his finger over the ticket. "I think it's cool."

"Because you're a child," she teased.

"Leave him alone." Trystan reached over and took a ticket. "I think they're cool too. Just because you're too cynical to appreciate the small joys in life doesn't mean everyone around you should be jaded too."

She took the ticket from Trystan, turning it over to inspect it. "It'd make a decent bookmark, I suppose."

"Does that mean you're going to lend me those books?" Kit asked.

"I'm still undecided." She managed a small smile, then finished her beer and declared she was hungry. They set off to the restaurant on foot and enjoyed good food and relaxed conversation. Mostly, Kit kept out of it and let Trystan and Seren chatter away.

He didn't manage to get any time alone with Trystan until after they'd got home from dinner and Seren had gone to the bathroom to get ready for bed.

"What the heck are you playing at?" he hissed at Trystan.

"How do you mean?"

"The sleeping situation for a start." Kit threw his hands up. "What happened to the air mattress? I can sleep on that and let Seren have the couch to herself."

"I'd forgotten about that thing." He gave an exaggerated shrug. "I'm not sure what happened to it. Maybe Jenny took it."

"Come on … do you think I'm stupid? Noah spoke to you, didn't he?"

Trystan winced. "It was mostly Keira."

"I should've known. That woman's a pest."

"I like her," Trystan said, leaning against the counter.

"Me too. But I don't like her interfering in my relationship with Seren … my *friendship* with Seren," he clarified. "I take it you don't really have to work tomorrow? You just said that to give me and Seren time alone?"

"I'll be working tomorrow. I could probably have put the client off until Monday, but three's a crowd."

"We're supposed to be here to cheer you up."

"I don't need cheering up. I'm fine."

"Are you?"

He pursed his lips thoughtfully. "I will be."

Kit glanced at the bathroom door, then at the pull-out couch. "I think we should abandon your sketchy sleeping arrangements. Tell Seren you remembered you have a mattress for me."

He shook his head. "I say we stick to the plan."

"It's creepy. And it makes no sense … how is sharing a bed going to make her suddenly attracted to me?"

"There's a lot to be said for physical proximity. Her leg brushes against yours in the night … she gets cold and cuddles up, then wakes to find herself wrapped around you and with a sudden desire to do naughty things to you."

"It's a stupid idea. And it's unethical. I'm not sure how you're okay with this given that it's Seren."

"I'm fine with it. Because I never said that sharing the couch was the only option. I just asked if it'd be okay … then I watched her reaction. If she'd have looked even a little hesitant I'd have got the extra mattress out, but there wasn't a flicker of discomfort on her face. She's absolutely fine with sharing a bed with you."

"Yeah, because it doesn't occur to her that sharing a bed with me could be anything other than completely innocent. She sees me as a child. Possibly even as a little brother."

"I don't think so."

"Didn't you hear her teasing me earlier … about the tickets and the Harry Potter stuff?"

"Yeah." Trystan glanced towards the bathroom. "I don't buy that for a second."

"How do you mean?"

"I mean it all felt a little forced. Like she was trying to make a point that you're just a kid. But who exactly do you think she was trying to convince?"

"I think she was treating me like a child because that's exactly how she sees me."

"And I think she was trying to convince herself that you're off limits. We can agree to disagree if you want."

"I'm not sure you and Keira have properly thought through this matchmaking business. You realise all that's going to happen is my heart's going to end up more battered than it already is?"

"Or the opposite could happen."

"Unlikely." Kit looked at the couch and sighed. "Did you think about how much torture it's going to be for me to share a bed with her?"

"Yes!" He slapped Kit's back. "I considered that … but torturing my little brother has been a pastime of mine for a while now."

"I hate you."

The bathroom door clicked and Seren wandered out in a tiny pair of cotton shorts and a skimpy vest. Kit tried not to stare.

"I really, really hate you," he muttered under his breath.

CHAPTER SEVEN

I f she had any sense whatsoever, Seren would have objected
to sharing a bed with Kit. She knew that if she'd have so
much as blinked too many times when Trystan had laid out the
sleeping arrangements they'd have figured out an alternative.

But Trystan had assumed they wouldn't mind sharing a bed,
and she didn't want anyone to think she was anything other than
fine with it. It *should* be fine. She should be able to sleep beside
Kit without her thoughts wandering. Unfortunately, that proved
impossible, and her thoughts wandered for most of the night. On
her frequent wakings she kept her back firmly towards Kit.

Finally, at the crack of dawn, she gave in to her desire to
shuffle onto her other side and watch his peaceful features as he
slept. He'd pushed the covers off, giving her a full view of his
bare torso. The rise and fall of his chest was hypnotic, and occasionally she let her eyes drift down to the waistband of his boxer
shorts. From there she snapped her eyes back to his face. When
Mirren had asked her to keep an eye on Kit she'd definitely
meant his general well-being and not his crotch area.

Seren was drifting back to sleep when she heard movement
elsewhere in the flat. It wasn't enough to fully wake her and she
dozed for the next hour, occasionally coming around enough to

hear Trystan and Kit chatting in the kitchen. Footsteps finally roused her and she blinked her eyes open as Kit set a mug of coffee on the table beside her.

"Thanks," she mumbled. "Is that a hint that I need to get up?"

"Trystan just left. If we want to go to the Warner Brothers Studios we need to leave to get the train in about half an hour, but we don't have to if you don't want to."

"You already bought the tickets," she said in confusion.

"I know, but I should have asked you first. I assumed you'd want to go, but I don't want you to feel you have to just because I was presumptuous. If there's something else you want to do, I don't mind."

God, he was so sweet it was unbearable. "I want to go," she said, reaching for her coffee. "I just need a minute to wake up, then I'll jump in the shower."

He went back to the kitchen and sat at the island, scrolling on his phone as he sipped his coffee. Seren mentally chastised herself for being insensitive the previous day. Kit had gone out of his way to plan a day that he knew she'd enjoy, and she'd completely thrown the gesture back in his face because she couldn't deal with her own feelings. To make things worse, he was still lovely to her even when she was awful to him.

Lost in contemplation, she almost jumped out of her skin when Kit's voice broke through the silence.

"Trystan's going to try and meet up with us for dinner tonight," he said from the kitchen, "but he's not sure what time he'll be finished with work."

"Okay." Seren swallowed hard, feeling daunted by the day ahead. It was crazy to be nervous about spending the day with Kit. She'd known him forever and should be completely relaxed around him, but she had the feeling that she had no idea how to act around him.

On the Tube ride and shuttle bus, Seren still felt half asleep and was grateful that Kit wasn't particularly chatty.

"You might have had a point yesterday," he said as they stood in a queue to go into the studios.

"About what?" she asked through a yawn.

"About needing a kid to come here." He looked pointedly at all the families around them, then raised an eyebrow. "Thank goodness you've got me."

"I was joking yesterday." Feeling the need to make amends for her previous attitude, she rested her chin on Kit's shoulder and slipped her arms around his waist. She'd always had a tactile relationship with Noah, and Trystan too, but not so much with Kit. She wasn't sure why. Now it felt unnatural. Pulling away immediately would seem weird, so she waited until the queue moved to extract herself from him and hoped he hadn't been able to feel the intense thudding of her heart.

"I'm sure it's fun for adults too," Kit said, sounding suddenly unsure of himself.

She smiled at him. "We'll have fun no matter what." At least if she ever fully woke up. Her night of disturbed sleep had left her feeling like a zombie.

Finally, it was their turn to go inside and they were ushered into a large room where a staff member welcomed them and gave them a rundown of the tour, then showed a video of the film's actors talking about their time filming.

Standing side by side, they waited before the massive, intricately carved wooden doors that signalled the start of the tour.

"I hope there's a cafe along the way," Seren whispered in Kit's ear as a couple of kids were chosen to open the doors.

"Are you hungry already?" Kit asked. "It's not long since we had breakfast."

"I need another coffee and something sweet to boost my energy levels."

Kit nodded and they followed the crowd into the Great Hall.

As it turned out, the excitement of being surrounded by all things Harry Potter gave her more of a boost than caffeine ever could, and her energy levels went through the roof as they moved through the various sets and exhibits.

All her previous discomfort around Kit vanished, and they excitedly pointed out details to each other while they explored. Seren could barely take it all in and gawked at everything. They took photos of each other pushing the trolley through the wall on Platform Nine and Three Quarters and then more photos in front of the gleaming red Hogwart's Express.

"Shall I get us a butterbeer?" Kit asked outside the Backlot Cafe.

"I guess it would be rude not to." Seren's cheeks were starting to ache from smiling as they moved inside.

"Do you want to have lunch too?"

Seren checked her watch and was shocked at how much time had passed. They agreed they'd eat there and Seren said she'd grab a table since there weren't many free. She instructed Kit to choose her something to eat.

"Can you get me one of those doughnuts for dessert?" she added, eyeing the display of mouth-watering treats.

He rolled his eyes and muttered about her sweet tooth as he walked away.

"I didn't know what you'd fancy," he said, when he arrived at the table with a tray of food and drinks. "I got a burger and a mac n cheese. Take whichever you want."

"They both look good." She helped to offload everything from the tray. "Shall we share?"

"Fine by me. And before you start complaining about dessert, I didn't forget... they've got peanuts sprinkled on them."

"All of them?" She craned her neck, not believing him.

"No." He took a knife to cut the burger in half. "But they're all in the same display case and they're using the same tongs to serve them. Let's not risk your life for your sugar addiction."

"That's annoying," she said, but was touched by how careful Kit was about her allergy.

He tapped his glass of butterbeer against hers before taking a long swig. "That's not what I was expecting."

"I like it," Seren remarked, setting it down and picking up a knife to cut the burger in half.

"Because it's probably mostly sugar," Kit said with a grin. "Do you still want a coffee, by the way? I can get you one if you want."

"No. Just eat," she instructed. "I completely forgot about being tired."

Kit took a bite of the burger, then looked at Seren with amusement. "Being here's really making me wish I'd read all of the books."

Laughing, she gave his shin a soft kick. "You've only got yourself to blame for that."

"That's not true. I'd say it's entirely your fault."

"Hurry up and eat," she said with a smirk. "We've still got more to see."

The day with Seren couldn't have gone better. Her bad mood from the previous day had vanished and her enthusiasm while she was surrounded by all things Harry Potter was infectious. Whatever awkward atmosphere had surrounded them before had been replaced by the usual banter and easy conversation. Kit wasn't sure whether it was entirely a good thing. His emotions were on a rollercoaster, and he couldn't decide whether the feelings were pleasant or not.

After dinner in a restaurant near Trystan's flat, they moved to a cosy traditional pub around the corner. He'd messaged Trystan to tell him to join them but given how much Seren was yawning he was about to suggest calling it a day and heading home when he finally arrived.

"You've just made me feel very under-dressed," Kit said as Trystan took a seat.

"You're always under-dressed," Trystan replied, looking down at his navy-blue shirt with a shrug. Pretty much everything Trystan owned was designer or tailor-made. "How was your day in the wizarding world?"

"Amazing," they replied at once.

"I loved it," Seren said. "We spent most of the day there and it absolutely flew by."

"Told you it was good." Trystan stretched his neck. "You weren't embarrassed at being there without a kid?"

Kit flashed Seren a cheeky grin. "Seren was acting like an over-excited child all day so it was fine."

"I *felt* like an over-excited child," she said, yawning again and finishing the last mouthful of her wine.

"I was going to suggest a nightclub and dancing," Trystan said. "But you look as though you're ready to drop."

Seren nodded, then laughed as she yawned again. "Do you mind if I go back to the flat? I need to go to bed."

"We can all go," Kit said.

"No." She stood and pulled her bag on her shoulder. "You two stay and hang out. I just need the spare key."

Kit handed it to her. "Are you sure you don't want us to come back with you?"

"Definite. Stay and have fun."

They called goodnight to her as she left, and Kit's eyes stayed on her until she'd disappeared outside.

"How are things between you two?" Trystan asked.

"Same as always." He took a swig of his beer. "Except I kept having to remind myself that it wasn't a date today. It kind of felt like it."

"That's good."

"I'm not so sure. I can't imagine anything will ever happen between us. I just don't think she sees me that way."

"Did you ever think about telling her how you feel?"

"Yeah. I think about it a lot. I guess it would be good to know once and for all that I have no chance. Maybe I could move on. But at the same time, living in hope isn't so bad."

"You seem to be forgetting the possibility that she might feel the same."

"Because it doesn't feel like a possibility to me."

"Of course it's a possibility. And there's a chance that knowing how you feel about her will change how she sees you."

Kit rubbed at his temple. "I think the most likely outcome to me telling her how I feel is an incredibly uncomfortable atmosphere between us for the rest of time."

"Slightly dramatic," Trystan said, shifting in his seat.

"Maybe," he said on a sigh. "Let's talk about something else. Tell me about work or something."

They spent an hour chatting about more neutral topics before they were interrupted by Trystan's phone.

"It's Jenny," he said, frowning as he accepted the call and moved the phone to his ear.

Kit watched Trystan's features to try and gauge the nature of the conversation, but he couldn't read him. After a short conversation which involved him agreeing to whatever she was saying, he ended the call and set the phone on the table.

"You don't mind me ditching you again tomorrow, do you?" Trystan asked.

"I hope this isn't another ploy to leave me and Seren alone, because I think that's unnecessary."

"No. Jenny wants to meet for lunch. She wants us to talk in person."

"Is that a good thing or bad?"

He rubbed at his neck. "I guess I'll find out tomorrow."

After finishing their drinks, they wandered back to the flat and crept through the living room where Seren was fast asleep.

"She sleeps very loudly," Trystan remarked as he poured himself a glass of water to the sound of Seren's gentle snores.

"It's not so bad." Kit ignored the look of amusement Trystan shot him and headed to the bathroom. When he came out, he walked softly to his side of the bed, trying not to stare at Seren with her silky hair fanned out on the pillow. Slipping under the covers, he smiled at the rhythmic sound of her snoring.

One of these days he was going to have to tell her how he felt. Maybe it would give him closure and he could move on.

Though he wasn't sure it was possible to get over someone when you even loved the sound of their snoring.

CHAPTER EIGHT

"I think there's something seriously wrong with your brother," Seren remarked as the front door closed behind Trystan. "Who goes to the gym on a Sunday morning?"

"He's stressed about meeting Jenny later." Kit handed her a croissant and a mug of coffee, then went back to the kitchen for his own.

"I could get used to this service," she said, shuffling the pillows behind her to get comfy.

Kit arrived back in the space beside her. "It's not a proper holiday if you don't get breakfast in bed."

"Thanks," she said, pulling the covers a little further around her midriff. Kit had already showered and got dressed, but she hadn't made it out of bed yet.

"What do you want to do today?" he asked.

She tore a fluffy piece of pastry and popped it in her mouth. "What are the options?"

"I dunno. I chose yesterday, so I reckon it's your turn to come up with something. My only requirement is that it's as much fun as what I planned for yesterday."

She gave his bicep a gentle shove with her own. "No pressure then?"

"Tons of pressure," he said with a grin.

"Will you hate me if I say I could do with going clothes shopping?"

"Yes." He had his coffee in his hand and almost spilled it when she nudged him again. "Was that the wrong answer?"

"I could always go shopping alone," she said with a hint of a pout. She'd really rather not go it alone. Mirren's insistence that Seren should go to London to keep an eye on Kit was pretty ironic considering it was Seren who was worried about getting lost in London.

"It's fine," Kit said seriously. "I could do with a couple of pairs of jeans anyway."

"Where's good to go shopping then?"

He smiled as he blew on his coffee. "I don't think you're grasping the concept of *you* being the one to plan the day."

"I don't know London!"

"Have you ever heard of something called Google?"

"I thought you'd know where to go," she said through a laugh. "And since you did such a good job of planning everything yesterday …"

He set his mug down and picked up his phone. "Fine. If the lady wants a day of shopping, I'll plan a day of shopping."

"You're the best!" She took a large bite of her croissant. "We probably don't need the whole day."

"I'll believe that when I see it," he said, without looking up from his phone.

Three hours later they'd settled themselves into the bustle of Oxford Street and were weighed down with bags. At least Kit was. He also had an armful of clothes that Seren had picked out to try on.

"Okay," she said, snatching another top from the rack and turning to take the collection from him. "I just need to find the fitting rooms."

"That way," he said, turning her in the right direction and following after her.

Once she'd wriggled into a pair of grey skinny jeans and buttoned up the shirt, she took a step back and connected with the curtain. They never did make changing rooms big enough.

"What do you think?" she asked Kit as she stepped outside for a better look.

"I like it."

"You say that about everything I try on. You just want me to buy stuff to get the shopping trip over with."

"Not true." He righted one of the shopping bags that had toppled over by his feet. "You just happen to look good in everything."

Her stomach fluttered and his bashful smile brought heat to her cheeks. "I think I'll get these and the T-shirt. Then I'm calling it a day. I'm running out of money anyway. Which reminds me, I owe you money."

"What for?"

Her eyes widened. "For the flights, and the tickets for yesterday and food yesterday. You keep paying for things."

"I don't mind. I'm just glad you came with me or I'd have spent most of the weekend alone."

"Our mission to check on Trystan has failed somewhat, hasn't it? Have you heard anything from him? I wonder how it's going with Jenny."

He pulled his phone from his pocket. "I haven't heard anything."

"Do you think we need to stay away from the flat for the day?"

"I dunno. Why?"

"Because I was thinking that shopping is exhausting and I'd quite like to chill out this afternoon, but if they're getting back together Trystan might want us to make ourselves scarce."

"He'd message if he wanted us out of the way."

"So, you think we can go and watch films for the afternoon?"

"Yeah."

She checked her watch. "We missed lunch. I'll get changed and pay for these things, then we can find jeans for you and grab something to eat before we head back. And while we eat, we can figure out how much money I owe you."

"You don't need to pay me back ... you can help me with my shopping and we'll call it quits."

"That doesn't seem fair."

"To who?" he asked, the corners of his mouth lifting to a smile.

"How bad are you at shopping?"

"Completely hopeless. Usually Trystan comes and picks everything out for me."

"Picking out clothes for you actually sounds like fun."

"You'll just have to tell me I look great in everything," he said, raising his voice as she slipped back into the changing room. "That way we can get it over and done with and get to the pub."

"Are we going to the pub?" she asked, unbuttoning the shirt.

"We are unless you're choosing where we go for food."

"I'll let you choose," she said, realising she'd paused in getting changed. Her reflection in the mirror was positively beaming. Spending time with Kit was far too lovely. There'd been a couple of moments when being with him felt so much like being on a date that she'd had to stop herself from pressing her lips to his.

Although it wasn't particularly like any dates she'd ever been on. Kit was sweet and kind and attentive, which didn't describe any guys she'd previously dated.

Peeling the jeans off, she silently cursed herself. Why was she thinking about dates? Kit was a friend and that was all. She needed to get a grip. It was just hard to do when he was so easy to be around.

Shopping for him was as enjoyable as shopping for herself, and the smile didn't leave her face as she waited outside changing rooms before giving her verdict. Being able to legitimately look him up and down without feeling like she was perving on her best friend's little brother was great. It wasn't doing anything to dampen her feelings towards him, but she decided not to worry about it while they were away. She'd figure out what to do when they were home and back to reality. Until then, she was determined to enjoy herself and not overthink things.

When they arrived back at the flat, Seren dumped the shopping bags and scooped up her pyjamas before heading for the bathroom.

"You realise it's only half past four," Kit said.

Turning, she grinned at him. "Are you commenting on me getting ready for bed?"

"It's a little early."

"We're not going out again. All we're going to do now is snuggle down and watch films. I'd like to do that in comfort." She had a hand on the bathroom door handle when she called out to him again. "Can you put the kettle on? And have a look through the cupboards to see if there's any popcorn …"

He was muttering something about slave drivers when she closed the bathroom door behind her.

They decided on a Harry Potter marathon and were an hour into the first film when Trystan arrived home.

"How did it go?" Kit asked, while Seren hit pause on the remote.

He sank onto the bed beside her legs. "She wants to sell the flat."

"What?" Seren asked, unable to hide her surprise.

"Things are definitely over." He put a hand across his forehead and rubbed at his temples. "She either wants to sell the place or she wants me to buy her out."

"Shit," Kit whispered. "Sorry."

"Are you okay?" Seren asked, putting her arms around him.

He rested his cheek against the top of her head and gave her a squeeze. "I have no idea. I still thought we might figure things out, but she was clear about what she wants. She was very matter-of-fact about it all."

"I'm really sorry," she said softly.

He made a pitiful attempt at a smile. "Hopefully your day was better than mine."

"Seren dragged me into most of the shops on Oxford Street."

"Approximately as bad as my day then?"

"Hey!" Seren gave him a playful shove. "We had a good day."

"What do you feel like doing?" Kit asked. "We can go out and get drunk if you want?"

Trystan didn't drink, so it was no surprise when he shook his head. "What are you watching?"

"Harry Potter," Seren told him.

"Shuffle up then," he said with a quick tilt of his chin.

"Are you sure you don't want to do something else?" she asked. "Or just talk?"

"I definitely don't want to talk." He kicked his shoes off and pulled the covers back to get in beside her.

Seren took the remote from him when he picked it up. "I really think you should talk about this," she said sternly. "We're here to support you. I don't think staring at the TV is very helpful."

"She's right," Kit said. "Pour your heart out, then we'll let you watch with us."

He leaned his head back and stared at the ceiling. "There's not a lot to say. Jenny doesn't want to be with someone who doesn't share her feelings about marriage and kids."

"I don't understand," Kit said in a strained voice. "If you're so upset about losing her, why couldn't you marry her?"

"I don't know. It doesn't matter any more though. She said that even if I changed my mind about marriage it wouldn't make any difference. She doesn't want to be with someone who she has to pressure into marrying her." He let out a long sigh. "I can see her point. I love her, but when it came down to it I'd rather not be with her than marry her. She deserves better than that."

"What will you do about the flat?" Seren asked.

"I don't know. I'm kind of used to living here without her, so I'll probably buy her out and stay here. It'll be easier than looking for somewhere new."

Seren put an arm around him and gave him a squeeze.

"Can we watch the film now?" he asked.

Seren looked to Kit for confirmation before pressing play. Wedged between the two of them, she adjusted the pillows behind her to get comfortable. Her leg was pressed against Kit's, and when her arm brushed against his it was an effort not to lace her fingers together with his.

"Sorry," he said, moving over a little. "Have you got enough room?"

"Yeah." *Too much now.*

As the film went on, Seren found herself concentrating less on the TV and more on the closeness between her and Kit. After they'd eaten takeaway pizzas and settled down to the second film, she discreetly moved in his direction, savouring the warmth radiating from his skin and the familiar scent of him, which suddenly seemed like some potent love potion. The thought of going home and back to real life the following day left her with a dull ache in her chest.

She drifted off while the film was still playing and woke sometime in the night to find the room in darkness. Quickly she fell back into a deep sleep that lasted until daylight seeped into the room. As the veil of sleep lifted, it took her a moment to register the arms wrapped around her. The warmth of Kit's legs nestled against hers felt wonderful. In the blurry moments between sleep and wake her instincts took over and she pulled his arms tighter around her while she wedged her back against his firm chest.

Turning in his arms, she could feel his breath on her lips and inched closer. She murmured his name and licked her dry lips. The grunt she received in reply made her pull back and blink rapidly.

"Oh my God!" she shrieked.

"What?"

"Get off me!" Roughly she shoved at the arms, which suddenly felt like an octopus. "Trystan! Get off!"

He shook his head and looked blearily up at her. "What did I do?"

"Nothing." She pulled the duvet up to her chest as she shuddered. "You didn't do anything. I just wasn't expecting you to be here. Where's Kit?"

"No idea." He sat up and dragged his fingers through his hair. "I must've fallen asleep before the film ended."

"Me too." Her heart was in overdrive, and she felt slightly nauseous at the thought that she'd very nearly kissed Trystan.

"Shit," Trystan said, pulling the covers back. "I didn't mean to sleep here." He checked his watch. "I need to go. I want to hit the gym before work. What time is your flight?"

"Eleven."

"You need to get moving soon, too." He stood and stretched. "I guess Kit's in my room," he said, walking in that direction.

Seren flopped back onto the bed and waited for her heart to settle back into a regular rhythm. If it had been Kit's arms she'd woken up in she'd definitely have kissed him.

She had no idea what to do with that information.

CHAPTER NINE

K it had switched the film off once Trystan and Seren had fallen asleep slumped against each other. He'd dropped onto Trystan's bed without bothering to get undressed, correctly guessing that he wasn't going to get a lot of sleep. The shadows in the room had become very familiar by the time the door inched open and Trystan wandered in.

"Morning," he said, giving Kit's leg a shove.

"Hey." His voice was croaky and he cleared his throat.

"I fell asleep in front of the TV."

"I noticed," Kit told him frostily.

"Why didn't you wake me up and kick me out?"

"What would have been the point of that?"

Lines deepened across Trystan's brow as he stared down at him. "Are you annoyed with me?"

"No," he said automatically.

"How come I don't believe you?"

"I've got no idea." He swung his legs off the bed and sat up. "Do you need to shower? Because we need to leave pretty soon."

"I'll shower at the gym."

"Okay," Kit said, standing. "I'm going to jump in the bathroom then."

"I'll be gone by the time you've showered." Trystan sidestepped to block Kit's path.

"See you soon," Kit said, giving him a brief hug. "Sorry about Jenny."

"You're pissed off with me, aren't you?" Trystan's hand in the centre of Kit's chest stopped him from moving any further. "I honestly didn't mean to fall asleep in there. Why didn't you wake me up?"

"Because it doesn't matter," Kit said on a sigh. "I spent the last two days kidding myself that maybe there could be something more than friendship between me and Seren. I kept getting these vibes and thinking she was giving me looks ... but when you came in last night, she was as affectionate with you as she ever is with me."

"She was affectionate because I was upset and she's one of my oldest friends. That's all."

"I'm not saying there's anything more to it. I don't suddenly think she has a thing for you ... I just realised she treats us the same. She sees us in the same way – as her oldest friends. I need to stop wishing for something else and get on with my life."

Trystan frowned. "Can you please not leave being angry with me?"

"I'm not angry with you." Kit took a deep breath and relaxed his shoulders. "I swear I'm not angry with you. I'm just tired."

"Good." Trystan smothered him in a bear hug. "Sorry I didn't get to see you much this weekend."

"No worries. I really am sorry about Jenny. Are you gonna be okay?"

"I think so." Trystan gave Kit a playful kiss on the side of his head, making him squirm to get away. It had been one of their dad's annoying habits, which Trystan would now occasionally inflict on him.

"Come over and visit soon," Kit said, pausing in the doorway. "And call anytime you want to chat."

"You too. Let me know you get home okay." Trystan gave him a quick smile. "Love you, baby bro."

"Love you too," Kit mumbled as he walked away.

When he came out of the bathroom, Seren had coffee and toast waiting for him and they sat side by side at the kitchen island and ate in silence. The weekend away had lost its shine, and he'd be happy to get back home and have space to think clearly.

On the journey his thoughts swirled madly. He couldn't keep on with his infatuation with Seren. That much was at least clear to him. He just wasn't sure what to do about it. Several times on the flight he contemplated telling her how he felt. It would be slightly awkward on the plane though. Raising his voice over the noise of the engines would likely guarantee that all the other passengers heard him too. It wasn't a conversation he wanted to have while shouting in each other's ears. Did he even want to have it at all?

Once they were in Seren's car for the final part of the journey, it felt like the perfect opportunity to say something. He'd tell her how he felt and then ... well, most likely she'd look at him as though he'd lost his mind. What would happen after she'd let him down gently?

He'd have closure and be able to start the process of getting over her, that's what.

"Kit!"

His head shot up as Seren nudged his leg.

"What?" Glancing outside, he realised they were at his place.

"You were miles away. I said you still need to let me know how much I owe you for the flights and rental car and everything."

"Yeah. I'll have to figure it out." Or just wait until she forgot about it. She was perpetually short on funds and the money made no difference to him.

"Thanks for inviting me," she said. "I had a great time."

"Me too." He reached for the door handle, then stopped and looked back at her. "I... um..." He closed his eyes briefly and opened them to find her looking at him, one eyebrow slightly raised. "I'm glad you came with me," he said, the words feeling disjointed. He couldn't find the right words and felt like a bumbling fool. If he told her how he felt, he couldn't take it back. She would know. Forever. Every conversation, every encounter would be awkward. They'd never be able to just hang out again. "See you soon," he said, pushing the door open and hopping out.

As he went into his flat, he told himself that keeping his feelings to himself had been for the best. His thoughts continued to whir regardless, and it didn't take long before he was restless and sick of his own company. Checking the time, he rushed out of the door and headed for the promenade at a quick pace. He made it to the train stop a few minutes before two o'clock, happy to find that Noah and Keira hadn't left.

"I didn't think you'd be back yet," Noah remarked, walking to the front of the train after collecting money from the passengers, who were all seated and waiting to go.

"We just got back. I thought I could take over."

"You don't have to," Keira said.

"I want to." It was preferable to sitting around at home feeling sorry for himself.

Noah slung his arm around Keira's shoulder. "I reckon Keira's going to be fighting you for train trips soon."

"I am," she agreed. "I love it."

"Have you been driving?" Kit asked her.

"Yes. And I'm feeling more confident about talking too. Noah did most of it, but there were a few times where I took over to give bits of information."

"That's great." Kit slipped into the driver's seat and had the feeling he was spoiling Noah and Keira's fun. He really needed the distraction of work though.

"How was the weekend?" Noah asked, with a meaningful look.

"Good," Kit said. "We had fun."

"How are things between you and Seren?" Keira asked.

Kit wished he'd never told Keira anything about the situation with Seren. "Same as always," he said, then glanced back at the waiting passengers. "I better go."

Keira gave him a sympathetic look before breaking into a spontaneous grin. "That woman from the tourist information was here looking for you yesterday."

"Holly? What did she want?"

"She didn't say," Keira replied. "She's sweet though."

"No doubt she wants to give me business advice or something."

"Or ask you on a date," Keira suggested.

"You should get a hobby." Kit shook his head, then turned the PA system on to welcome the passengers and launched into his quick safety speech as he set off through the town.

Seren collapsed on the couch when she got home, covering her face with a cushion as though she could muffle her thoughts, which were too loud and annoyingly disorganised. As though her own feelings weren't enough to deal with, she now had Kit's to contend with. She was sure his bad mood on the journey home had been caused by her and Trystan falling asleep together. She was also convinced he'd been gearing up to say something momentous when she'd dropped him off.

The moment in the car had been excruciating. She hadn't had time to decide whether she'd wanted him to broach the subject or not. What she'd really wanted was for him to lean over and kiss her. That didn't seem like Kit's style though. She'd briefly contemplated kissing him but had managed to control herself. It was a good thing too. And a good thing that he'd left the car without saying anything. If he said something, she'd be forced to tell him she didn't feel the same.

The best thing to do would be to avoid each other for a few weeks until the feelings passed, which they no doubt would. They were probably both lonely and that was manifesting as an inappropriate crush. They'd get over it.

At the sound of the doorbell, she flung the cushion aside and stood up. Once upon a time she'd have assumed an unannounced guest would be Noah, but it was a long time since he'd shown up at her door without warning. After spending ages looking forward to him moving back from Bristol, it hadn't quite worked out as she'd expected.

Kit had been right that Noah didn't have time for her now that he had a girlfriend. Not that she was complaining … she liked Keira and was glad that Noah was happy. Maybe that was partly why she'd suddenly developed feelings for Kit. Her best friend was all loved up, and it looked like an appealing prospect.

Annoyingly, there was no intercom system to her flat. Answering the door involved descending the steep flight of stairs to the door that opened directly onto the street. She was halfway down them when the doorbell sounded again, and she muttered that she was coming, not loud enough for her impatient visitor to hear.

"Sort of wishing I'd stayed on the couch," she said as she clapped eyes on her cousin. "Hi, Cadan."

"What kind of greeting is that?" Stepping over the threshold, he wrapped her in a hug which lifted her off the ground. He was about a foot taller than her.

"Get off me." She gave him a playful shove. Underneath her air of hostility, she was secretly happy to see him. At least he could distract her from thoughts of Kit. "When did you arrive?" she asked as they set off up the stairs.

"Saturday. How was London?"

"Good."

"You were with Noah, right?" Upstairs he went straight to

the kitchen and opened the fridge. Without asking he took out two beers, then searched the drawers for a bottle opener.

Seren watched him in amusement. "I was with Kit. Visiting Trystan."

"Oh, that's right … Noah's cheating on you with some bird he met in Bristol."

"I'm not going to dignify that with a reply." She leaned on the counter and took the beer that he held out to her. "Are you really staying all summer?"

"That's the plan."

"What about work?"

"I'm between jobs, so I'll work on my CV and take a few shifts in the pub."

She had the bottle to her mouth and almost choked on her beer when she laughed. "As if you'll work in the pub." He'd never had any interest in working in the pub, but his dad was usually willing to pay him to stand around not doing much.

"I'll keep you company while you work," he said with a mischievous glint in his eyes.

"That sounds more like it."

"The weather's been amazing this weekend. If it stays like this it'll be a fantastic summer. You need to tell me where the good parties are these days."

"I have no idea. I can't remember the last time I went to a party." She'd hazard a guess and say it was some time before Terry Treneary died. No one she spent time with had been in much of a party mood since then.

"Where do you hang out?"

"The Mermaid Inn."

He laughed. "We need to find somewhere further away from my dad. Felix's place will do, I suppose."

"Felix is back?" The hairs on the back of her neck stood on end at the mention of her ex-boyfriend.

"I'm staying at his place." Cadan's lips twitched to a smirk. "I'm sure I told you that."

"We both know you didn't mention that. What's he doing back?" The last she'd heard he was in London, though she wasn't sure what exactly he did there.

"His parents have gone away for a couple of months. Some business thing in the States. Felix said he'd come and keep an eye on Rebecca and the house."

"Isn't his sister old enough to look after herself?"

"Yeah, and she's fairly hot these days too. She grew up well."

Seren rolled her eyes. "Please tell me you have more sense than to go there?"

"Yeah." He chuckled. "Felix would kill me. Anyway, he's taking a working holiday over here."

"What does he do these days?"

"Web design or something."

"Shouldn't you know? Isn't he your best friend?" It annoyed her immensely that Cadan had kept up his friendship with Felix after he'd broken things off with Seren. Out of loyalty she thought Cadan should have dropped him.

"I know what he does … something to do with web design." He checked his watch. "Do you want to go over there?"

"To Felix's place?"

"Yeah. We're going to drink some beers and smoke a joint."

"Oh, god. Dad was right … you'll never change, will you?"

"Let's hope not. How is Uncle Benji? Still not my biggest fan?"

"No. And he never will be if you insist on calling him Benji."

"Ben's boring."

"*You're* boring," she countered.

He drained his beer and set the empty bottle on the counter. "Let's go. Either come with me or give me a lift over there."

"Don't get any ideas about me being your personal taxi service for the summer."

"I was going to talk to you about that ... how would you feel about lending me your car?"

"Is that your first beer of the evening?"

He pursed his lips. "It's my first beer since I got to your place. But I wasn't thinking about tonight. I meant in general. Lend me your car for the summer ... you live in town, what do you even need a car for?"

"You're not having my car."

He narrowed his eyes. "Are you ever going to tell me what happened between you and Lowen Treneary?"

"Nothing happened between me and Lowen Treneary," she told him through gentle laughter.

"So, the guy bought you a brand-new car and had it shipped over here ... and you're still claiming you never slept with him?"

"I've never slept with Lowen Treneary."

"So why did he buy you a car?"

She shrugged. "Because I asked him to." It wasn't only him she'd asked; after the Trenearys all inherited money a few years back, she'd jokily suggested that one of them ought to buy her a car. If she'd had to put money on which one of them might have done it, she'd have gone for Noah. But it had been Lowen who'd shown up on her doorstep with a shiny new Mini. She'd cried happy tears, then driven over to her dad's house and then to Mirren and Terry's place to show off her pride and joy.

"Lowen lives on Bryher now, right?" Cadan asked. "Maybe I could rock up there and ask him to buy me a car."

"I don't think that'd work out well for you."

"I heard he's turned into some grumpy recluse?"

"He's not grumpy or a recluse," she argued without conviction, thinking she ought to go over and see Lowen soon. She tried to get over there every few weeks, not that he particularly seemed to welcome her visits.

"Are you coming over to Felix's?" he asked, gearing up to leave.

"I'll give you a lift over there." She set her almost full beer down. "I'm not staying though." If Felix was around for the summer and Cadan was staying with him, she wouldn't be able to avoid him for long, but her head was spinning enough for one day.

She'd leave the awkward reunion with her ex for some other time.

CHAPTER TEN

To her annoyance, Seren didn't have to wait long before she encountered Felix. He wandered into the pub with Cadan on Tuesday evening, not long after she'd started her shift. Her eyes had already been checking the door every time it opened, hoping to see Kit. She told herself it was an experiment more than actually wanting to see him. She wanted to know if she was right about him engineering ways to see her. If she wasn't on a day shift, she didn't pass him on her way to work, so he came in for a drink instead. At least that was her working theory, but maybe she was delusional.

The sight of Felix with his mop of thick, dark curls put her on high alert. Her shoulders rose towards her ears as her muscles tensed. Glancing behind her, she looked at the door through to the back. Noah had just gone to speak to the chef. If he could reappear quickly she'd appreciate it.

"Seren!" Felix's cocky tone was irritatingly familiar as he and Cadan slipped onto stools at the bar.

In reply, she muttered his name.

"How are you?" he asked, resting on the bar to show off sleeves of interwoven tattoos on both forearms.

"Fine," she replied curtly. "What do you want to drink?"

They ordered beers and she felt Felix's eyes on her the whole time she poured them.

"It's nice to see you again," he remarked when she set his drink in front of him.

"I'm not sure the feeling's mutual."

Cadan punched Felix's arm. "Told you she's still pissed off at you."

"Aw, come on." Felix gazed at her intently. "That was all a long time ago. We had some good times, didn't we?"

"Debatable," she said. "But I definitely didn't enjoy watching you snogging Cindy Taylor in that corner" – she pointed – "on my twenty-first birthday. With all my friends and family around."

His smirk annoyed her immensely. "I got confused. Thought it was you."

"You went home with her," she pointed out, her voice hostile as the emotions from the past enveloped her. It would be better to pretend she was well and truly over it, but she didn't seem capable of that.

"That was a mistake." His lips lifted in amusement and he kept his dark eyes on her as he took a swig of his pint. "It's my biggest regret," he said in an eerily quiet voice.

"That's hard to believe, given that I never even got an apology."

"I'm sure I said sorry."

"Not that it would have made any difference, but you didn't."

He sat up straighter, pushing his hair off his face. "Well, wasn't I a jerk?"

Cadan cracked up laughing and Seren wandered away from them, wishing the pub was busier so she had other customers to distract her. As it was, there were only a couple of tables in the back occupied. She was thankful when the door opened. Her smile came naturally for Kit and he grinned at her in return.

"Long time no see," he joked.

"It's like you can't stay away from me." The flirting was automatic and it didn't even occur to her to care.

"Seems like it, doesn't it?" He held her gaze for a moment, making her insides flutter. "Can I have a bottle of lager, please?"

"You can." She'd only just turned away from him when she heard Felix and Cadan chatting loudly. The mention of the train made her stomach lurch.

"You're the train guy, right?" Felix asked, leaning in Kit's direction. "Noah's baby brother."

Kit's eyebrows hitched slightly. "That's me."

For a moment, Felix seemed as though he'd leave it at that. Unfortunately, only for a moment. "You own the bus too, don't you?"

"Yep." Kit nodded a greeting at Cadan as Seren put his beer on the bar.

"So, it's like a transport fetish?" Felix asked.

Resisting the urge to slap the stupid smirk off his face, Seren glared at Felix instead. "It's a successful business, is what it is. Probably not something you'd know anything about." She was fairly sure that Felix's work in web design was his own business and only hoped he wasn't particularly successful.

"You're very feisty with me this evening." His eyes moved slowly to Seren. "Glad to see our old spark is still there."

"You're pathetic." Her heart raced and she hated how easy it was for him to get under her skin.

"So, how fast does your train go?" Felix asked Kit, his tone making the innocent question sound like an insult.

"Will you either shut up or get out?" Seren snarled at him.

"It was only a question," Felix said, laughter in his eyes. "How come you're so protective of Baby Treneary? Can't he speak for himself?"

"I don't want him to have to waste his breath talking to you."

The door behind the bar opened and Noah wandered out, his brow creasing as he clocked Felix. "Did you forget the rule about keeping dogs on leads?" he said to Cadan.

Felix slapped a hand to his chest. "Ouch. That hurt, Noah. I see the staff in this place are as friendly as ever."

"You're welcome to find somewhere else to drink," Seren told him.

"I was looking forward to hearing about the train," Felix said, looking at Kit.

Kit took a slug of his drink, his Adam's apple bobbing when he swallowed. "What do you want to know?"

"I was wondering what effect it has on your sex life." He ran his tongue along his bottom lip. "Does the train attract the ladies … or is it more like the opposite?"

Before Kit could respond, Noah parked himself on a stool, creating a barrier between him and Felix. "How was your day?" he asked Kit, then took a sip of his Sprite.

"Aren't you supposed to be working?" Cadan called out to him.

"Yes." Noah span around on the stool. "Aren't we supposed to sit at the bar and chat to customers? That always seemed to be your approach."

"It's different when you own the place," Cadan replied, but his confidence had vanished.

"I'm sure it is," Noah told him. "But the last time I checked, you don't own the place."

Cadan cocked his head. "I will one day."

Noah turned back to Kit while Seren wandered around the bar, trying not to think about Cadan's words. There was no way he'd ever take over the pub from Charlie, but it reminded her that her plans to buy the pub from Charlie one day were fading fast. For one thing, her attempts to save money felt futile, and for another, she suspected her plan to get Noah to go into business with her was less likely to happen since Keira had come on the scene.

Standing beside Cadan, she pulled on his arm to whisper in his ear. "Can you guys just leave?"

"Why?" he growled back. "This is my place. What gives

your friends the right to treat me like crap?"

"Because *your* friend treats everyone like crap."

"Can you just get us another beer?"

She kept her hand on his arm and waited until he looked her in the eyes. "Please," she said quietly.

"Fine." He sighed and stood up, then slapped Felix on the arm. "Let's get out of here."

"How come? I was enjoying myself."

"Just finish your drink and let's go."

Felix dutifully drained his beer, then winked at Seren as he stood.

As soon as they'd gone, Noah moved back around the bar and began tearing open rolls of change to fill up the till. He didn't say anything, which made his feelings as clear as if he'd launched into a rant.

"Sorry about them," Seren said to Kit.

He shrugged. "Who is that guy?"

"Felix," she told him. "An old friend of Cadan."

Realisation flashed in his eyes, and her momentary hope that Kit wouldn't connect the dots vanished.

"Didn't you used to date him?" he asked.

"A long time ago." Her cheeks flushed at the humiliation of the night of her twenty-first birthday. Even Kit must remember that night.

Noah closed the till with too much force. "I'll never know what you saw in that guy."

"He's got nice hair." It was supposed to be a joke, but it fell flat. "Do you want anything to eat?" she asked Kit.

"No, thanks. I think I'll head home."

"The chef's got risotto on special this week ... it's really good." She wanted him to stay around, but he slipped off the stool, clearly not tempted.

"Have a good night," he called before he walked outside, leaving Seren with a misplaced feeling of guilt over the way Felix had spoken to him.

CHAPTER ELEVEN

Seeing Seren's idiot of an ex-boyfriend in the pub riled Kit up. The guy was obnoxious and cocky and clearly intent on making a move on Seren. After the way he'd treated her when they'd been dating, Seren surely wouldn't give him the time of day, but Kit hated the thought of Felix sniffing around her. Mostly he was panicking that some guy was about to swoop in between the two of them, which was ridiculous considering there was nothing between him and Seren.

On Thursday, he was debating whether to go ahead with his afternoon train ride despite the drizzle when the heavens opened, making the decision easier. There was a note on the timetable at the beach saying that the train didn't run in heavy rain so he didn't have to do anything – he just got the afternoon off. The relief at not having to entertain tourists was only momentary. Until he realised he had nothing to do except mope around his flat, thinking about Seren.

After whiling away a couple of hours mindlessly playing on his PlayStation, he got a beer and drank it standing at the window, looking out at the dreary grey car park. Usually he could glimpse the sea between the buildings, but the view was impeded by mist and rain. He'd just sent a message to Trystan, checking how he was doing, when his phone rang.

"Something's been bothering me since you and Seren were here," Trystan said without preamble.

"What?"

He paused for a moment. "I'm kind of a cuddly sleeper."

"I really don't want to know." Kit's heart rate picked up and he paced in front of the window.

"No, just listen to me … I woke up with my arms around Seren and I'm fairly sure she was about to kiss me."

"Well, that's lovely," he growled in reply. "Thanks for telling me."

"She thought I was you," Trystan said forcefully. "She didn't care that I was cuddled up to her until she realised it was me. When she thought it was you, she was going to kiss you … at least I think she was …"

"Maybe she was just going to kiss *you?*"

"Definitely not. I was half asleep and I'm not entirely sure what happened, so I wasn't going to mention it, but it's been bothering me all week, and the more I think about it, the more I think she wanted to kiss you. She said your name. Then she completely freaked out when she came around and realised it was me."

"Was there a point to you telling me this?" Kit asked wearily.

"Yeah. I think you should tell her how you feel."

He took a long pull of his beer. "I've been thinking about that too, but what if it ruins things between us?"

"Wouldn't you rather know one way or another?"

"Kind of, yeah. But I also like hanging out with her. I don't want to lose her as a friend."

"So you're going to carry on with things the way they are? Indefinitely?"

"What's going on with you? Why are you suddenly so keen for me to make an idiot of myself?"

"I don't know. Maybe you're right and you should keep your

mouth shut. I just keep thinking about Jenny … maybe some-times it's better to jump in with both feet than do nothing and wonder what might have been."

"You miss her?"

"Yeah. We were together for ten years. I thought I'd always be with her."

"Sorry."

"I'll survive. How come you're not working anyway?"

"It's raining." Kit looked out at the trees blowing in the gusty wind. "I think you might be right …"

"About what?"

"Telling Seren. It's pathetic spending years pining after someone. If I talk to her, I might be able to put all this behind me and stop obsessing over her."

"I think you should go for it."

He blew out a breath. "I'm going to."

"When?"

"Now. Before I change my mind."

"Are you serious?"

"Yeah." He was already at the door and shoving his feet into his shoes. "I'm going to her place now."

"Wow. Okay."

Kit swapped the phone from hand to hand as he put his jacket on. "Wish me luck."

"Good luck. Let me know how it goes."

He promised he would, then ended the call and raced out of the door. When he'd been out with the train that morning, he'd seen Seren on her way to work and had chatted to her for a few minutes. She hadn't mentioned working a double shift, so she should be home again by now. If not, he'd take it as a sign to keep his feelings to himself.

The rain eased slightly as he walked over there and his hood kept him mostly dry. Shortly after he rang the doorbell, he heard footsteps on the stairs.

His heart was hammering when Seren opened the door, her eyebrows twitching upwards in surprise.

"Hi," he said. "How are you?" As his chest clenched, he shoved his hands in his pockets and leaned against the door frame, then immediately stood up straight again.

"Fine." She glanced up and down the road. "How are you?"

"Good. Thanks." He flashed her a nervous smile. "I wanted to talk to you … if you have time. Can I come up for a bit?"

"Sure." Standing aside, she gestured for him to come in and closed the door behind him.

Being in her flat felt strange. He'd been there before on occasion, but most of the time they spent together was at his mum's house or Noah's house or at the pub. They weren't often in each other's homes. The open-plan kitchen-living room was a little messy with the sink full of dishes and a couple of plates and glasses sitting on the coffee table.

"Do you want a drink or anything?" Seren asked.

"No. I'm okay, thanks."

"I presume you got the afternoon off with all that rain?" She moved to the couch and shifted a basket of washing to the floor.

"Yeah. Was the pub busy today?"

"Not really." She took a seat and he did the same. The small talk felt uncomfortable, and he knew he should get to the point of his visit.

"I had a really good time last weekend," he said, his voice slightly too loud.

"Me too."

"It was great to spend so much time with you." He wiped his clammy hands on his jeans. "I wanted to tell you …" Oh god, what was he doing? He should have prepared what he was going to say. Declaring that he loved her felt dramatic, but the alternative was to say he liked her or fancied her … which was nowhere close to how he felt.

"Tell me what?" she asked when the silence stretched on. "Is this about the money I owe you? Because I—"

He cut her off. "It's not about the money. I actually wanted to pay for you."

"I don't need you to pay for me, Kit."

"I know you don't." He stood up and paced the room, needing to release some of his built-up adrenaline. "You can give me money for the trip if it'll make you feel better. Or not. I don't care. That's not what I wanted to talk to you about."

She rubbed at her temples as though the conversation made her weary. "What did you want to talk about?"

"It's a bit awkward … maybe … I'm not sure … I just wanted to tell you …" He stopped dead, shoving his hands in his pockets as he looked at her. "I love you."

She stared up at him for a moment, not a trace of surprise in her features.

The silence dragged on and every second felt unbearable. He cleared his throat. "I'm fairly sure you don't feel the same, but I just thought I'd tell you and then … I don't know. I just love you. I'm in love with you, I mean."

Tilting her head, she gave him a sympathetic smile. "Do you know Noah had a crush on me once? It lasted a few weeks and then he was over it. This is probably the same."

"I didn't know that," he said, slightly disturbed by the notion. "But I don't have a crush on you. It's not like that. I'm in love with you. I have been for a while."

She stared at her hands in her lap, nodding lightly as though digesting the information.

"I had to tell you," he said, needing to fill the silence. "I'm not sure what I was expecting, but it's been eating away at me. I needed to get it off my chest." He paused, but she only put her head in her hands. "Can you say something?" he asked gently.

She didn't look at him. "I don't know what to say."

"You don't seem surprised," he ventured. "Did you already know how I felt?"

"No." She shook her head. "Maybe. I sort of suspected … but I didn't *know*."

"And now that you do know?"

"Oh god, Kit," she whispered, wiping her fingers under her eyes. "I'm sorry."

"Sorry for what?" The conversation didn't seem to be going his way, but he needed her to spell things out for him. After she'd smashed his heart to smithereens, he could set to work putting it back together for someone else.

"The last thing I'd ever want to do is hurt you."

He let her words sink in for a moment. "I guess that tells me everything I need to know."

"I'm sorry," she said, tears shining in her eyes when she finally looked at him. "You're so sweet …"

"But you just don't see me that way? It's okay. You can't help how you feel. Or *don't* feel in this case."

"You're such a good friend," she said sadly.

He pushed the heels of his hands into his sockets, then dragged his fingers through his hair. "I've messed everything up, haven't I? I suppose it's not possible for us to pretend this conversation never happened?"

Standing, she put a hand on his arm, and he made an effort not to withdraw immediately. He wasn't sure he could cope with her sympathy as she ripped his heart out of his chest. "You can do so much better than me."

"I can't," he said, locking eyes with her. "There isn't anyone else for me." It hit him with a jolt of certainty. If he could scrape the pieces of his heart back together, the broken mess would still belong to her. Always.

"You only think that now." Her words were condescending, but the pain in her eyes was earnest.

"I think that now and I'll think it forever." His confidence was borderline comical, but he didn't care. There was no real difference between making a fool of yourself and making a *massive* fool of yourself. He was all in. "I love you," he said, taking the opportunity to say it once more before he left. He took a few steps towards the door.

"Kit," she sniffed, tears falling down her cheeks as she followed him. "I feel terrible."

"Don't." He wanted to wrap her in a hug but knew that wasn't a good idea. "I didn't come here with any expectations. I just needed you to know. We don't need to speak about it again." He squeezed her arm but couldn't look directly at her. "I'll let myself out."

Down on the street he waited for the crushing sensation in his chest to pass. Then he inhaled deeply and set off for home in the pouring rain. By the time he got there he was drenched and only paused to fire off a quick message to Trystan, saying that things hadn't gone well, before stripping off and getting in the shower. The hope that he'd been carrying with him for more than two years had gone and now he didn't feel much at all. Just a horrible numbness that no amount of time in the shower would wash away.

When he finally dragged himself out, he pulled on a pair of jogging bottoms and a T-shirt, then sat on the couch with his phone in his hand, registering missed calls from Trystan and Noah. It rang again after a moment and he hit the button to answer.

"Hi," he said to Noah. "I take it you've been in touch with Trystan?"

"He was worried when you didn't answer your phone. I was about to come over."

The concern of his brothers almost tipped him over the edge and he blinked back tears. "I'm okay," he said hoarsely.

"What happened?"

"I told Seren how I feel about her. It didn't go well."

"Shit," he replied.

Kit closed his eyes for a moment. "You knew, didn't you?"

"Knew what?"

"That she didn't feel the same. That's why you've never pushed me to talk to her. You knew it'd only mess things up between us."

His hesitation spoke volumes. "I didn't know for sure."

"Well, I've completely messed things up now anyway."

"No, you haven't. It'll probably be a bit awkward for a while, that's all."

"Can you go and check on her?" His chest clenched when he thought about her tear-streaked face. "She was upset when I left."

"I'm sure she's all right. I'll message her, but I'm going to come over and see you."

"I'm fine. Please go and see her."

"Keira's here. I'll send Keira to check on Seren and I'll come to you. I'll bring beers."

Kit sat up straight and tried to keep his anger under control. "She won't want to see Keira. You're her best friend. She'll want to talk to you. Please just go over there."

"Fine. I'll check on Seren, then I'm coming to you."

"Thank you." He ended the call and dropped his head to his hands.

CHAPTER TWELVE

Seren had known as soon as she'd opened the door to Kit what he was going to say. She wished he hadn't. Them denying their feelings for each other wasn't ideal, but it was better than the current situation. Hurting Kit was the worst thing she'd ever done. All she'd wanted to do was kiss him and tell him she was confused and scared but she felt the same.

The tears wouldn't let up as she perched on the edge of the couch, cradling her head in her hands. It would never have worked, she reminded herself. She had a track record of messing up relationships, and with Kit she'd be risking too much.

The sound of the doorbell spurred her to dry her eyes, not that she intended to answer it. When it rang again, her resolve dissipated and she made her way down.

Anger coursed through her at the sight of Noah standing out in the rain, though she wasn't sure why she was angry. "What are you doing here?" she snapped.

"Nice to see you too," he said with a sheepish smile. "I brought crab cakes from Tanglewood Kitchen."

The fact that he'd brought her favourite food should have softened her mood, but all it did was remind her of the times they'd hung out at her place eating takeaway from the Tangle-wood Kitchen. Now it never happened.

"Considering you never come to my place any more, I'm assuming Kit sent you?"

His eyebrows drew together. "Are you annoyed with me?"

"No," she said unconvincingly.

"It seems as though you are. And I can understand why. I promised we'd still be friends and I've been a really crap friend … I'm just trying to help Keira settle in and—"

"I'm not annoyed with you. At least I wasn't until I saw you. And I guess that's because I'm generally annoyed. Everything is going to annoy me today."

"Can I come in so the whole town doesn't hear our conversation?"

She didn't budge from the doorway. "Kit told you to come over here, didn't he? I can't believe him. I upset him and he still told you to check on me."

"He was worried he'd upset you …"

Her chest hitched involuntarily before her face crumpled and more tears came. "*I* upset *him*," she said, her words garbled by a sob.

Noah stepped inside and closed the door behind him before embracing her tightly. She let herself cry into his shoulder for a few minutes before pulling herself together and leading the way upstairs.

"I feel horrible," she said, slumping against the sideboard in the kitchen. "He looked so hurt. You should have gone to check on him, not me."

"I'll do that next." He put the takeaway packages on the counter and moved to fill the kettle. "I take it you don't feel the same way he does?"

She stared at her feet, wishing things were that simple. "It's *Kit.*"

"What's that supposed to mean?"

"It means he's the little kid who followed us everywhere with his constant annoying chatter."

"He *was,*" Noah pointed out unhelpfully. "He's not a kid any more."

"He practically is," she mumbled.

Noah folded his arms over his chest as he waited for the kettle to boil. "Do you really still see him as a kid? Half the time I feel as though he's more mature than me with the way he coped with Dad's death and how he's supported Mum. At the same time, he never takes his eye off the ball with his business. Not many twenty-two-year-olds are as dedicated to their job as he is."

"He's pretty much family," she said, taking a different tack since she couldn't argue with anything he'd just said.

Noah quirked an eyebrow. "No, he's not."

"You know what I mean. We grew up together."

"You've known him his whole life, but you grew up in different houses with different parents. The fact that you spent a lot of time together as kids doesn't mean you can't have a relationship with him as an adult."

"Why does it sound as though you want me to get together with Kit?" she asked accusingly.

"I'm just surprised by the way the conversation's going. I thought you'd say you don't feel the same, but instead you're making up excuses for why you can't be with him ..."

"I'm not making up excuses."

"It sounds as though you are. If you have feelings for Kit you can say so."

"That would be convenient for you, wouldn't it? If I got together with Kit you wouldn't need to feel guilty about the fact that you completely ditched me when you got a girlfriend."

He opened his mouth but clearly thought better of it and got on with making tea instead. Seren's whole body felt tense as she grabbed a fork and the container with the crab cakes and went to the couch.

"Sorry," she whispered when Noah placed two cups of tea on the coffee table and sat beside her.

"I'm not entirely sure what you're so upset about. Is it to do with Kit or me? I'm pretty confused."

"Me too." She leaned into his chest when he put an arm around her. "I'm not annoyed with you. I promise."

"What's going on then?"

"I'm not even sure myself." She took a moment to calm down and get her thoughts in order. "I spent loads of time with Kit while you were away in Bristol. He was always around … in the pub or at your mum's place. I don't think I appreciated what a good friend he's become … I hate that I've hurt him. And I don't know how things will be between us now. I don't want to lose him as a friend."

He squeezed her shoulders. "You won't."

"I feel as though I will." Opening her takeaway box, she stabbed a piece of crab cake and shovelled it into her mouth. It tasted better when she was in a good mood, but it made great comfort food too. "How can it not be awkward between us?"

"It might take a little while, but this will all blow over and everything will be fine. I don't think he expected you to tell him you feel the same. I reckon part of him just wanted to check he had no chance so he can move on."

The thought made her stomach lurch and she set the food aside. She wasn't sure what was worse: the idea of Kit being heartbroken because of her or the thought of him casually getting over her and moving on to someone else. With her head nestled against Noah's chest, she let herself imagine how different her day would have been if she'd been brave enough to tell Kit how she really felt.

Quickly, she put the brakes on that train of thought. A relationship with Kit would mean risking her relationships with every member of his family. There was too much to lose, and she couldn't stand the thought of any more loss in her life.

"Can you go and see if Kit's okay?" she asked, wiping tears from her cheeks as she sat up.

"Can I drink my tea first?"

She sighed heavily. "I'd rather you didn't. I want to be alone. And I'll be happier knowing Kit's not on his own."

"Are you sure you're not annoyed with me?" Noah asked as he stood.

"I'm not."

He looked at her sadly. "I'm sorry I haven't been around much."

"I see you at work often enough."

"That doesn't really count."

She gave him a hug. "Honestly, it's fine. You want to spend time with Keira and that's completely normal. I'm happy for you. I shouldn't have snapped at you. It's just been a long day."

"Call me if you need anything?"

"I will. Let me know Kit's okay."

He kissed her forehead and she flopped back onto the couch when he headed for the door.

CHAPTER THIRTEEN

I t shouldn't have come as a surprise to Seren that she didn't see Kit the following day on her way into work. Every time the door to the pub opened, she held her breath, hoping it might be him. She'd messaged him the previous evening while she lay awake in bed, telling him she was sorry and hoped he was okay. He'd replied with two words: *I'll survive.* It did nothing to make her feel better. Desperately, she wanted some reassurance that he was okay and that they could still be friends. That was probably optimistic, but she couldn't stand the thought of not seeing him regularly – or of not having him in her life.

When Felix wandered into the pub in the middle of the afternoon, her jaw clenched.

"What do you want?" she asked.

He leaned on the bar. "Depends what's on offer?"

Unceremoniously, she handed him a menu.

"How about a date?" he asked, setting the menu aside.

She walked away, going over to chat to a couple of regulars at the table by the window. To her surprise, Felix left a few minutes later. With the coast clear she went back around the bar and spotted a napkin where he'd been sitting, the word sorry written on it in a large scrawl. The guy really was pathetic. Seren balled up the napkin and tossed it in the bin. If nothing else, Felix was a good reminder of how terrible Seren was at relationships. Every relationship she'd ever been in had ended in disaster.

By the time her shift came to an end she was itching to get away from the pub. Noah was on the late shift and was chatting inanely while she inched towards the door.

"Did you hear from Keira?" he asked. "She was going to see if you wanted to hang out with her tonight."

"She messaged me earlier but I didn't have a chance to reply. I'll call her when I get home." She flicked her hand in a wave and hurried to the door. Kit would have finished for the day and be cleaning up the train before heading home. A smile and a wave was all she needed. Just some indication that their friendship wasn't completely dead.

After powerwalking through the town, her stomach dropped when she glanced along the promenade. There was no sign of Kit or the train.

At the sound of her name, she pushed down her emotions and turned around, forcing herself to return Keira's smile.

"I was just on my way to your place. Did you get my message earlier?"

"Yeah. I was going to call you in a bit."

She screwed her nose up. "Are you okay?"

Seren glanced back to where the train would usually be parked. "I was hoping I might catch Kit but he's already left. Have you seen him today?" One of the reasons she hadn't replied to Keira's message was because she didn't think she could face spending the evening chatting about Kit. Now having someone to talk to was appealing.

"I called him this morning to see if I could go out on the train with him, but he didn't answer the phone. When I messaged him, he fobbed me off."

"Let's go to my place. I've got wine." They fell into step together. "I guess you heard what happened?"

"Yeah." Keira's smile was full of sympathy, but she didn't say anything more.

"He's going to avoid me from now on and things will be weird between us forever."

"I'm sure things will be fine eventually. It's understandable that he wants to hide away and lick his wounds for a while."

"I feel like crap," Seren admitted as they wandered along. "He's the last person in the world I'd ever want to hurt."

"It's not as though you set out to hurt him." Keira fell silent for a moment. "I have a confession to make," she said when they were almost at Seren's place.

"What?"

"I knew Kit liked you, and I encouraged him to tell you how he felt." She looked genuinely remorseful. "I should have kept my opinions to myself, but I thought maybe you felt the same. I'm sorry."

"It's not your fault." Seren fumbled for her keys in her pocket. "Kit's not easily led. He wouldn't have said anything unless he'd come to the decision himself."

"It's a shame you don't like him back," Keira remarked, following Seren inside and up the stairs. "Kit's such a sweetheart. He'd make a great boyfriend."

Seren's heart pounded and she was terrified that her feelings were written all over her face. "I think so too," she said weakly.

"You just don't feel that way about him?"

"It's hard to think of him as anything other than a friend." She went to the fridge and busied herself with the wine. "He's also really young."

"Very mature though." Keira leaned against the counter. "I'm probably being paranoid, but I'm concerned that he's annoyed with me for encouraging him to speak to you. I've been telling myself that him not wanting me to go on the train with him today is only because he wants to be alone and not that he's angry with me. It's hard though. Kit's been so welcoming and I was excited about working with him … now I'm not sure that will happen."

Seren shook her head. "Kit won't blame you. Even if he did, he'd forgive you in a second. He doesn't hold grudges." She passed Keira a glass of white wine. "He's loyal. If he's your friend, he's your friend for life." She smiled lightly. "I need to remember this too. Kit's not going to avoid me forever. It's like you said, he just needs some time. Who wouldn't?"

"You're right." Keira clinked her glass against Seren's. "Everything will be fine eventually."

"How are you settling into island life?" Seren led the way to the couch, then listened as Keira chatted away, talking about the research she'd been doing to prepare for giving tours on the train. Enthusiasm radiated from her as she jabbered away.

Talking to Keira about Kit had made Seren feel more rational about the situation. It felt huge now but in time things would settle.

That's what she told herself when she didn't see Kit the following day, or the day after that. By Sunday, she was starting to think she might have made the worst decision of her life. With Kit on her mind constantly, she couldn't help but think about the possibility of telling him the truth of how she felt. Would it really be so bad?

She messaged him again, saying she hoped he'd had a good week. It took him an hour to reply and then it was only with a thumbs up emoji. Her fingers hovered over the keypad, tempted to tell him that she missed him and couldn't stop thinking about him. She even typed the words, then deleted them almost immediately.

To distract herself, she set off to visit Mirren. In the back of her mind, she thought Kit might be there or call up at some point. When she arrived, there was no sign of him, but she was on tenterhooks thinking he might arrive at any moment. That was if he didn't see her car parked on the lane and turn around quick.

Sitting on the patio with Mirren under a dazzling blue sky, Seren wondered if she had any idea of the situation with her and Kit.

"Have you seen Kit?" she asked tentatively. "I thought he might be up here scrounging food from you."

"Whenever I speak to him at the moment he's busy. I'm pleased that Keira's going to be helping with the train this summer. It should give him more of a break. Although he was talking about helping more at the lifesaving club. I guess he likes being busy."

"I haven't seen him much this week." Seren pulled her sunglasses down her nose to peer at the friendly house sparrows hopping around beneath the table.

"Have you seen anything of Cadan since he's been back?"

"Not much. He comes in the pub sometimes, but that's about it."

"I heard Felix is back too?"

"Just for the summer, not for good." Seren really didn't want to get into a conversation about Felix. After pushing her sunglasses into place, she gazed out to sea for a moment. The vastness of the blue-green water made her problems feel slightly less overwhelming. Finally, she snapped her eyes back to Mirren. "Can I ask your advice about something?"

"Always."

Seren inhaled deeply. The situation with Kit was made more frustrating by having no one to talk to about it. But there was no reason she couldn't ask Mirren's advice if she didn't mention who they were talking about and kept things vague.

"I take it from the look on your face that it's man trouble?" Mirren prompted.

"Yes." She caught a drop of condensation that slid down her water glass. "There's someone I like, but it's a bit complicated."

"Who is it?"

Seren chuckled. "I'm not telling you that."

"It was worth a try," she said with a smile. "Do I know him?"

Seren did her best to look thoughtful. "You've probably seen him around."

"Why is it complicated? Is he with someone else? Please tell me he's not married or anything?"

"No! Of course not."

"Does he like you?"

"He says so."

"If you like him and he likes you, why is it complicated?"

"You know me and my habit of falling for the wrong guys. I'm worried it would end up being a lot of drama and upset."

The corners of Mirren's lips twitched upwards. "That doesn't usually stop you."

"True. But I think it's time I started being more sensible in my choices." She winced. "I can't stop thinking about him, but it feels all wrong."

"Trust your instincts," Mirren said. "If it feels wrong it probably is. When you find the right person, you'll know without a doubt."

"Maybe."

She didn't like to mention that it wasn't the thought of *being* with him that felt wrong. It was the fact that their lives were already so intertwined that being with him felt like too much of a risk. Any previous drama with guys would pale into insignificance if she got together with Kit and things didn't work out.

CHAPTER FOURTEEN

On Tuesday Seren was on her way to the supermarket when she checked her watch and realised that Kit's afternoon train ride was due to set off. Without much thought, she walked in the direction of the beach, wondering if she might make it in time to at least catch a glimpse of him. She was almost there when the train pulled up the road towards her. The fact that Kit was in a moving vehicle meant she couldn't speak to him, but it felt good to set eyes on him.

He was speaking to the passengers over the PA system but smiled at Seren and lifted his chin in acknowledgement. Her heart felt like it was being crushed and she stood rooted to the spot as she watched him go by.

Seeing him in passing was nowhere near enough. It never would be. She needed to hang out with him and joke around like they always had done. She wanted to touch him. To kiss him. She wanted everything, and increasingly she couldn't remember why she thought she shouldn't be with him.

At work that evening, she moved on autopilot. Her body was in the pub, but her mind was elsewhere, flitting between excitement at the idea of admitting her true feelings to Kit, then shrouded with doubts about the possible ways things could go wrong.

After spending most of the evening and a restless night chewing things over, she was still no closer to deciding what to do. To make things worse, it was her day off so she had nothing to do but contemplate. At the rate she was going, she'd drive herself crazy thinking about it.

With a rush of restless energy, she walked down to the harbour and waited for the inter-island ferry to take her to Bryher. The wind whipped at her hair, pulling strands from her ponytail as the boat trundled over gentle waves.

Once she'd disembarked at Anneka's quay, she wandered slowly through the town and emerged at the opposite side of the island to look out over the beach at Great Par. Seabirds sailed on the breeze, filling the salty air with their squawks and cries. The sun on her face made Seren's cheeks tingle and she pulled her hoodie off to tie it around her waist before continuing down to the beach. Slipping her sandals off, she squished her toes into the cool sand with every step.

It was at least a few weeks since she'd last been to visit Lowen. She felt a pang of guilt that she didn't visit him more often. He wasn't the easiest person to be around though, and to be fair she saw him more often than some members of the family. Noah and Kit didn't go over to Bryher often at all. Her stomach knotted to a ball of tension as she thought about how close the Treneary brothers had been a few years back. The falling out between Lowen and Mirren had caused a ripple of tension, and Seren wasn't sure they'd ever get past it.

She wasn't surprised to find the pottery shop empty. It was too isolated to attract much in the way of passing trade – which was only part of the problem. Lowen also didn't make much effort to attract customers. He didn't advertise the presence of his shop, and the place wasn't exactly welcoming. From the outside it was hard to know it was even open. There was no bell over the door to alert Lowen of her arrival. If she were a legitimate customer, she'd be left wondering if it was okay to come in at all. As it was, she had a quick browse of the shelves, taking in the beautiful mugs, plates, bowls and vases. They deserved to be displayed in a more artful fashion.

"Hi," she said when she walked through the open archway at the end of the room, following the whir of the pottery wheel.

Lowen switched the wheel off and wiped his clay-covered hands on a towel draped over his shoulder. "Hi. How are you?"

"Fine, thanks. How are you?"

"Same old. Busy." He glanced pointedly around at the various pottery projects on individual wooden boards.

"Don't let me stop you."

She stroked the ginger cat curled up by Lowen's feet, then hopped up onto the sideboard across from him. It was her usual spot to sit and witter away while he worked. The one-sided conversations used to bother her, until she found that it could be therapeutic to chatter away as though no one was listening. Most of the time she was sure he *wasn't* listening. With the look of concentration on his face as he worked the clay, she was certain he wasn't thinking of anything else.

After pressing the foot pedal to turn the wheel on again, Lowen dipped his hands in water before getting back to work. Seren studied his profile, remembering a time when he'd taken pride in his appearance. Now, his dark blonde hair was in dire need of a cut and his jaw was covered in an unkempt beard with flecks of grey, which she'd never noticed before. He'd lost weight in the last couple of years, but he didn't look well for it. Seren's gaze shifted to his hands, mesmerised by the way they moved so instinctively over the clay.

"What's going on with you?" he asked, as though the silence bothered him.

"Not a lot." She started by telling him the mundane stuff – the regulars at work, the number of holidaymakers, the weather. She went on to tell him how her dad and Naomi and Charlie were, even though he hadn't asked.

"I was in London a couple of weeks ago," she told him eventually. "Kit and I went to stay with Trystan for the weekend."

"How is he?"

"Not great. Jenny broke up with him."

"So I heard. I presumed they'd have sorted things out again by now."

She swung her legs back and forth like a small child. "Jenny wants him to buy her out of the flat, so it's definitely over."

"Seriously?" He stopped the wheel to look up at her and she nodded in reply. "How's Trystan taken it?"

"He was a bit upset when we were there. But you know Trystan – he puts on a brave face. He doesn't talk about it much." She searched his features, surprised at how Lowen didn't bother to hide his concern. "You should call him. If he'd talk to anyone, it'd be you."

He ran a finger over the clay in front of him, making some tiny adjustment. "Are you hungry? We could go up to the hotel for lunch."

"Sure. If you're paying. I'm skint."

"I'm paying," he said, amusement in his voice. He plucked a hoody from a rickety wooden chair in the corner.

"Aren't you getting changed?" she asked, looking him up and down. His jeans and T-shirt were covered in smears of clay.

"Wasn't planning on it." He treated her to a small smile. "You embarrassed to be seen with me or something?"

"Nope. Just wasn't sure they'd let you in the place like that."

"They're quite used to me and my casual attire."

"Casual?" she said amid a burst of laughter. "What I'm wearing is casual. What you're wearing is scruffy."

"I might change my mind about buying you lunch in a minute."

"Let's go quick then."

They didn't speak as they ambled along the beach with the warm wind blasting their faces. There wasn't another soul to be seen, and Seren was reminded of how much more remote Bryher felt than St Mary's.

On the restaurant's terrace, Seren turned her chair to face the sun. She asked Lowen about work, managing to get him chatting about the projects he'd been working on and some new techniques he'd been trying out with glazes. He could be quite chatty if you steered the conversation in the right direction. Unfortunately, it took a fair amount of patience. Most of the time he was unapologetically monosyllabic.

"How's everything with Noah's girlfriend?" he asked when they'd finished eating and were sipping coffees.

"Good. He's all loved up and everything seems to be going well."

"It seemed that way when they came over here the other week. She was saying Kit had offered her a job on the train."

"Yes. He's been training her up."

He smiled lightly. "If Kit gets on with her she must be all right."

"That's how you judge people? On whether Kit likes them? That seems like a poor way to judge, considering Kit likes everyone."

"I know. But if Kit *doesn't* like someone that's a very bad sign."

"True." She felt her smile slip and took a sip of coffee as her chest tightened. Her plan for the day hadn't been to sit around discussing Kit's virtues.

"I take it Kit's doing well?" Lowen asked.

She pursed her lips and fought off tears. "I don't really know. We've hardly spoken since we got back from London."

"Did you fall out or something?"

"Kind of … not really … I don't know."

He waited for her to say more, then shrugged when she didn't. "I'm sure he's fine. Kit's about the happiest person I know."

Every muscle in Seren's body tensed. "As far as I know he's actually pretty miserable."

"Why?" His tone was suspicious, as though she might be trying to trick him.

"He's your brother. Ask him yourself."

"Did you come here today to make a point about me not calling my brothers enough?"

"*Not enough?*" she asked with a humourless laugh. "Do you ever call them?"

"We message now and again. I talk to them when I see them."

"Which is like once in a blue moon!"

He stared at her. "What's your problem?"

"You," she spat. "You're my problem. Why can't you swallow your pride and sort everything out? You can't claim not to care about your family and then sit here quizzing me about how your brothers are doing."

His jaw tightened as he stared out to sea, then his gaze dropped to the sand dunes and the long grass which leaned with the wind. "I never claimed not to care about them," he muttered as he pushed his chair back and stood up. "I need to get back to work."

When he stalked inside the restaurant, she waited for a moment, blinking back tears until her legs finally got into gear. He'd paid the bill by the time she walked inside, and she had to hurry to catch up with him as he left through the front door. On the front path he upped his pace and ignored Seren's pleas for him to slow down.

Finally, she gave up and stopped in her tracks. "Don't you miss them?" she shouted after him, fully expecting him to march on without looking back. To her surprise he stopped and looked back at her in concern.

"What's going on with you?" he asked.

Fat tears pooled on her lower lids. "Don't you miss how it

used to be? When we were one big happy family and the best thing in the world was having all of us together."

"It was never like that," he said, walking back to her. "Not for me."

"It was for me. I miss it." She didn't believe that he didn't miss being part of his brothers' lives and knowing what was going on with them from day to day. "I miss *you,*" she said sadly.

He slung an arm around her shoulders and they set off again, walking slowly across the island in the direction of the quay.

"Is Kit okay?" Lowen asked when they rounded the bend and the stone jetty came into view.

"Probably," she said with a shrug. "I honestly don't know."

He blew out a breath. "Are *you* okay?"

"Not really, no."

"Can I do anything?"

"No. I'll be okay. I just need to figure some things out."

He stopped and looked out at the day tripper coming into view. "Thanks for visiting."

"Are you serious?" She wrinkled her brow. "I cost you lunch and annoyed the heck out of you!"

He kissed her cheek. "I'm always happy to buy you lunch and listen to you rant at me."

"I'm not sure that's true."

"The part about lunch is," he said, taking a few steps backwards. "Take care."

"You too," she whispered, then watched him walk away.

As the wind whipped around her on the ride back to St Mary's, all she could think was how much she didn't want to end up like Lowen: cut off from everyone she cared about and seeing each other occasionally to exchange polite conversation while pretending nothing had changed.

She'd been right about her decision not to start anything with Kit.

All she needed to do was make sure she stuck to it.

CHAPTER FIFTEEN

A voiding Seren wasn't difficult on a practical level. Kit's main difficulty was overriding his *desire* to see her. She wasn't an easy habit to break. A few times he considered pretending he hadn't declared his undying love for her so he could continue his routine of ensuring their paths crossed multiple times a day.

It wouldn't do any good though. Besides, he was reserving all his fake happy vibes for his paying customers, so there was no way he could manage to convince Seren he was fine. Even passing her while he was driving the train had been hard. His forced smile had felt as though it might break him.

It wasn't only Seren he was avoiding. He'd happily hide from the whole world if he could, but the more he retreated, the more his family closed in on him. Noah and Trystan called and messaged him regularly. While he appreciated their concern, he'd rather they left him alone. Thankfully his mum hadn't got wind of the situation or he'd never get any peace.

He was sitting at his kitchen table on Wednesday morning when his phone vibrated with a call from Keira. He answered it with a wry smile.

"You're persistent," he said. "Anyone ever tell you that?"

"I'm worried about you … and …"

"And you want to come with me on the train?"

"Can I?"

"I thought you were back to your office job now."

"I am, but it turns out I'm much more efficient away from the office. And I'm only supposed to be working twenty hours a week, so I have loads of free time."

Kit massaged the nape of his neck. "How about you come with me this morning?"

"Perfect! I'll see you at the promenade in a bit."

When he arrived there an hour later, Keira was already waiting and flung her arms around him when he stepped out of the train.

"I was worried you hated me," she said, her brow wrinkled.

"Of course I don't hate you."

"You've been avoiding me."

"I've been avoiding everyone," he told her. "It was nothing personal."

"I'm sorry anyway. I've been feeling pretty bad about the whole thing."

"It was me who got my heart broken." He managed a smile. "How come you were feeling bad?"

"Because I pushed you into saying something to Seren. I should never have involved myself."

"I think I knew you'd encourage me to do something about it. I'd been wanting to tell her for a while. I needed someone to give me a nudge. And to be fair, it was Trystan who convinced me to say something in the end, so you really needn't feel bad."

She arched an eyebrow. "It would've been nice if you'd told me that a week ago."

"Excuse me for being too busy nursing my broken heart to worry about how you've been doing!" He laughed and the release felt good.

Her eyes widened dramatically. "I didn't mean to sound so self-centred. It's just that you've been so nice to me, so I hated the thought of falling out with you. I was honestly concerned about you too."

"I was winding you up." He gave her arm an affectionate tap. "We're all good, I promise."

A family with two kids approached and Kit opened a door for them to board before continuing along the train to open all the doors.

Keira smiled brightly as she followed him. "I have a surprise for you."

"What is it?" he asked dubiously.

"I've been swotting up," she told him at the back of the train. "So I can do everything now."

"What do you mean?"

"I can drive the train and give the tour. I can collect the money too and welcome the passengers. It can be like a job interview today. You can observe me and then decide if you want me to work for you."

"Today? Like now?"

"Yes."

"Um … okay… if you're sure you want to?"

"Yes." She nodded firmly. "I'm all prepared." Pulling a sheaf of paper from her back pocket, she unfolded it and scanned the pages. "Oh god. There's a lot of information. My mind's going to go blank."

"You don't have to take the tour today," Kit said, wavering over the thought of having someone working for him on a regular basis.

"I can do it." Keira took a breath and shoved the papers back into her pocket before she swung around to greet the customers, who were arriving in a steady trickle.

Hanging back and letting Keira take the reins wasn't easy. Once they set off it took a few minutes of speaking into the microphone before her nerves faded. Even then it was difficult for Kit to quell the urge to jump in and add information that she'd missed. At one point he reached to take the headset from her, but she slapped his hand away and switched off the PA system as she shot him a frosty glare.

"You said I don't have to give the tour exactly as you do," she reminded him. "If I'm going to work for you, you won't always be here to jump in. Can you just let me do it?"

"Sorry," he whispered sheepishly. She was doing a great job anyway, so there was really no need to intervene. It was only habit. Sinking lower in his seat, he let Keira get on with it.

By the time they arrived back at the promenade and the passengers had dispersed, she looked as though she might burst with excitement.

"How did I do?" She bounced on the balls of her feet as she waited for a response.

"Great."

"Really?"

"Yes. You were brilliant."

She put her hands together in a prayer-like gesture and pressed her index fingers to her lips. "Does that mean I can have a job?"

"I guess so." He nodded slowly.

"You don't sound very enthusiastic. If you don't want me to give me a job you can say so."

Kit sank onto the passenger seat, sitting sideways so he faced Keira, who stood beside the train. "Sorry," he said, raking his hands through his hair. "When we first talked about you working with me, I thought taking a couple of days off each week sounded pretty nice ... but with everything with Seren ..."

"Work's a good distraction?" she asked.

"Yeah." He'd even been thinking of adding another tour into the daily schedule to keep himself busy.

"It's totally fine," Keira said in a rush, smiling through her evident disappointment. "I understand. At least I know what I'm doing now, so I can jump in if you ever want time off or if you're ill or anything."

"Yeah. I'm really sorry."

"Don't be." Her smile looked forced, and he was slightly worried she might start crying. "I had fun today anyway," she said firmly. "I got lots of tips too." She pulled a bunch of notes and coins from her pocket and held them out to him.

"That's yours," he said, when he registered that she was waiting for him to take the money.

"All of it?" she asked. "Don't we share it?"

"I didn't do anything. Why should I take your tips?"

"It's quite a lot of money." She looked down at it thoughtfully. "Do you get tips like this every time you take a tour?"

"It varies, but that looks pretty standard."

Keira dropped the coins into her pocket, then straightened out the notes. "I'm sorry to tell you this, but I'm probably going to spend a lot of time hoping you get ill. Nothing serious, of course, just a head cold that forces you to spend a few days in bed."

Kit shook his head in amusement. "Sod it, you can have a job."

"But you just said you want to work more."

"I know, but I'd already offered you work. It's pretty crap of me to go back on it after you've spent so much time memorising facts about the island. Working seven days a week isn't going to help me get over Seren anyway. I'd be better off finding something else to do with my time."

"Like what?"

He shrugged as he stood up. "I volunteer at the lifesaving club and I'm always saying that if I had more time I'd help out more. They're desperate for swim instructors and for people to help run the kids' clubs over the summer." He pondered the idea for a moment and decided that would keep his mind much more occupied than just doing the train tours. Teaching local kids about water safety always felt fulfilling too – like he was doing something worthwhile.

"You're a swimming teacher?" Keira asked in surprise.

"Yeah. I got certified when I was eighteen and offered

classes for a while before I bought the train. Sometimes I give private lessons if someone specifically asks, but it's not something I do regularly any more. Which is a shame. I enjoy it."

"So, it would be useful for me to help with the train?"

"Yeah. Would it be okay for you to work every morning from Monday to Friday in August? That would free me up to help with the kids' club."

"I'd love to. My other work is flexible. I can do that in the afternoons."

"Perfect. We'll have to figure out a schedule for the rest of the time. See what's best for us both."

Keira beamed from ear to ear and smothered Kit in a hug. "Thank you so much. I've never been this excited about a job before." She released him and took a step back. "I've worked in marketing for the past eight years, so if you need any help with the advertising and marketing side of things just let me know."

"I'll bear it in mind."

"When should I start?"

"I'll need to draw up a contract and make sure we have everything set up officially. I'll get on that as soon as I can. How about we discuss everything again next week and go from there?"

She grinned. "I can't wait to tell Noah."

"You better go and tell him then."

"Wait … what do you do in between trips? I need to know everything."

"I wipe the seats down and check for any rubbish that's been left behind. That's about it."

"I can do that," she said eagerly.

"You don't need to do it now. Get back home and see Noah."

She hugged him again before hurrying away.

Keira's enthusiasm left him feeling a little more upbeat. Getting more involved at the lifesaving club would be good for him, and with the height of tourist season just around the corner he'd soon be too busy to dwell on his heartbreak.

By the end of the day, his newfound positivity had dwindled slightly. He checked his watch after saying goodbye to the last of his passengers. If he waited half an hour, Seren would emerge after her day shift. It was easy to kill half an hour chatting to whoever was around the promenade or grabbing a coffee in one of the cafes. Cleaning up the train took a bit of time too if he chose to do that at the promenade rather than back at the garage.

He needed to break away from his old habits though. It was time for him to start looking to the future. His days of stalking Seren were over.

Lost in his internal motivational speech, he didn't notice Holly until she called his name. Her blonde curls bobbed around her shoulders as she quickened her pace.

"Hi," he said as she neared him. "How are you?"

"Good thanks."

He squinted. "Keira said you were looking for me a couple of weeks ago ... I only just remembered."

"It wasn't important." She shook her head as a blush hit her pale cheeks. "I just wanted to ask you something ..." She bit down on her lip and drummed her fingers against her thigh.

"If it's about the train tickets again, I'm really not interested in selling tickets from the tourist office. For several reasons."

"No. It wasn't about that."

"Do you want to give me a clue then?" he asked, sounding curter than he'd intended.

"Yes. Sorry. It's nothing ... I just wondered ..." She glanced around. "I was wondering if I could come on the train with you sometime?"

"If you're looking for a job, you're a few hours too late. I took someone else on this morning."

"It's not that," she said in a rush. "It's only that I spend a lot of time recommending your tour to sightseers. Everyone says it's great and your online reviews are fantastic. But I thought it might be nice to have actually experienced it."

"Oh. Yeah sure. You're welcome to come along whenever

you want. Free of charge, of course. I'll even let you ride in the front with me."

"Thank you." Her shoulders sank and she gave him a small smile.

"I'm afraid you've missed the last trip for today though."

"Yes. Another day would be great. I'll look forward to it." She took a couple of steps backwards, then stopped abruptly. "Are you single?" she said in a rush, her voice rising in pitch.

"What?" He'd heard her, he was just slightly confused since the question seemed to come out of nowhere.

"Are you seeing anyone?" She winced. "I just wondered."

He swallowed hard, hoping she wasn't about to ask him out. "No. I'm not seeing anyone." He scuffed the toe of his shoe on the concrete when she didn't say any more. "Are you still with …" The name escaped him. "You were seeing the guy who works in the hotel, right?"

"Yes." She nodded, then switched to shaking her head. "We were together, but we're not any more."

"That's why you don't work at the hotel any more?"

"Yes." Her cheeks turned a deeper shade of scarlet. "Working together was difficult after we broke up."

"I can imagine." He took a deep breath and stepped into the driver's seat of the train. "I'm heading home if you need a lift somewhere?"

"No. I'm fine, thank you. I'm meeting a friend for a drink in the pub."

"Have a good night." He flashed her a smile and started the train, keen to avoid giving her a chance to ask him out. She seemed sweet, if slightly awkward. If it weren't for Seren he'd probably have been quite happy to go on a few dates with her and see what happened. It was bad timing though. Before he turned the corner, he glanced in the rear-view mirror.

Maybe it was actually perfect timing. Going on a few dates could be just the distraction he needed. It would also be a good way to get his brothers to accept he was fine and stop checking up on him. There was a possibility it would also ease the awkwardness with Seren. He could laugh off his declaration of love as a crush and get back to being friends with her. Not that he was sure he could cope with being friends with Seren.

With a quick shake of his head, he concentrated on the road again. Dating anyone now would be unfair to them and would only cause more complications in his life.

He definitely didn't need that.

CHAPTER SIXTEEN

When Keira came into the pub on Thursday, jabbering away about her new job, Seren schooled her features to an acceptable amount of enthusiasm. It wasn't easy with Keira cooing about how great Kit was and how excited she was about working with him.

To be fair, Keira *should* be excited – Kit *was* great, and working with him *would* be fantastic. Seren felt sick with jealousy that Keira had been spending time with Kit. And would continue to do so.

On Friday, she managed to convince herself that the only reason she couldn't stop thinking about Kit was because she never saw him any more. Just because they couldn't be in a relationship didn't mean they could never see each other.

She told Charlie she needed to leave work early and set off to catch Kit before he went home for the day. At Porthcressa Beach, gusts of wind lifted the top layer of sand, sending it swirling along before setting it down again. The warm air tasted of salt and seaweed as Seren marched along determinedly. Spotting the train at the end of the promenade, she picked up her pace but was intercepted by someone calling out to her before she got near the train.

She turned to see Felix and Cadan sitting outside a cafe, both with their legs stretched out in front of them.

"Hi." She flashed a smile but had no intention of stopping.

"We were about to come and look for you in the pub," Cadan called out.

"I'm not there, so you don't need to bother."

"Wait up …" Felix chased after her and she sighed in annoyance. "Did you get my message the other day?"

"Yep. I got it and I ignored it." He'd asked her out for a drink and the only emotion she could muster was annoyance at Cadan for giving Felix her number.

"I only wanted to catch up with you properly."

Up ahead, Seren could see Kit by the train. Around his legs were a gaggle of children of varying sizes, all of them looking up in wonder as Kit expertly twisted a long blue balloon into the shape of a sword. He tapped a blonde-haired girl on the head with it before handing to her and getting to work on the next creation.

Wearily, she flicked her eyes to Felix. "What makes you think I'd want to catch up with you?"

"Just let me take you out on one date …"

She rolled her eyes. "That's never going to happen so you can stop wasting your breath."

"Come on." He stepped into her personal space and lowered his head to her. "I apologised."

She took a step back. "I've never heard the word sorry cross your lips. I suspect it's not in your vocabulary."

"I thought writing it in a note would be more romantic."

"A note?" She couldn't help but laugh. "You scrawled one word on a napkin. It was hardly a heartfelt letter."

Stepping closer again, he rested a hand on her hip and tilted his head. "I'm sorry," he whispered.

"What exactly are you sorry for?" She peeled his fingers from her hip, but he seemed to take it as an invitation to hold her hand.

"Everything." He managed to look earnest as he gazed into her eyes. "I know I was a terrible boyfriend—"

She snorted a laugh. "Really? You think so?"

"I was young and stupid and didn't appreciate what a good thing I had."

"For once we agree on something."

"Give me another chance."

"No." Seren glanced along the promenade, thankful to find Kit facing the opposite direction, deep in conversation with a group of middle-aged men and women – presumably the parents of the kids who were proudly playing with their balloons.

"Why don't we go for a drink?" Felix asked. "Have a proper chat."

She yanked her hand from his grip. "Because you're the last person I'd want to go for a drink with."

"Give me a chance to show you I've changed."

"I know you haven't changed. Not that it matters. I've grown up and moved on. I have zero interested in stepping back into the past."

"Don't be like that."

"Please just go away." She really didn't want Kit to spot her talking to Felix.

A high-pitched whistle made them both turn. Cadan stood outside the cafe.

"Are we going for a drink or are you intending to hang around out here all night?"

"Come for a drink with us at least," Felix said to Seren.

"I've got things to do." She waved at Cadan before stalking away.

Kit stood by the train looking out over the water, his thick blonde hair ruffled by the breeze. She called out to him when she approached, and he turned slowly to look at her, his expression blank.

"How are you?" she asked brightly.

He pushed a hand through his hair to tame it. "Fine, thanks. How are you?"

"Not too bad, you know."

His gaze drifted over her shoulder, then he lifted his arm to check his watch. "I need to go," he said. "I'm meeting someone."

Seren's chest clenched and a lump formed in her throat.

"I'll see you later," Kit muttered as he moved around her.

Anger coursed through her and her blood pumped hard. "Kit," she shouted, her voice brittle.

He stopped and turned his head to one side, not far enough to look at her.

"How long are you going to ignore me for?"

"I'm not ignoring you," he said sadly. "I just have some-where to be now."

Kit felt as though he'd been punched in the gut when he saw Seren laughing with Felix. It'd been bad enough to be turned down by her, but to think she'd go for someone like Felix made it ten times worse. He'd had to look away when Felix put his hands on her. It had been a colossal effort to focus enough to chat to the group of parents who'd cornered him after the tour.

When Seren came over to him he could barely look at her. Seething, he told her he was meeting someone and stormed away. He wasn't meeting anyone – at least he hadn't arranged to – but a thought had popped into his head, and in his emotional turmoil he'd latched onto it. His determination increased as he strode to Porthcressa Road. He was going to ask Holly out.

There was no reason not to. Why should he mope around over Seren when she had absolutely no consideration for his feelings? Surely she knew how hard it would be for him to see her with Felix?

Well, he didn't owe her anything. So what if he immediately

moved on and started dating someone? That had been the point of telling her how he felt after all. To give him closure so he could move on.

His surge of adrenaline fizzled out when he reached the tourist information to find the sign on the door turned to closed. He didn't have Holly's number or know where she lived, so there was no way for him to get in touch with her.

At least the brisk walk had calmed him down a little. He blew out a long breath and was about to start back the way he'd come when a head of distinctive blonde curls stepped out of the supermarket further up the road.

Breaking into a jog, Kit crossed the narrow road at a diagonal, calling out to Holly as he went.

"I thought I'd missed you," he said, breathing hard when he stopped in front of her. "I went to the tourist office but it had already closed."

She held up her shopping bag. "I was just getting something for dinner before I head home."

"I keep thinking about our conversation the other day…" He shifted his weight from foot to foot. As his adrenaline faded, his confidence went with it. "When do you want to come out on the train?"

Her smile brought colour to her cheeks. "I don't," she said, shaking her head and pulling a stray strand of hair from her face.

"But you said you wanted to come so you could recommend it to people."

"I just said that." She looked slightly bashful. "It was pretty good for a spur of the moment excuse. Because it's genuinely a good idea."

"I'm lost," Kit said, utterly confused.

She moved her shopping bag to the opposite hand. "I came to ask you out on a date. I imagine that was obvious. But I lost my nerve, so I asked about the train trip instead. Then I was about to ask you out, but in my panic I realised that I didn't even know if you were single, so I asked that instead. And you looked so freaked out by the question that I knew there was no way you'd want to go out with me, so I gave up on the idea."

"Sorry." Kit found her honesty oddly endearing. "You took me by surprise. I haven't dated anyone in ages. My social skills are probably a bit rusty when it comes to dating."

They stood looking at each other for a moment before Holly broke the silence.

"I'm glad we've sorted that out then. We seem to have cleared all the awkwardness."

Kit chuckled at her teasing. "Do you want to go out sometime?"

"I thought you'd never ask." She beamed. "I'd really like to."

"How about dinner tonight?" As he said it, he remembered he had a gig race. Considering he hadn't raced the previous two weeks due to being in London and nursing his broken heart, he really ought to go. The physical exertion of the intense rowing would no doubt be good for him too. "I'm racing," he told her. "But I won't hang around after, so we can still have dinner at a reasonable hour."

"Well, I did have big plans to cook myself some pasta." She peered into her bag. "But I suppose that will keep. I presume you were thinking we'd go out for dinner … you weren't angling for an invite to sample my cooking? Because I'd advise against that."

"No. I can definitely take you out. Where do you fancy? The food at the hotel is pretty good …" He put a hand on her arm as she bit her lip. "That was a joke … sorry, it was pretty bad."

She inhaled a sharp breath then laughed loudly. "I'd actually love to see the look on Gavin's face if I went on a date at the hotel. I'm not sure I'm ready for that yet, though."

"How about Juliet's Garden? Any ex-boyfriends work there or are we safe?"

"Safe," she said happily. "I love it there."

"Good. I'll pick you up after the race." He squinted at her. "I've no idea where you live."

"Just over on Church Street. Near the museum." She gave him her phone to put his number in and told him she'd message him the address. As she took the phone back, her nose wrinkled. "Do you have a car?"

"No. I hope this doesn't sound like bragging, but I do have a train and a bus. Which one would you prefer I pick you up in?"

"I really hope that's another joke."

"Yeah." He smiled widely. "I also have a golf cart, but it looks as though it'll be a nice evening if you feel like a walk."

"A walk sounds good." She glanced over the road and winced slightly. "Is that your mum over there?"

"Great," Kit muttered, catching his mum's eye as she lingered outside the post office. "Now I'll have my mum asking me twenty questions about you."

Holly told him she'd see him later and looked amused as she wandered away.

Kit crossed the road to greet his mum.

"Who was that you were talking to?" Mirren asked.

"Holly. I went to school with her."

Mirren nodded. "I thought I recognised her. She works in the tourist information now, doesn't she? I didn't know you were friends with her."

"I see her around sometimes," he said vaguely.

"She looked as though she was flirting with you. I could hear her laughing from here."

"I'm a funny guy," Kit said flatly. "And I'm not sure why you sound so surprised by the idea of someone flirting with me."

"Is there something going on with the two of you?"

"No. She's just a friend." He wasn't about to tell his mother he was taking her out on a date later. "I have to go," he said, kissing her cheek and rushing away.

CHAPTER SEVENTEEN

Kit's enthusiasm for the evening with Holly waned before he even picked her up. After the exertion of rowing he could happily have gone and lazed around at home for the evening but reminded himself that going for dinner with Holly was a better option than feeling sorry for himself.

Conversation felt slightly strained as they walked up the hill to Juliet's Garden. The highlight of the casual cafe was the view over the harbour. They grabbed a table outside to enjoy the sunset, which had turned the sky a wonderful shade of peach and dappled the sea with flecks of red and orange.

"This is way better than what I had planned for dinner," Holly remarked as she tucked into a seafood salad.

Nodding, Kit swallowed his mouthful. "I really like the food here."

Usually, he was much better at keeping conversation flowing, but he was in the wrong frame of mind and was wishing he hadn't been so hasty with his decision to ask Holly out. Staying at home wallowing in self-pity suddenly felt like a decent plan for the evening.

Once she'd finished her food, Holly took a long swig of her wine and looked at him intently. "I was sorry about your dad."

Her words took him by surprise and he only managed to murmur an unintelligible reply.

"This is probably a weird thing to say, but I think about him often. I guess that's normal when someone dies in such tragic circumstances."

Again, Kit couldn't find words. He shrugged and wondered how to change the subject. Chatting about the weather and the view and the food had felt strained, but talking about his dead dad didn't seem like an improvement in the conversation.

"I spoke to him a day or two before he died," she said. "He was in the hotel doing some jobs." Her face cracked into a smile. "I'll never forget it. He stole food for us from the kitchen."

Kit tilted his head. "He did *what?*"

It took her a moment to stop giggling. "He was renovating a couple of the hotel rooms and I was supposed to hold the ladder while he hung the curtains. After that I was going on my lunch break. I made some comment to Terry about the owners not being very generous with the staff food. We could order food from the kitchen but only soup or sandwiches."

She put a hand over her mouth as she stifled more giggles. "Your dad started complaining about George – saying how he was always so grumpy. He agreed it was a bit naff that we couldn't get a decent meal while we were working, so he called down to reception from the hotel room and put on this stupid posh voice to order two lots of steak and chips to be sent to the room."

"Seriously?" Kit asked, amused.

She caught a tear at the corner of her eye as more laughter came. "I didn't believe for a second it would work. But the receptionist didn't think to check that there was someone staying in that room. I guess if you get a call for room service it doesn't even occur to you to check it might be a hoax.

"Anyway, fifteen minutes later there was a knock at the door and your dad put on his posh voice again and told them to leave it outside the door. I could hardly eat for laughing." She held her stomach and took deep breaths. "Your dad joked about calling down again for dessert, but we decided that might be pushing our luck. I swear that was the best meal I'd ever had."

"I never knew that," Kit said wistfully. "It totally sounds like something Dad would have done though."

"I couldn't tell anyone about it because I couldn't let anyone at the hotel find out. I felt a bit guilty a couple of days later when Kirsty on reception got into trouble for charging two steak dinners to a room that didn't have anyone staying in it."

"You still didn't say anything?"

Slowly, she shook her head. "Your dad had gone missing the previous day. People were still out looking for him. A couple of steak dinners seemed completely insignificant. At least as far as the hotel was concerned. They will always be significant to me. I came to the funeral. Didn't get a chance to speak to you though."

"It was a weird day." The day he'd said goodbye to his dad and fallen head over heels for Seren. *Weird* pretty much summed it up.

"Sorry," Holly said. "I probably shouldn't have brought it up."

"It's okay. I like hearing new stories about him. Especially the funny ones."

"I told him that I went to school with you, so he was chatting about you a lot. Saying how well you were doing with the train, and how impressed he was by how much you'd accomplished so young."

Kit took a swig of his beer. "He was the one who always encouraged me. Mum was supportive too, but I'm sure she thought the idea of buying a train to give tours of the island was slightly mad. Dad always saw the potential and was as enthusiastic as me."

Holly gazed out over the water. The sun sank lower on the horizon, causing the vibrant colours in the sky to fade to more muted tones. "He told me another story, about getting called into school one day because you'd thrown a doughnut at the teacher."

Kit cracked up laughing. "Mr Thompson! Do you remember that?"

"Yes." She put a hand in front of her mouth as she snorted a laugh. "He had a huge nose and the boys were all joking that he could be a fairground attraction … people could try to hook a ring on his nose!"

"I can't believe I threw the doughnut. In my defence, there was a lot of peer pressure. And it wasn't me who brought the doughnuts into school, so I think it was unfair that I took all the blame. Jim Courts threw one too – the only reason he didn't get into trouble was because he's a bad shot."

"The poor teacher," Holly said, not looking at all sympathetic. "Your dad said when he got called in he could barely keep from laughing. He had to pretend to take it seriously and told them he'd think up a suitable punishment, but really he just found it hilarious."

"I didn't get punished at all. Mum tried to give me a lecture about it, but at the dinner table that night we were all in hysterics. Even Mum gave up on trying to be stern about it. It was mean though. I wonder what happened to Mr Thompson. He left not long after that. I tell myself it wasn't me who drove him away."

Holly was silent for a moment. "Maybe he went to join the circus."

Once they'd stopped laughing, they got more drinks and spent another hour chatting about their schooldays and old school friends, exchanging information about the people they'd stayed in touch with.

The walk back into town was infinitely more relaxed than the way up there.

Casually, Holly slipped her arm through his. "I'm going to have to ask. Why are you so against the tourist office selling tickets for your train tours?"

"This again," he said on a sigh.

"I'm curious as to why you're so against it."

"It'd cause a lot of unnecessary hassle. What happens if it rains in the afternoon and you've already sold a load of tickets in the morning?"

"I hadn't thought of that."

"It also means I'd have to print physical tickets. Which is a massive waste of paper."

"You don't have tickets?"

"Nope. Being eco-friendly is part of my brand. One of the only reasons I was approved for the train was that it's electric and because I was replacing the bus with an electric one. We live on this amazing island and I think we have a duty to be conscientious about the environment."

"I wasn't expecting that answer." She bumped her shoulder against his. "I actually thought I might dig up some dirt about the owners of the tourist office. Like maybe you didn't want to work with them."

"Wyatt seems to think I'm being awkward. I've tried to explain to him, but I think I'm wasting my breath."

"He's pretty set in his ways."

"Do you like working there?"

"Yeah. The work is pretty nice. It definitely beats working for my ex-boyfriend's parents."

"Oh!" Kit winced. "Gavin is the owners' son?"

"Yeah. You can imagine how awkward that was after we split up."

"No wonder you looked for a new job."

"I think it all worked out for the best. I was ready for a change. Sometimes moving on to a new chapter of your life is exciting … that's what I keep telling myself anyway."

"The problem with change is that often you only realise it's a good thing with hindsight."

"Very true. Hopefully one day I'll look back on this time of my life with much more positivity than I feel now."

"Maybe." Kit mulled the idea over, wondering if one day he'd be able to look back on this part of his life and see that it was a necessary transition. Maybe finding out he had no chance with Seren would be the catalyst for something good.

"I had a really nice evening," Holly said when they arrived at her door.

"Me too." The evening had been a lot more fun than he'd anticipated.

"Do you want to go out again sometime?"

"Yeah," he said automatically. "That would be good." He had a momentary panic over how to end the evening. Even though he'd enjoyed himself, it'd felt more like hanging out with a friend than a date. He felt no desire for a goodnight kiss.

Thankfully Holly moved towards the door before he had time to think too much about it.

"I'll talk to you soon then," she said briskly, avoiding any mention of who would get in touch with who.

As he wandered on through the quiet town, Kit felt slightly lighter. An evening out had been refreshing. Wallowing was doing him no good, and he needed to get out of the habit. He just wasn't sure dating was the right thing for him at the moment.

Holly was sweet. The last thing he wanted to do was hurt her.

CHAPTER EIGHTEEN

The following Thursday evening Kit went over to Noah's place to drop off the contract he'd drawn up for Keira.

"Do you want to stay for dinner?" Noah asked, turning from the chopping board when Kit walked into the kitchen.

"Yeah okay." He perched on the stool at the island while Keira stood beside him, scanning the contract. "I've just adapted the contract I have with the bus drivers," he told her. "But I'm happy to make changes if there's anything you're not happy with."

"I'm sure it's all fine."

"Take some time to look over it. I've put fifteen hours based on you doing the morning tours in August. I probably won't need you that much generally, and definitely not in the winter. There'll be a few months where I won't need you at all, but I'll pay you year-round anyway."

"Are you sure?"

"Yeah. The hourly rate isn't that great, but with the tips it's pretty good money."

"I'd be quite happy to do it just for tips, so anything else is a bonus."

"Don't tell him that," Noah said. "He'll change the contract."

"I've put the start date as next week, but if you want to do a few more trips with me before going it alone, you can."

"Maybe one or two more times with you would be good, if that's okay."

Kit nodded. "That's fine. I'm quite happy to relax and take in the view."

"You didn't look very relaxed last time," Keira said, shaking her head. "It seems pretty excruciating for you to watch someone else giving the tour."

He grinned. "That's no reflection on you. I told you, the train's my baby. It's weird having someone else take the tour."

"What do you want on your pizza?" Noah asked, taking a step back from the cutting board, which was covered in an array of chopped veg, ham and salami.

"Everything," Kit said while Keira moved to put her own toppings on the dough.

"Have you been up to anything fun recently?" Noah asked Kit once he'd put the pizza in the oven.

The question sounded fairly loaded, but Kit wasn't sure what reply Noah was expecting. "Not really."

"Not been on any dates or anything?" Noah leaned back against the counter, his lips twitching to a smirk.

Kit groaned. "What's Mum been saying?"

"Not a lot. Just that she spotted you chatting to some pretty blonde chick."

"Holly?" Keira asked in surprise. "The girl from the tourist office?"

"Yeah."

Noah grinned. "Mum reckons she was fluttering her eyelashes and flirting outrageously."

"She wasn't," Kit insisted. "Mum's delusional."

"So, there's nothing going on?" Noah asked.

Kit rocked his head from side to side. "We went out for dinner last weekend."

"You went on a date!" Keira sucked in a quick breath. "Where did you take her?"

"Juliet's Garden. It wasn't really a date though. I don't think."

"Sounds like a date," Noah said, plucking a piece of tomato from the salad bowl and popping it in his mouth. "It's good that you're getting out and seeing people. I thought you'd mope around over Seren for ages."

"It's not as though I suddenly got over Seren. I'm just bored of feeling sorry for myself. Holly's good company, and I like hanging out with her. Anything that takes my mind off Seren is a good thing, but Holly and I are only friends."

"When are you seeing her again?" Keira asked, seeming completely oblivious to his comment about them just being friends.

"I don't know. We didn't make any definite plans."

She dropped her elbows to the counter and propped her chin on her hands. "Are you going to call her?"

"Maybe. I'm not sure." If he was going to call her, he probably should have done it by now. Almost a week had passed since they'd been out.

In a bid to change the subject, Kit asked Keira how she was finding life on St Mary's and how she was enjoying living a stone's throw from their mum. She was cheerful and positive about everything and chatted away until the pizza was ready.

Kit didn't stay long after they'd eaten. Driving home in his golf cart, he thought about Seren at work and the times when he'd have detoured to go and prop up the bar and keep her company. A pang of sadness hit him at the thought of not being able to do that any more.

Back at home, he perched on the edge of his bed with his phone in his hand, staring at a message from his mum asking him to go over for lunch on Sunday. No doubt Noah and Keira would have been invited too. And Seren. After a couple of minutes, he replied to his mum, saying he'd be there. He'd have to start seeing Seren again eventually. May as well start easing himself back into it.

As his mood spiralled, he contemplated messaging Holly. That would be unfair though – getting in touch with her to distract himself from thinking about Seren. On balance, the kindest thing he could do for Holly would be to stay away from her.

Of course, that was easier said than done. He was on his way to work on Saturday morning, driving the train through the town, when Holly waved at him. Slowing the train, he felt a pang of guilt that he hadn't been in touch with her. He should have at least messaged to say he wasn't in a good place for dating at the moment.

From her bright smile he got the impression she wasn't concerned by his lack of contact.

"How's your week been?" she asked, leaning into the train.

"Not bad." Surprisingly, that was the truth. Things were starting to feel more normal and his heartache wasn't quite so raw. "How about you?"

"It was fine. I'll be glad when I finish work today."

"Got much planned for the weekend?"

"No." She looked thoughtful. "I was supposed to be going out tonight, but I'm thinking about cancelling."

"How come?"

She waved a hand dismissively. "It's my friend's twenty-first birthday. Petra's lovely and I promised her I'd be there … but we worked together at the hotel. I'm not sure who else is invited."

"You're worried about your ex being there?"

"Yeah. I don't know if he will be, and I don't think bumping into him would be too terrible. It's bound to happen at some point. I'm just not overly thrilled by the idea. I'm also not sure how many people I'll know at the party." She screwed her nose up. "I'll probably just call in for half an hour to wish her a happy birthday."

"Where is it at?"

"The Old Town Inn. Her parents own the place."

"Sounds like fun."

"Yeah. I should at least go along for a while. Hiding away to avoid bumping into Gavin is a bit pathetic." She smiled lightly. "What are your plans for the weekend?"

"Mainly work. And a family lunch at my mum's place tomorrow. That's about it."

She arched an eyebrow. "I don't suppose you feel like coming to the party with me tonight?"

"Um … I guess I could."

"Don't feel obliged. Clearly I'd just be using you for moral support. You can absolutely say no."

He tapped the steering wheel as he pondered it. Again, it felt like a much better option than staying home alone. It would be a pleasant distraction, and that was exactly what he needed. Besides, it wasn't a date – just two friends hanging out.

"Okay," he said with a smile.

"You're the best. I'll look forward to it now I know I have someone fun to hang out with."

"I'm looking forward to it too," he said earnestly.

They agreed that Kit would call on her at eight and they'd walk over there together. When he left her, he was running slightly late for the train tour. To his relief, Keira was down at the promenade, reassuring the passengers that the train would be there shortly.

She gave the tour and they went out for lunch together afterwards. Having company for the day as well as plans for the evening made the day go quickly. It was only when he got home that he realised he'd hardly thought about Seren at all.

That was definitely progress.

CHAPTER NINETEEN

Three weeks had passed since Kit's big declaration and Seren had only seen him when he'd been passing in the train. Each time, she'd gone out of her way to be there, and each time he'd acknowledged her with a smile and a tip of his chin but never stopped to chat.

Mirren had invited her over for lunch on Sunday, and she was hoping Kit would be there too. She didn't like to get her hopes up, though. There was a chance he'd stay away just to avoid seeing her.

On Saturday she was utterly fed up with the whole situation and was struggling not to snap at customers while she worked. To make things worse, Cadan and Felix were sitting at the bar. For once they were keeping to themselves and managing to act like respectable human beings. Even *that* annoyed Seren. Venting her emotions at someone might be a good release, and Felix would usually be the perfect target. Trust him to be amiable when she'd rather he gave her a reason to bite his head off.

"What time do you finish?" Cadan asked when she set a fresh pint in front of him. Felix was drinking soft drinks, which was completely out of character. Presumably he was driving.

Seren didn't like to ask for fear of giving the impression she was interested in his life.

"Half an hour," she replied, checking the clock on the wall.

"Got any exciting plans for the evening?" Cadan asked.

"No." She glanced at Felix, expecting some cocky remark, but none came. Maybe he was ill.

"We're going back to Felix's place after this." Cadan indicated his beer. "There's a bottle of Laphroaig that needs drinking. Come with us if you want."

"I'd rather do anything other than spend an evening drinking whisky with you two." She fully expected to get a rise out of Felix, but he looked around the room, seemingly uninterested.

"Maybe you'd *rather* do something else," Cadan said with a teasing glint in his eyes. "But considering you have no other options for the evening it looks like we're your best choice."

"And I didn't think I could feel worse about my social life," she replied, smiling and dodging out of the way as Cadan reached across the bar to give her a friendly shove.

She went to serve customers at the other end of the bar and only came back when Cadan and Felix got up to leave.

"Sure you don't want us to wait for you?" Felix asked.

"No thanks."

As they left the pub, Noah arrived for his shift, along with Marty, another of the bar staff, meaning Seren could go home.

"Are you going to Mum's for lunch tomorrow?" Noah asked as she lingered by the bar.

"Yes. Who else is going?"

"Me and Keira, and Kit. I thought Trystan might come over this weekend since he hasn't been back for a while, but he says work's busy."

The mention of Trystan made Seren think of her weekend in London with Kit. Her stomach twisted at the thought of how much time she'd got to spend with him. At least it seemed as though she'd finally get to see him the following day. The way she was feeling, she was tempted to have it out with him and tell him to stop avoiding her. Not that she'd get the chance with everyone around.

"See you tomorrow," she said to Noah before she headed for the door.

Wandering through town, the idea of confronting Kit stirred in her mind until she redirected her course. Going over to have a go at him might not be her best idea ever, but she'd get to see him at least. The thought made her stomach flutter.

He buzzed her into the building, and she walked inside to find him standing in his doorway in a pair of jeans and a checked shirt. His hair was damp as though he was getting ready to go out.

"Hi," he said hesitantly.

"Hi."

His lips twitched to a bemused smile. "Is everything okay?"

"No." The butterflies were replaced by irritation over the fact that he'd spent three weeks acting as though she no longer existed. "Everything *isn't* okay."

"What's wrong?"

"You're avoiding me," she stated, her voice rising in pitch and volume.

"What?"

"You're avoiding me and I don't like it."

Idly, he fastened the button on his cuff. "I'm not avoiding you. Not really."

"Yes. You are," she practically shouted at him. "It's not fair. I didn't do anything wrong, but now you're avoiding me." As tears sprang to her eyes, she stepped back, realising she'd lost control of her emotions. It was tempting to bolt before she made a complete fool of herself.

"I'm sorry," he said, venturing barefoot into the hallway.

"You don't need to be sorry. Just don't pretend you aren't avoiding me." She wiped at her cheeks with trembling fingers. "I used to see you every day. For as long as I can remember I've seen you every day. Then you tell me you love me and disappear."

She blinked tears away to bring him into focus, and the sadness in his features almost made her cry even more. "I understand why you don't want to see me," she said slowly, "but I hate that we're not friends any more. I feel as though you're punishing me when I haven't done anything wrong."

He tilted his head and looked at her intently. "It's not that I'm going out of my way to avoid seeing you. I've just stopped going out of my way *to* see you."

She sniffed and her voice came out squeaky. "What?"

"The reason you used to see me every day was because I made sure I'd see you as often as possible. If you were having dinner with Mum I'd call around there. I timed going to work so I'd pass you on your way to work." He swallowed hard. "If you were working the late shift, I'd call in to see you after work."

She chewed on her lip but couldn't find any words.

He took a deep breath and flashed her a sad smile. "We're still friends. We'll always be friends. But for the sake of my sanity I've stopped going out of my way to see you."

"Okay," she said quietly.

"I never wanted to upset you," he said, his brow creased. "I definitely never wanted to jeopardise our friendship."

"I hate not seeing you."

His features scrunched up. "I think I need a bit of space. Seeing you all the time is too hard for me at the moment. And things feel weird now that you know how I feel about you."

"I can pretend I don't know," she suggested weakly.

He gave her a lopsided smile. "I'm not sure how well that would work. Just give me a bit of time. We'll figure out how to be around each other again eventually."

She nodded. "Are you going to your mum's for lunch tomorrow?"

"Yeah."

"Even though I'll be there?"

"Fortunately my love of Mum's cooking outweighs my discomfort around you."

"Glad to hear it." She smiled through her tears.

"Are you all right?"

"I think so." She sighed as the embarrassment at her outburst hit her. "I'm sorry to turn up here and rant at you. I could probably have messaged you."

"I don't know …" His shoulders hitched slightly. "If there's a choice between messaging someone or turning up on their doorstep and shouting at them, I think you should always opt for the latter."

"Don't tease me." She gave his arm a gentle shove, which only served to remind her of the fact that he was wearing a shirt and looked as though he was on his way out. "Where are you off to?" she asked, hoping she sounded casual.

He glanced down at his shirt. "Just meeting a friend."

That sounded like code for a date, but she decided she was probably being paranoid. And if he *was* going on a date, it was none of her business. She could hardly be annoyed with him for dating when she'd turned him down.

"Have a good night then," she said, forcing herself to back away.

Going home to spend the evening in her own company didn't appeal in the slightest. Automatically, she wandered in the direction of Old Town. She could have gone to her dad's place, but hanging out with her dad and Naomi didn't quite provide the same comfort that being with Mirren did. Whenever Seren was upset, it was Mirren she was drawn to.

The sun was setting as she walked along the beach at Old Town Bay. Light spilled from the windows at Noah's place, and Seren reminded herself that even if it weren't for Keira, she wouldn't go to him with this problem. There was no one she could confide in about her feelings for Kit.

As she slipped in through the backdoor of Mirren's house, Seren had a flashback to the days when the boys still lived at home and the place was constantly abuzz with chatter and noise. Now the house was eerily quiet as she kicked her shoes off in the utility room. She called out to Mirren, who answered her from the kitchen, where she was sitting at the table with a glass of wine in front of her.

"Hi," Seren said, a wave of sadness hitting her as she kissed Mirren's cheek. Once upon a time, Mirren had probably longed for peace and quiet, but from the look on her face there was no way she wanted it now. "Are you okay?"

"Yes. Fine. How are you?"

"Not bad. I hope you've got more wine."

"In the fridge. Help yourself."

"Do you think you'll rent out rooms in the house again this summer?" It had been something they'd done after the boys had moved out, before Terry had died. Mirren hadn't done it since, but it occurred to Seren that it might be a good thing to have some bustle around the place.

"I'm trying to avoid it. I don't like the idea of having strangers around these days."

"What about returning customers? So you already know them."

She shook her head. "I might seem sad and lonely, but I'm okay."

"That's not what I meant."

"I'm fairly sure it is," Mirren said as Seren sat across from her. "Anyway, I might be forced to have people to stay in the house this summer since Trystan's causing havoc with the bookings for August."

"Why? What's the problem?"

"Jenny wants to stay in the London flat in August. She's staying with a friend for now and has found a place of her own from September, but there's some problem with staying at her friend's place in August."

"So Trystan's coming back here for the whole of August?"

"Yes. I already had his place free for him for the first two weeks, but there was a couple booked in for the end of August."

"Why can't Trystan stay here with you? There's loads of room."

"He begrudgingly suggested the same, but he doesn't want to. And I can't blame him. He has his own place and he wants to stay there, not be under his mother's feet."

"Will you offer the couple a room in the house instead?"

"Maybe. I'm trying to find them alternate accommodation elsewhere on the island, but we'll see."

"It'll be nice to have Trystan around anyway. How's he doing?"

"Says he's fine, but I don't suppose he'd say otherwise." She took a sip of wine. "What's going on with you? There used to be a time when your social life was too hectic to visit me on a Saturday night."

"Times have changed," Seren said with a sigh.

"Kit's out with Holly Burton. Do you know her? They went to school together."

Seren's stomach twisted sharply, but she kept her features neutral as she shook her head.

"Second date apparently," Mirren said. "Not that Kit told me anything about it. I saw him chatting to her outside of the supermarket, then I pried the information out of Noah. Their first date was last weekend. He took her to Juliet's Garden." She twirled the stem of her wine glass. "I'm not sure where they've gone tonight."

Unable to formulate a response, Seren pushed her chair back and casually walked across the kitchen. "Have you got any chocolate?" she asked, opening the snack cupboard. Picking up a bar of Dairy Milk, she held it up. "Can I?"

Mirren nodded. "I can't imagine it will last between Kit and his new friend anyway."

"Why not?" Seren asked, as though the conversation was of barely any interest to her.

"She's very young." Mirren reached over and snapped off a square of chocolate.

"I thought they went to school together? Aren't they the same age?"

"Yes, I suppose they are, but Kit's mature for his age. She's quite … giggly. You probably know her by sight – she used to work in the hotel, now she works in the tourist information."

"Curly, blonde hair?" Seren asked.

"Yes. And an annoying laugh."

Seren cracked a smile. The fact that Mirren wasn't a fan made the situation marginally easier. "Don't be mean," she chastised her mildly.

"I suppose it's good he's dating, even if I think he can do better."

"I suspect no one would be good enough for your baby."

"You might be right." She bit the chocolate and chewed slowly. "What about you?"

Seren's eyes widened as her heart rate increased. "What about me?"

"How's your love life?"

That made more sense. For a crazy moment, she'd thought Mirren was making some comment about her and Kit. Just because *she* couldn't stop imagining the two of them together didn't mean anyone else was. Least of all his mum.

"I don't have a love life," Seren said, her mind flicking to Kit telling her he loved her. Then to him out on a date with giggly bloody Holly.

"I heard Felix is still hanging around you."

Seren rolled her eyes. "Did you hear that from Noah? He seems to have turned into the town gossip."

"He's concerned about you."

"He needn't be. I'm not daft enough to get involved with Felix again." Something niggled at her though; he'd been quiet in the pub that evening, and it reminded her of how he used to be when she was first with him. Before his ego had grown and he'd smothered his softer side with his cocky persona. She'd almost forgotten that she'd liked him once.

The landline rang and Mirren went to answer it, leaving Seren to her thoughts. Knowing that Kit was on a date would no doubt keep her mind whirring all night. Taking a long swig of wine, she had an overwhelming desire to get drunk. Maybe she should have taken Cadan up on his offer to hang out with them.

On impulse she took out her phone and messaged Felix, casually asking how the whisky was.

As dots pulsed over the screen to show he was typing a reply, she waited anxiously. He said he hadn't started drinking it yet. Nothing more. She'd expected him to invite her over, but it didn't seem like an invitation would be forthcoming.

Taking the bull by the horns, she asked if she could come over.

When he offered to pick her up she told him she was at the Trenearys' place.

Some things never change, he replied. *I'll be there in ten minutes.*

Seren was still staring at the phone when Mirren came back in, complaining about the strange times people called to enquire about booking the cottages.

"Do you mind if I head off?" Seren said when she could get a word in. "Cadan messaged me, wanting to hang out. I feel a bit bad that I haven't made time to see him since he got back." While she wasn't overly comfortable with lying, there was no way she could admit that she was in such a bad place that she'd got in touch with Felix.

"Do whatever you want," Mirren said. "Where are you going with him?"

"His place," Seren said, hoping she wouldn't ask any more questions.

"Is that Charlie's place?" She arched her eyebrows. "Or Felix's place?"

"Felix's. But don't look at me like that. They're practically joined at the hip, so if I want to hang out with my cousin I have to hang out with Felix. It doesn't mean I have to like him."

"Just be careful," Mirren warned.

"I will." After finishing her wine, Seren put the glass in the dishwasher.

"How are you getting there?"

"He's picking me up."

Mirren gave a small shake of the head. "I suppose it's better if I don't ask which *he* you're referring to."

"Probably not." Seren gave her a quick hug. "Thanks for the wine and chocolate."

"I'll see you tomorrow," Mirren said. "Lunch is at one. Don't be late."

CHAPTER TWENTY

A hum of chatter and music filled the Old Town Inn. The twenty-first birthday party was a low-key affair with an eclectic mix of the birthday girl's friends, family and co-workers, who ranged in age from eight to eighty.

Kit knew most people, by sight if not by name. Thanks to his job, everyone on the island knew him.

He and Holly happily mingled with the other guests for the first hour or so, then filled their plates at the buffet and found a table to themselves outside. The low stone walls around the patio were overrun with agapanthus and the striking tall blue flowers cast eerie shadows as the daylight faded.

"I'm sure we said we wouldn't stay long," Holly eventually said, looking at her watch. "It's almost midnight."

Surprised that so much time had gone by, Kit checked his watch too.

"Don't you believe me?" Holly gave his foot a gentle kick. "Or do you think I can't tell the time?"

"Bit of both," he replied cheekily. "You got it right though. Do you need to get home before you turn into a pumpkin or something?"

"It was the coach that turned into a pumpkin, Cinderella just went back to being scruffy." She yawned. "I wouldn't mind going though. It seems as though things are winding down."

"I wish I'd driven," Kit remarked as they stood. "Why did you insist we walk?"

"Trying to get you drunk," she said lightly. "To be honest, I thought you were just being gentlemanly offering to drive. I assumed you'd want to drink, but you don't drink much, do you?"

"Not really."

"Maybe I should take a leaf out of your book." She put a hand on his arm as she wobbled slightly. "I drank too fast because I was nervous of seeing Gavin, but that was pointless since he didn't show up."

"How long ago did you guys break up?" Kit asked.

"A couple of months. I haven't really seen him since. I feel as though I need to get the first time over with, then I can relax."

They sought out Petra to thank her for the party and wish her happy birthday again. As they made their way out they called goodbye to a few more people too.

Walking along the dark road, Holly veered to the side. Kit pulled her hand into the crook of his elbow so he could keep her in a straight line.

"Your mum lives around here, doesn't she?" Holly asked when they approached the sandy bay at Old Town. The silver moon was large, making the surface of the water sparkle beneath it.

"Over on the headland," Kit told her, nodding in that direction.

Holly squeezed his arm as she giggled. "Remember your sixteenth birthday party on the beach down there?"

He smiled at the memory. "That was fun."

"It was until the police turned up."

Kit laughed loudly. "It wasn't the police."

She cast him a puzzled look. "We had a barbecue on the beach and everyone got drunk. People kept turning the music up until someone called the police. Everyone made a run for it."

"It was my dad." Kit grinned at her. "He got sick of the noise but didn't want to embarrass me by coming down to break up the party. So him and my brothers came out and shone torches on the beach and shouted 'police'. After everyone had done a runner, I stayed on the beach drinking beers with my dad and Trystan and Lowen and Noah. Dad thought it was hilarious that a bunch of drunk sixteen-year-olds were so easy to get rid of."

"Oh my goodness. That party went down as legendary because the police broke it up."

"Definitely better than my dad coming down to get rid of everyone."

"Your dad was really cool, wasn't he?" She swayed and her shoulder bumped against his.

"Yeah," he said through the tightening in his chest. "He was."

"How many brothers do you have?"

"Four."

"I know Noah from the pub. Lowen's the guy who makes the pottery, right? I've had people in the tourist office asking about his studio, but I didn't twig that he was your brother until recently."

"He lives on Bryher. We don't see that much of him. He's eighteen years older than me, so we didn't exactly share a childhood. He'd already moved out when I was born."

"That must be weird. Is he more like a father figure?"

"No. We're not close. Trystan can be kind of paternal sometimes."

"He lives in London?"

"Yeah, but he comes back here pretty often. He and Noah are quite protective of me."

"That's nice. Who's the fourth brother? I'm missing one."

"Jago."

"I've never heard of him. Not that I recall anyway."

"He's also a lot older than me. He moved out of home when I was about four. Over to the mainland to go to sixth form, then uni. After that he moved to London for a while, then France, then New York. He doesn't get back to visit much, so I don't feel like I really know him at all."

"That must be so weird."

"It is a bit. He came over for Dad's funeral but only stayed for a few days and that time was all a bit of a blur."

She squeezed his arm again and they continued in silence for a couple of minutes.

"There's something I wanted to ask you," she said hesitantly. Kit had the distinct impression that whatever she was going to say was something she wouldn't bring up when she was sober. "It's about Lowen. There are a lot of rumours floating around about him …"

Kit's jaw tightened. If there was one thing he hated about island life it was the gossip. Over the past few years, his family had been at the centre of a lot of it. Mostly he ignored it or just refused to comment.

"Is it true that he's a millionaire?" Holly asked.

That hadn't been the question he'd expected and his shoulders relaxed. "I don't actually know. Maybe."

"But he's your brother. You must know."

"I know he has a lot of money. He's never told me how much."

"How do you get to be a millionaire from making pottery?"

"He didn't. He used to be an investment banker. He knows a lot about the stock market and made some good investments. I think the pottery is more like his retirement project."

"There are other rumours too," she said, tightening her grip on him as she stumbled slightly.

"Oh, I'm sure there are a lot!"

"Are you going to get annoyed with me for asking questions?"

"No." He chuckled. "I just won't answer any questions I don't like."

She cast him a sidelong glance. "Where did you get the money for the train and the bus?"

"I inherited some money," he said, hoping she wouldn't dig any further on the matter.

"From who? I heard some people say it was from grandparents and some people say it was some long-lost relative who you never even knew."

"Something like that." He breathed a sigh of relief that they were almost at Holly's place and he could wrap the conversation up.

"Which one is it?"

"I can't tell you," he said lightly.

"Why not?"

"Because if the truth got out, no one would have anything to speculate about. It'd ruin everyone's fun of making up stories."

"Kit!" she chastised with a hint of a pout.

"Sorry," he said, sounding utterly unapologetic. "I told you I won't answer questions I don't like. But you can be assured that it's a long and boring story and I'm doing you a favour by not telling it."

"I don't believe that for a minute!"

He smiled, glad she didn't seem annoyed with him for being mysterious. It was no reflection on her that he didn't want to tell her about how he and his brothers had come into money. It just wasn't something he spoke about. Even within his family there seemed to be an unspoken rule that they didn't talk about it.

"I can't thank you enough for coming with me." Holly pressed a kiss to his cheek. "I had a great time."

"Me too. Thanks for inviting me."

She looked him right in the eyes and he had a horrible feeling she was going to try and kiss him properly. He took a discreet step back, and Holly turned to let herself inside. "See you soon," she called over her shoulder.

"Night," he replied as he set off for home.

By the time he clambered into bed, his mind was a jumbled mess. Spending time with Holly was far more enjoyable than he'd anticipated. She was easy company and fun to be around. If the timing wasn't so bad he suspected there could be something between them. As it was, his heart belonged to Seren, and he felt increasingly guilty that he hadn't been clear with Holly about the situation.

Felix peered over the dashboard to look up at the Treneary house when Seren slipped into the passenger seat.

"It's a blast from the past, picking you up from here," he remarked, turning the car to set off back down the lane.

"Is it?"

"I think you were over there more than you were at home when we were dating. Pretty much every time I called you were at their place."

"I was still living at Dad's." She thought back. "Naomi had moved in and things were a little awkward."

"Do you get on with her better now?"

"Yes. We got on fine as soon as I moved out."

Felix glanced in the rear-view mirror. "How's Mirren these days?"

"Fine." Seren shot him a sidelong look, surprised by the question. It felt as though there was an agenda to everything with Felix.

"It must be hard for her, on her own." He geared down at the junction. "I remember hearing about Terry's death from Cadan. So tragic."

"Yeah." Somehow, having a normal conversation with Felix was more unsettling than him being obnoxious. "How is it being back on St Mary's? Are you enjoying it?"

"*Enjoying* is probably the wrong word. It's nice to chill out for a while. Good to have a proper catch-up with Rebecca too."

His sister had been in Kit's year at school. Seren remembered Rebecca hero-worshipping Felix. Sometimes she'd tagged along with them for day trips to the off islands or come out for lunch with them.

"Have you been working a lot while you're here or are you taking some time off?"

"I have a few projects on the go, but it doesn't feel so strenuous when I'm sitting out on the patio with a sea view."

"I imagine that's nicer than your office in London."

"I have a home office, but the view definitely isn't as good as it is here."

His parents' place was on the northwest side of the island, standing alone on high ground, overlooking the sea.

"The house is beautiful," Seren commented, taking in the wraparound patio, which was a new addition since she was last there.

"Mum and Dad have done a lot of work on it."

She followed him around to the back of the house. Cadan sat on the patio with his feet up on a chair and a glass of whisky in his hand.

"Decided to grace us with your presence after all," he said, leaning his head back to look up at her.

Before she could answer, Rebecca stepped out of the kitchen. "Thank goodness you're here," she said, surprising Seren by hugging her tightly. "These two are terrible company."

"Thanks a lot," Felix said, giving her a friendly shove. "What do you want to drink?" he asked Seren. "If you're not up for whisky, there's wine ... or pretty much anything. My parents keep the place well stocked with alcohol."

"I'll have white wine if there is some."

"Me too." Rebecca beamed at Seren. With her long dark curls and big brown eyes, she was a softer, feminine version of Felix. "I haven't seen you properly in ages."

"Yeah." Sometimes Rebecca came into the pub with her friends; they always greeted each other warmly but never really chatted. Seren had always seen her as a reminder of Felix, and she hadn't wanted to be reminded.

"You could help me with something … I'll be back in one sec." Rebecca waltzed away inside.

Cadan shrugged when Seren looked at him questioningly. "Party-planning would be my guess."

"Where did she go?" Felix asked, coming outside with two glasses of wine in his hands.

Rebecca reappeared with a notepad and pen. "I need some advice about my birthday," she said, pulling the chair out from under Cadan's feet with a look of glee. "It's in two weeks and I'm going to have a party here, but I can't decide what to do about food."

Cadan cast her a look of amusement. "I keep telling you, no one will care about food. It's a load of twenty-two-year-olds. If there's alcohol, they'll be happy."

"I want to make food," Rebecca said adamantly.

"You're causing yourself a headache for no reason," Cadan told her.

Rebecca glared at Felix. "Can you tell your idiot friend to shut up?"

"Leave her alone," Felix said. "It's her birthday, she can do what she wants." He nodded at a seat for Seren, then sat down himself.

"I can't decide what to cook," Rebecca said. "I guess I'll do finger foods and make it a buffet."

"I can order food in if you want?" Felix offered.

She insisted she wanted to cook, then rattled off a list of potential foods, asking for their opinions as she jotted down ideas. With her rosy cheeks and incessant chatter, she sounded about twelve. It made Seren feel old. With an uncomfortable jolt she realised Rebecca was the same age as Kit. She'd started to convince herself that the age gap between them wasn't such a huge deal, but sitting with Rebecca it seemed fairly monumental.

"Thirsty?" Felix said, drawing her from her trance.

She snapped her gaze to the empty wine glass in her hand.

"I'll bring the bottle out," Rebecca said, then slipped inside.

Cadan lit a cigarette and inhaled deeply. "Are we going to have to hear about this bloody party for the next two weeks?"

"You're welcome to find somewhere else to stay," Rebecca told him, returning and refilling Seren's glass.

"And miss the party of the century?" he said with a smirk. "No chance."

"Who said you're invited?" she fired back. When he didn't reply she turned to Seren. "Will you come?"

"To your birthday party?" She took a large swig of wine.

"Yes. You should come."

"I probably wouldn't know many people, and I think I'd raise the average age considerably."

"Don't be silly, you should come. It'll be fun."

"Maybe," Seren said, then realised how miserable she sounded. "Thanks for the invite."

Cadan stubbed his cigarette out and stood up. "All this scintillating conversation is tiring me out. I'm going to bed."

He shouted goodnight as he left.

"What's up with him?" Seren asked Felix. "He's not exactly cheerful this evening."

"I think he had an argument with Charlie this afternoon."

"What about?"

He shrugged. "He didn't say, but he went up to talk to him and came back in a foul mood. I'm guessing he asked for money and his dad told him he needs to start working."

"What makes you think that?"

He stretched his legs out in front of him. "He asked me for a loan this morning and I turned him down. I've given him a place to stay and constant supply of food and alcohol. I'm not giving him money as well. Especially since he still owes me from the last time I lent him money. It's not as though he can't find a job, he's just too idle to work."

"Can you be quiet for a minute, please?" Rebecca said, her eyes fixed on her phone.

Felix's lazy smile was full of affection. "What are you doing?" he asked Rebecca.

"Writing a message to invite people to the party."

"You need silence for that?"

"I need to concentrate while I figure out how to word it."

Felix's smile widened. "Perhaps you could do that inside instead of getting annoyed with us for speaking?"

She didn't reply but wandered inside bent over her phone.

"She's sweet," Seren commented after she'd gone.

Felix quirked an eyebrow. "Mum and Dad wrap her in cotton wool. She's sweet and kind, but she's also scarily innocent and naive. The only reason I'm here for the summer is because she's scared of staying in the house on her own."

Seren looked out over the lawn, which stretched for fifty metres before falling away gradually to a long crescent beach. With no neighbouring properties in view, all that could be seen to either side of the house was heathery moorland.

"It is quite remote," Seren remarked.

"I suppose so. Anyway, what's going on with you?"

"How do you mean?"

"You seem sad."

"I'm okay." Wine glugged out of the bottle as she topped her glass up.

Felix laughed and the sound annoyed her. "If downing wine like it's water wasn't enough of an indication that you're not in the best headspace, there's also the fact that you messaged me this evening. That's a sure sign there's some serious self-loathing going on."

A smile tugged at her lips. "I suppose I can't deny that."

"Are you going to tell me what's wrong?"

"No."

"You're just going to sit there and drink yourself into oblivion?"

"That was my plan."

His eyes were full of sympathy and he'd just opened his mouth to speak when Rebecca reappeared, asking him to read her message before she sent it. Then she hung around discussing who to invite to the party.

The conversation faded to background noise as Seren gazed out over the dark water that swept onto the shore with a gentle hushing sound. Overhead, millions of stars decorated the awe-inspiring sky. Contemplating the vastness of space made her head spin. Or maybe that was the wine. The glass in her hand was empty and she reached for the bottle only to find it was all gone.

"I'm going up to bed," Rebecca said. "Nice to see you, Seren."

"You too," she murmured, tiredness making her words sound thick and sludgy.

"Want me to drive you home?" Felix asked when they were alone.

"Not particularly. Did you say there was whisky?"

"I don't think you need whisky," he said, an intensity to his gaze that irked her.

"Why aren't you drinking?" she asked, standing and walking into the kitchen. Her legs felt wobbly after sitting for so long and she swayed a little.

"So I can drive you home." He followed her inside. "What are you doing?"

"Getting my own drink since you're a terrible host." She opened three cupboards before she found glasses. The bottle of whisky was easier to find, standing out on the countertop.

"I think it's probably better if you go home," he said while she poured whisky into two tumblers in a jerky motion.

"It's Saturday night. Everyone is out having fun. We should

do the same." Annoyingly, he didn't drink when she handed him a glass, just set it back down on the counter.

"Okay. I'm guessing someone didn't invite you to a party or something? That's why you're upset?"

"No." She thought of Kit out with Holly and downed the whisky, wincing when it burned her throat. As she began to unscrew the lid to pour herself another, Felix's hand closed over hers, then peeled her fingers away to take the bottle from her. "What are you doing?" she demanded.

"You've had enough."

"Just give it to me." She lurched at him but he moved backwards, holding the bottle away from her. She glared at him defiantly before reaching for his untouched glass and knocking it back.

He shook his head. "You're a mess, Seren."

"Well coming from you that's pretty offensive." She laughed, then covered her face with her hands as her chin began to twitch uncontrollably. He was right; she was a mess. Her life was a mess, and she had no idea what to do about it.

"Hey." Felix wrapped his arms around her and she didn't have the energy to protest. Instead she leaned into his shoulder and sobbed. Rubbing her back, he whispered gentle reassurances into her hair. "Do you want to tell me what's going on yet?" he asked when she finally calmed down.

"No," she sniffed, backing away from him.

"Let me drive you home then."

She swiped her fingers under her eyes. "I don't want to go home."

"Why not?"

"Because getting drunk on my own is pathetic."

His smile was condescending. "Is this about Noah, by any chance?"

"What do you mean?"

"I heard he's got a new girlfriend and they're living together."

"So?"

"So, I thought maybe that would be difficult for you …"

She screwed her nose up and shook her head. "I'm very happy for Noah."

"Sure you are." He rolled his eyes. "Clearly you don't want to share your problems with me. If you don't want to go home, you can stay here, but I think you should go to bed."

She blew a raspberry as she laughed. "There's no way I'd ever sleep with you again. I might be drunk but I'm not *that* drunk. I could never be *that* drunk."

"Oddly enough, that wasn't me trying to seduce you."

"You could never seduce me," she said, narrowing her eyes.

He squeezed the bridge of his nose, then reached for his car keys. "Get in the car, please. I'm taking you home."

"Sure." More tears flooded her eyes as she stepped out through the patio door. "Even *you* don't want to hang out with me. That's how much of a mess my life is."

She could hear him muttering to himself as he followed her outside, but she didn't look back, just strode towards the car with tears streaming down her face.

CHAPTER TWENTY-ONE

S unlight rudely woke Seren. Her brain felt as though it was throbbing inside her skull, and her tongue felt like an intruder in her dry mouth. Blinking her eyes open, she brought the room into focus. Everything was wrong, but at the same time it was vaguely familiar.

Her mind whirred, trying to piece together the previous evening. Felix had wanted to take her home and she'd got in his car … then she'd started crying again. It was all a bit of a blur after that, but evidently she'd slept in Felix's bed. Thankfully, she was alone, and still fully dressed.

Sitting up brought on a wave of nausea that swept from her stomach and up her throat until she retched. With a hand over her mouth, she leaped from the bed and onto the landing. She just made it to the bathroom in time to hunch over the toilet bowl and bring up the contents of her stomach.

After swilling out her mouth and splashing water on her face, she straightened up and caught sight of herself in the mirror. Her deathly pale skin and dark eye circles were a ghoulish combination. The house was quiet as she crept down the stairs. In the living room, she found Felix sprawled out on the couch, fast asleep.

Her stomach roiled again and she just wanted to be at home. It crossed her mind to wake Felix and ask him for a lift, but that would mean having to face him. She was too embarrassed.

In the kitchen she located her shoes and bag and slipped outside into the early morning light. Sunlight shone too brightly from the clear blue sky, and birdsong assaulted her ears to exacerbate the pounding in her head. Her mind tormented her as she walked – with thoughts of Kit and Felix and how stupid she was for turning to alcohol to try to block everything out. All she'd done was make herself feel worse. Something she hadn't considered to be a possibility.

As soon as she got home, she went straight back to bed, only pausing to set an alarm so she wasn't late for lunch at Mirren's place. Hopefully sleep would perk her up, because the way she was feeling now she couldn't stomach food, and she wasn't sure she was emotionally stable enough to be around Kit.

Keira had joined Kit on the train on Sunday morning. After his initial discomfort at being a passenger on his own train, he was getting quite used to sitting back and taking it all in. Watching Keira grow in confidence was good too.

They left the train down by the beach after the morning tour and ambled over to his mum's place, where Noah was waiting for them. Seren would be there soon, and Kit wasn't sure how he felt about that. Hanging out with Holly had lifted his spirits and he was feeling much more positive generally. He had the sense that spending time around Seren would be okay, but he could be completely wrong on that score.

"I've made lasagne and salad," his mum said as she bustled around the kitchen. "We can eat out on the patio."

They all moved out there to wait for Seren. Kit was setting the table but stopped abruptly when his mum spoke.

"I'm worried about Seren," she said, frown lines etched on her face as she rested back in her chair.

"Why?" Noah asked.

"She's hanging out with Felix again."

"I don't think so." Noah discreetly flashed Kit a sympathetic look. "He's been hanging around her, but she doesn't have any time for him."

"She had time for him last night," Mirren said wearily. "He picked her up from here. She said she was only going up to his place so she could hang out with Cadan, but I don't buy that for a minute."

"I take it you're not his biggest fan?" Keira asked Mirren.

She shook her head. "He treated her terribly when they were together, then ruined her twenty-first birthday – completely humiliated the poor love and broke her heart while he was at it. She was devastated. I can't understand why she'd have anything to do with him." Her eyes flicked to the lane where Seren's car was approaching.

"Seren seems pretty level-headed," Keira said. "Maybe she really is only seeing him because her cousin's staying with him."

"I hope so." Mirren sighed. "Otherwise she's going to get her heart broken again."

As Seren walked towards them, the conversation died away and Kit forced himself to continue setting the table. Maybe he wasn't okay with spending time with Seren after all. The thought of her seeing Felix made every muscle in his body tense.

"Hello!" Seren called out as she approached. She went around kissing everyone's cheeks. Kit's heart raced when she got to him, but she didn't hesitate in dropping a kiss on his cheek as she'd done with everyone else. "I'm not late, am I?" she said to Mirren. "Were you waiting for me to eat?"

"No. You timed it perfectly," she replied, standing and moving towards the kitchen. "The lasagne should be about ready."

"My mouth's watering already." Seren caught Kit's eye and

smiled. It hit him like a blow to the solar plexus and his appetite vanished. Apparently he was never going to be okay enough to casually hang out with her now that she knew how he felt.

"Have you managed any solo train rides yet?" Seren asked, touching Keira's arm as she sat beside her.

"So far Kit's always been with me."

"I don't actually do anything," Kit said. "She's a natural."

Noah draped his arm around Keira's shoulders. "It's funny how adamant you were that you'd never manage to do the tour and how much you love it now."

"I'll never be as good as Kit," Keira said. "But I really enjoy it. I just feel a bit bad for the people who get stuck on my tour instead of Kit's."

Kit smiled at her. "Remember, Noah used to take tours sometimes. Think about those poor people."

"Hey!" Noah chuckled. "I might refuse to drive for you again if you keep on like that."

"It doesn't seem as though I'll need you to. Keira's stolen your job."

Noah tilted his head. "I actually liked working on the train."

"Food's ready," Mirren called through the kitchen window. "Someone come and give me a hand."

Kit jumped up and carried the lasagne out while his mum brought the salad and serving spoons. He ended up sitting next to Seren to eat and was constantly aware of her arm close to his.

"You're quiet," she remarked when he didn't speak for a while.

"Are you hungover?" his mum asked. "You usually devour my lasagne in a matter of moments."

"I'm not hungover." His brow wrinkled as he tried to figure out why she'd jump to that conclusion.

"Did you go out last night?" she asked.

"Yeah," he said slowly, then noticed Keira and Noah both had their eyes fixed on their plates. He glared at them as he realised his mum knew full well that he'd been out – and who with. Kit had mentioned it to Keira, who'd obviously passed the info on to Noah. Presumably he'd been the one to loop their mum in.

"Did you have a good night?" Seren asked when no one else spoke.

"It was fine," he said. "I'm definitely not hungover. Just tired. I didn't get a lot of sleep."

"Really?" Noah said with a mischievous glint in his eye.

"Shut up! Not like that …" His cheeks felt as though they were on fire and he didn't dare glance in Seren's direction. Not that she'd care; she'd most likely be glad to hear he'd spent the night with someone. That way she could stop worrying about him following her around. He was still mortified by his confession about his stalker-like behaviour towards her. Why on earth had he thought it was appropriate to tell her that he timed going to work so he'd bump into her?

He focused on his food, hoping for a change in conversation. Racking his brain, he failed to come up with anything himself. Sleep really had been in short supply the previous night. He'd lain awake after his evening with Holly feeling terrible for leading her on. She was sweet and easy to chat to – both times they'd been out had been perfectly enjoyable – but his feelings were completely platonic, and he was guilt-ridden that she might think there could be anything more between them.

"I should hurry up," he said, swallowing a mouthful of lasagne. "I have to get back to work in a bit."

His mum glanced at her watch. "I thought the next train ride wasn't until three?"

"It's not." He only did one morning and one afternoon trip on Sundays. "I just need to nip home first."

"What for?"

He put his knife down and rubbed at his jaw while he searched for a reason. *Because he needed to get away from Seren* didn't seem like an appropriate response. "To pick something up," he mumbled, then felt a wave of relief when his phone rang.

Holly's name flashed up and he caught his mum leaning over to look at the screen. He moved away from the table to answer it.

It was too much to hope that the conversation around the table would continue. He was sure they all kept quiet specifically to eavesdrop on his phone call.

"Hi," he said, wandering to the front of the house and watching a butterfly land in the flower box under the kitchen window.

"Hey." She sounded nervous. "How are you?"

"Good, thanks. You?"

"I'm good too. I was just wondering if you're free this afternoon?"

"Um …" He'd been hoping to avoid seeing her for a few days to give himself time to figure out how to let her down gently. "I'm working later."

"Right. Yes. I knew that." There was a short pause and he turned in time to see all the faces at the table whip back to their food as though they hadn't been watching him. "Could I come with you?"

"What?"

"On the train? I told you I wanted to check it out so I can recommend it from personal experience … Maybe we could go for a coffee afterwards?"

He tried hard but couldn't come up with a reason why not. "Sure," he said. "That'd be nice."

"Great. Three o'clock, right?"

Had he mentioned that yesterday? Or did she know his work schedule like some obsessive stalker? Not that *he* could comment on that. Besides, she probably had it memorised for work.

"Yes. Exactly. I'll see you there."

When he ended the call and went back to the table, everyone remained silent.

"Sorry," he said, directing the apology at his mum. "I have to go."

"Already?"

"Yes." He couldn't face sitting down with them again. Sitting next to Seren while his family quizzed him about his dating life was too excruciating for words.

"At least finish your lunch. You've got loads of time before the train."

"I know, I've just got stuff to do."

Noah was staring at him. "Are you going to meet Holly? I didn't think things were that serious between you two."

"We're just friends," he said.

"So how come she calls wanting to meet you and you go running off?"

"Could you hear that?" he asked, holding up his phone.

"No, but it was pretty obvious."

"I told you I have to go home before work." He bent to give his mum a quick hug. "Thanks for lunch. I'll see you in the week."

"I was thinking we could have lunch next Saturday. Celebrate your dad's birthday ..."

Kit swallowed hard but managed a tight smile as he nodded. "I'll be here."

"Can we make it dinner?" Noah asked. "I'm working during the day."

"Ask Charlie for the day off," Seren suggested. "He'll understand."

Noah shook his head. "I'd rather work."

"Dinner's fine," Mirren said. "Come up whenever you finish work."

"See you later," Kit said as he backed away.

Forcing himself to look at Seren, he flashed her a smile, then made a dash for it.

CHAPTER TWENTY-TWO

Lunch at Mirren's place couldn't have been more painful for Seren. As though her hangover wasn't enough to contend with, she also had to listen to conversations about Kit and Holly. The whole situation would be funny if it wasn't so hurtful. Only a few weeks ago he'd told her he loved *her*. And now he was already seeing someone else. Someone he'd go running off to meet as soon as she called.

The only upside to Kit rushing off was that Seren didn't feel so bad for not hanging around after lunch. She made an excuse about having washing to do and headed home.

She'd just got back when Felix called her. Overriding the temptation to ignore him, she sank onto the couch and answered hesitantly.

"What time did you sneak off?" he asked.

"Early." She sucked in a breath. "Sorry about last night."

"No worries."

"It's a bit of a blur," she admitted. "I thought you were going to drive me home."

"I was. But you kept crying. It felt wrong to take you home in that state so I persuaded you to get in my bed."

"Sorry," she said again.

"I just wanted to check you're okay."

"Aside from my hangover?"

He chuckled. "Aside from that."

"I suppose I'll survive," she said as tears burned the back of her eyes.

"I can come over if you want? We can hang out and watch TV or something …"

"No thanks." She shook her head as she realised what he was up to – pretending to be concerned but really using her misery to get close to her.

"Okay. Give me a shout if you need anything."

"Thanks," she said without feeling.

"I hope it's not annoying having me tag along," Holly said, as the train set off.

"No." Kit glanced in his rear-view mirror, making sure his passengers were sticking to the rules and keeping in their seats. "It's fine."

"It won't distract you?"

"No. To be honest, I'll probably forget you're here." He winced. "Sorry. That sounded bad. I tend to get so absorbed that I don't notice if anyone's beside me or not."

Thankfully, she didn't seem offended by his lack of tact. "I'm surprised you don't slip into autopilot since you make the exact same trip day after day."

"I try not to work on autopilot. Even though the maximum speed is fifteen miles an hour and there's barely any traffic, I still don't like the idea of losing concentration." He surreptitiously checked that the PA system wasn't accidentally broadcasting to the passengers. "The chances of there being an accident are slim, but it would kind of wreck my livelihood if I put the train in a ditch."

"That's true," she said brightly.

"I also try to not give the exact same tour every time. It's more fun for me that way, and I feel as though passengers would be able to tell if I said the same thing every time."

"You've got one of those voices that is easy to listen to anyway. You could recite the alphabet and people would be enthralled."

"Thanks," he said, smiling self-consciously. "Let's hope you still think so in an hour." After putting on his headset, he switched the PA system on and directed his passengers to look to their left, then gave them information about the police station and the housing for the police officers beside it.

Just as he'd said, he pretty much forgot about Holly beside him as he chatted to his passengers. That was how it felt – as though he was chatting to them rather than reciting information. Catching their smiles in the rear-view mirror when he told a joke always gave him a buzz.

An hour later they were back at the beach with satisfied customers discreetly handing over tips while Kit deftly modelled balloon animals for the kids waiting patiently around his legs. It wasn't long before the crowd dispersed and Kit turned his attention to Holly. She'd remained in the passenger seat and seemed lost in thought but beamed at him when he went over to her.

He held up his balloon pump. "Can I tempt you to a giraffe? Or an elephant?" He tilted his head. "Maybe just a coffee?"

"Coffee sounds good …" She sighed and looked suddenly weary.

"Are you okay?" Kit slipped into the driver's seat and looked at her in concern.

"I don't think we should go for coffee. I'm sorry. The reason I wanted to meet up with you was to tell you in person that I can't see you any more."

She paused for a moment but kept talking when Kit didn't comment. "You're so lovely, and I enjoy spending time with you … I *really* enjoy spending time with you, so this feels completely stupid, but I've just come out of a relationship and I don't want to jump straight into another one."

She wrung her hands in her lap. "If I'm honest that's not even the real reason … I think you're great but I'm just not attracted to you … not in any kind of romantic way…"

He drummed on the steering wheel. "That's okay."

"I'm so sorry. I feel terrible."

"It's fine." He turned to face her, his smile coming naturally. "I feel the same."

Her eyebrows shot up. "You do?"

"Yes. I like you, but I'm not attracted to you."

She pressed her lips together. "It's crazy how offended I am by that."

"Sorry," he said, amused. "It's nothing personal. There's someone else I like."

She narrowed her eyes. "Were you using me to try and get over them or to make them jealous?"

"Definitely not to make her jealous. I don't have any chance with her. I guess I thought dating might be a nice distraction. But then I immediately felt bad that I might have given you the wrong idea."

She smiled warmly. "Looks like we're pretty much in the same boat. I'm glad there are no hard feelings. I was dreading speaking to you."

"I really did enjoy going out with you," he said. "Which I was pretty surprised by. I thought it'd be a disaster."

"Me too." She straightened her spine. "Any chance you still want to date me? But like platonically … as friends?"

"I'm not sure you'd call that dating … isn't it just friends hanging out?"

"Yes." She laughed. "Can we do that?"

He nodded. "Shall we get that coffee then?"

"Yes. And I can get a massive slice of cake without worrying that you'll think I'm a pig."

He hopped out of the train and walked around to her. "I'm

going to think you're a pig."

"That's fine." She slipped her arm through his. "It's not a date, so I don't care what you think!"

"Women are weird sometimes, you know?"

"Yep. Speaking of which ... who's the mystery women who you've got a crush on?"

"I'm not telling you."

She gave him a sidelong glance. "Which means it's someone I know ..."

"I don't want to talk about it. I'm trying to put the whole thing behind me."

"Okay. But is it all right if I drone on about my horrible break-up?"

"I suppose I can endure that ... if there's enough cake."

"We might need to order a whole cake!" She laughed, then looked at him excitedly. "Did you get a message from Rebecca about her birthday party?"

"Yes."

"It'll be the old gang from school and I wasn't sure I wanted to go, but it'll be fun if you're there."

"I didn't say I was going." He'd dismissed the message as soon as he'd read it, partly because he wasn't overly keen to hang out with the people he'd gone to school with, and partly because Rebecca was Felix's sister and he'd no doubt be hanging around the party too.

Holly squeezed his elbow. "You're going."

"Really?"

"Yep. Protest all you want, but I've got two weeks to wear you down. You may as well just say you're going now and skip the part where I badger you about it."

"I thought we'd agreed to be friends only. You sound like a nagging girlfriend."

"Just say you'll go to the party!"

"Fine. I'll go." He had two weeks. Plenty of time to come up with an excuse to get out of it.

CHAPTER TWENTY-THREE

Once she recovered from her hangover, Seren was left with a deep sense of self-pity. Her head felt fuzzy for the entire week and all she really wanted to do was hide away in her flat. The only person she wanted to see was Kit, but that wasn't an option. While he was happily getting over her and moving on with his life, she felt completely stuck.

Whenever she worked with Noah she put on a show of cheerfulness. It was exhausting, but better than having to deal with sympathetic looks and questions about what was going on with her. She had enough of that from Felix, who'd taken to messaging and calling her frequently. Mostly she ignored him, but a few times she'd engaged in some mundane message exchanges. She shouldn't encourage him, but with nothing else to occupy her mind she'd got drawn into it.

On Saturday, she had the whole day off and nothing to do until she went over to Mirren's place for Terry's birthday dinner. By late morning she was sick of her own company. For once, her thoughts weren't purely on Kit – she couldn't stop thinking about his dad. Her mind wove elaborate stories about how the day would be if Terry was still with them. Lowen would no doubt have joined them for dinner too. The day would've been joyful and filled with laughter.

With tear-soaked eyes she typed out a message to Kit, asking how he was doing. She added another, saying she was missing Terry. If she felt bad, she imagined he'd be feeling a hundred times worse.

When he didn't reply she checked her watch. He'd be out giving a tour on the train. It should be over soon and she kept an eye on her phone, waiting for the ticks to turn blue to indicate he'd read the messages. No matter what was going on between them, she was certain he'd reply to her message as soon as he saw it. Except the ticks didn't change colour. An hour after she sent the message, she tried calling him but got no answer. Maybe he'd left his phone at home.

With nothing else to do and a niggling worry in the pit of her stomach, she set off down to the beach when it was almost time for his next train tour. Seeing the train parked in its usual spot eased her anxiety.

"Where's Kit?" she asked Keira, who was collecting money from the passengers.

Keira moved away from the train before replying. "He wanted the day off. I'm going it alone for the first time."

"That's great," Seren said, registering Keira's nervous excitement. "Is Kit okay?"

"He called this morning and asked me to take over for the day. I think his dad's birthday was getting him down. Noah wanted to keep busy, that's why he made sure he was working." She smiled gently and tipped her head towards the train. "I need to get on."

"Yeah. Of course. Did Kit say what he was doing?"

"No. I guess he's at home." She went back to the customers and Seren wandered away. As she walked in the direction of Kit's place she tried calling him again but wasn't surprised to get no reply. When he didn't answer the door either, her niggling worry increased to a knot of anxiety.

Instinctively, she set off to the Mermaid Inn. Most of the tables were occupied, and there was a hum of voices in the air. Noah was pulling a pint while chatting to one of the regulars who was sitting at the bar. When he saw her, he set the pint in front of Jim and moved along to her.

"How are you doing?" she asked, with a slight tilt of her head.

His chest expanded as he drew in a breath. "Okay."

"You haven't seen Kit, have you?"

He shook his head. "As far as I know he was planning on chilling out at home. He didn't feel like working so asked Keira to take over the train."

"I know. I've just spoken to her. I went to Kit's place but he didn't seem to be there. He didn't answer his phone either."

"He's probably with Mum."

"Maybe." Seren pulled her phone out to call Mirren, then let out a low growl when she didn't answer either. Almost immediately a message came through to say she was at the hairdresser and wouldn't be able to hear anything over the noise of the hairdryer but asked if everything was okay. Seren replied that she was fine and would see her at dinner.

"Kit's not with your mum," Seren said to Noah. "I'm worried about him."

"He'll be fine. Maybe he's with Holly." He frowned. "Except I guess she works on Saturdays."

"She works at the tourist information on Porthcressa Road?"

"Yeah."

That seemed the obvious place to check next. If Kit was with Holly, Seren really didn't want to know, but she at least needed to know he was okay.

"I'll see you later," she said to Noah, before going outside again. If nothing else, traipsing around the town was good exercise.

Holly was easy to spot with her bouncy blonde curls and bright eyes. She stood behind a desk chatting to a middle-aged couple about the ferry crossings to the off islands. Seren shifted her weight from foot to foot and tried to catch Holly's eye to no avail. It felt like ages before the couple finally left.

"How can I help you?" Holly asked, smiling at Seren.

"I'm looking for Kit."

Her smile remained but frown lines appeared on Holly's brow. "I'm sorry?"

"You're friends with Kit, aren't you?"

"Yeah." She blinked a couple of times. "You work in the pub, right?"

"Yes. I'm Seren." She felt a pang of sadness that Kit had clearly never spoken about her to Holly. "I'm friends with Kit. With all the Trenearys… I can't seem to track him down and I'm a bit worried about him. I wondered if you knew where he might be?"

She leaned across the desk and lowered her voice, which seemed a bit dramatic considering they were the only ones in the room. "It's his dad's birthday today. You know his dad died, I suppose?"

"Yes," she said through gritted teeth. "That's why I'm worried about Kit. It'll be a hard day for him."

Holly nodded. "I spoke to him this morning. He didn't feel like working, so he'd got someone to cover for him."

"Do you know what he was planning on doing for the day?"

"It sounded as though he was going to stay at home. He said he didn't feel like being around people. He's going to his mum's house for dinner later. Have you tried calling him?"

It was an effort for Seren not to snap at the annoyingly smiley woman. Of course she'd tried calling him. What kind of an idiot did she think she was?

"He's not answering," she said calmly.

"I'll bet he's fallen asleep. They say grief is exhausting, don't they? Try calling him again later."

Seren forced a smile. "I'll do that. Thanks."

Back outside, she let out a frustrated sigh, but realised she had one last place left to look for him. Just because Mirren wasn't at home didn't mean Kit wasn't there. It was only a fifteen-minute walk, but she went back home for her car and drove over there.

Finding the backdoor locked wasn't a good sign. If someone was at home the backdoor was always unlocked. Nevertheless, she used her key to let herself in, calling out to Kit as she did a sweep of the quiet house. Feeling defeated, she wandered back to the car.

Gazing out over the turquoise water, she racked her brain, thinking of where Kit might be. All she could come up with was that he was alone at home, missing his dad and shutting out the world. The thought brought tears to her eyes, and she blinked them away as she looked at her phone again.

The messages she'd sent Kit were still marked as unread. She hit dial and held the phone to her ear to listen to it ring. As she was about to give up, a noise from the garage drew her attention, just a small bang which she could have imagined.

The garage was large enough for three cars, but what it actually housed was Mirren's car and golf cart, plus an assortment of boats, bikes, fishing equipment and goodness knows what else. Seren's eyes did a quick sweep, but she didn't notice anything obviously out of place. The golf cart wasn't there but presumably Mirren had driven that into town.

Running a hand over the side of the dinghy, Seren thought of how excited they'd all been when Terry and Mirren had bought it, back when she and Noah were teenagers. Prior to that, they used to borrow Terry's little sailing boat for their adventures around the islands, but a boat with an engine was way more fun.

At the thought of the sailboat, Seren looked to the far end of the garage, where it had been left as a morbid reminder since the day Terry didn't come back on it. As far as Seren was aware, no one had taken it out since his death.

She froze when she noticed it was missing, then her heart rate increased at the thought of Kit taking it out alone. Her foot hit something and her gaze fell to his phone on the floor. Presumably that was the source of the noise – it had probably fallen off the side of the boat when she called. She slipped it in her pocket before marching back outside and scanning the horizon. There was no sign of Kit, and she wasn't sure there was much sense in going after him given that she had no idea which direction he'd have gone in.

What else was she going to do though? Pace around waiting for him to get back? Turning on her heel, she pulled the dinghy out and manoeuvred the trailer easily along the tarmac. The job became more strenuous when she hit the sand, but she trudged on regardless.

Once the trailer was in the shallows she floated the dinghy off it. Dragging the trailer back up the beach, she parked it beside the one for the sailing boat, which she hadn't noticed until she'd got onto the beach.

The cool water felt refreshing as she splashed through the waves. In the boat, she scraped her hair back to a ponytail, then started the motor and headed for deeper waters. Turning east was instinctive. Kit would be thinking about his dad, and that would likely mean sailing over to the Eastern Isles, where Terry would've been on his last sailing trip.

Her eyes constantly scanned the water as the boat bounced over gentle waves. A couple of yachts were anchored out to sea, and there were a fair few paddle boards closer to the shore. Out of courtesy, she slowed near a group of wind surfers who weren't getting anywhere very fast. She nodded a greeting before ramping up the speed again.

Just passed Toll's Island, a large grey seal caught her eye, lazing on a rocky outcrop. Distracted, she almost didn't see the sailing boat that was bobbing around a little further out to sea. With its sail down Seren had trouble identifying it, but from the way her stomach twisted she would've bet anything it was Kit. As she sped towards it, the boom swung wildly to starboard, stopped only by the main sheet reaching its limit.

There was no one on board.

Seren felt her blood pumping harder and tried to keep her breathing even. He'd have gone for a swim, that's all. Slowing, she searched the water and began to mutter his name repeatedly.

She'd almost reached Terry's boat when she cut the motor. The dinghy rocked when she stood, and her eyes frantically darted all around, searching the crystal-clear water for any sign of Kit. Any minute now he'd swim up to her and make her jump. It'd been his favourite trick when he was younger. He'd always found it hilarious. She'd laugh now too … if he'd just appear and splash her with water.

Panic gripped her and her voice sounded strange when she called his name at the top of her lungs.

CHAPTER TWENTY-FOUR

As her shout faded, her attention was drawn to movement in the sailing boat.

"What are you yelling for?" Kit asked, sitting up so quickly that he almost cracked his head on the boom.

"Oh my god." Seren slapped a hand over her heart, then leaned precariously far out to try and get a hand on Kit's boat. When she couldn't reach, she threw him the rope instead.

"What are you doing here?" Kit asked.

Seren didn't answer as she hopped from her boat to his. "I couldn't see you," she said, her voice raspy as her emotions threatened to overwhelm her. "Don't ever do that to me again!" Grabbing his lifejacket at his shoulders, she pulled him close. "Promise me."

He looked at her in confusion, their faces so close she could feel the warmth of his breath on her skin. "I don't know what I'm promising …"

"I could see the boat," she explained. "But I couldn't see you."

"Oh." Realisation flooded his features. "I'm fine."

"I can see that … but you just took about ten years off my life." She loosened her grip on him and tried to move away, but the sway of the boat propelled her into him and she didn't fight it. With their noses touching, she instinctively pressed her lips to his. For the briefest moment the waves ceased and everything was perfectly still.

As she pulled back, she caught the shock in Kit's eyes. It was an effort not to jump back over to the dinghy and make a quick getaway.

Instead, she moved to sit by the tiller and glared up at Kit. "What the hell are you playing at?" she demanded.

"What am *I* playing at?" Deftly, he tied the rope from the dinghy onto the mast, then ducked under the boom to sit at the other side of the tiller.

"Yes," she snapped. "You teach kids about water safety for goodness' sake. You know the rules. You don't go out on the water alone without taking precautions. Someone needs to know where you're going and when you expect to be back. And you have your phone with you, *always*. What were you thinking? Did you decide safety rules don't apply to you or what?"

He looked her right in the eyes. "I went to visit Lowen," he said calmly. "I called him to say I was on my way, but then I left my phone in the garage. Lowen knew I was coming though … and I messaged Mum from Lowen's phone when I was setting off back. I told her I'd be taking it slow and didn't have my phone but I was on the way home."

"Oh," she said sheepishly.

"I'm also wearing a life jacket, which is more than I can say for you." He raised an eyebrow. "Did *you* let someone know where you were going and when you'd be back?"

She ran her teeth over her bottom lip. "I was in a rush."

"Why?"

"I wanted to check how you were doing, but you didn't answer your phone or your doorbell, and no one seemed to know where you were. I was worried …" Their eyes locked and all she wanted to do was kiss him again. If he moved so much as a millimetre in her direction she wouldn't be able to help herself.

He didn't though. He shifted his gaze to his hands as his brow wrinkled with a frown. "Sorry you were worried. I'm fine."

"Are you?" she asked gently. "What the heck were you doing having a nap in the bottom of the boat?"

"I wasn't sleeping. I was looking at the sky." He gazed at the plump white clouds overhead. "When I was a kid, Dad would bring me out on the boat and I'd lie down and watch the clouds floating by. I thought it'd be nice to feel that carefree again … just for a few minutes."

The muscles in his jaw tightened as he continued looking heavenwards.

"Sorry," Seren said, reaching for his hand. "I knew you'd be missing him today. That's why I wanted to check on you."

"I'm okay," he said, swallowing hard.

The shriek of gulls broke the silence for a moment, then died away, leaving the sound of the waves slapping against the boat to fill the void.

"There's something I can't get out of my head," Kit said, giving her a sidelong glance.

"What?" She swallowed, thinking he was going to bring up the fact that she'd just kissed him. Except it was clear from the serious set of his features that he had a lot more on his mind than her springing kisses on him.

He chewed on his lip for a moment, then shook his head. "It doesn't matter. Forget it."

"Just tell me."

"I saw Dad on the day he died," he said after a pause. "I'd taken the train out in the morning, and I was walking up to see if I could scrounge lunch from Mum before I took the afternoon tours." He paused and looked down at Seren's hand, which was still curled around his. Turning his hand over, he intertwined their fingers, the action making Seren's heart flutter. "I saw Dad putting the boat in the water as I walked along the lane, and I remember thinking that if I hurried I could catch him and go out with him for an hour." His breath caught in his throat and tears filled his eyes. "But I was hungry …"

She squeezed his hand as he turned away from her. "You couldn't have known," she said quietly.

"I slowed down." His voice was choked with emotion. "I knew that if he saw me he'd ask me to go with him … I could never say no when he asked me to go out on the boat with him, so I slowed down so he wouldn't see me … I watched him sail away on his own, and it was the last time I saw him."

"Oh, Kit," she breathed, leaning over the tiller to wrap her arms around him.

"I should have gone with him. If I'd have gone with him he might still be here."

"There's no way of knowing what might have been if things had gone differently that day. But beating yourself up about it isn't going to change anything. And you know your dad wouldn't want you to."

"I never told anyone that I saw him," he sniffed. "Not even Mum. I feel so guilty."

Seren's throat was so thick it was difficult to speak. "He asked Noah to go out sailing with him that day," she finally managed. It wasn't her secret to tell, but she was sure Noah wouldn't mind, given the circumstances.

"What?" Kit pulled away from her, searching her features.

She nodded. "He told your dad that he didn't have time. He also thinks he should have done things differently."

"Who knows about that?"

"Me and your mum. Possibly Keira now … I don't know."

He leaned on his knees with his head in his hands.

"Noah felt terrible," Seren said. "He blamed himself. Thought that everything would be different if he'd just gone with him."

"What did Mum say?" Kit asked sadly.

Seren swallowed the lump in her throat. "What do you think she said?"

It took him a minute to speak. "That it wasn't his fault and he shouldn't blame himself ..."

"It was definitely something along those lines." Reaching over, she slipped her fingers into his again. "Are you okay?"

He nodded but gazed out to sea, pointedly avoiding eye contact. "I keep telling myself that there's no point in dwelling on it. What's done is done and I can't do anything to change it. But it seems crazy that I slowed down to avoid talking to him. Or that I chose not to go out on the boat with him." He took a breath. "All I want to do now is go out sailing with him."

"I know," she said, resting her head against his shoulder. "I'm sorry."

After a couple of minutes, he sat up straighter, pulling his hand from hers to wipe tears from his cheeks.

"We should probably get back," he said, ducking under the boom and moving to untie the rope from the mast.

"We could lie down and watch the clouds for a bit if you want?" Anything to keep her on the boat with him a little while longer.

"Thanks." He flashed a smile without looking at her. "But I don't want Mum to worry."

With a twist of disappointment in her gut, she handed him his phone, then stepped back over to the dinghy while Kit held the boats level. "Want me to tow you home?" she asked.

"I'm okay. There's enough of a breeze to get me back." He threw the rope back to her, causing the boats to drift apart. "Thanks for coming to look for me."

"Of course." She gave him a sympathetic smile, then switched the engine on, the noise breaking the atmosphere.

With a quick wave, she set off, following the shoreline all the way back to Mirren's place.

CHAPTER TWENTY-FIVE

M irren was busy in the kitchen when Seren arrived at the house. Her hair was freshly cut and styled, and she seemed determined not to let the emotions of the day get to her.

"I'm just making chicken legs and baked potatoes and salad," she told Seren. "That's all right, isn't it?"

"Sounds great to me. What can I help with?"

"There isn't much to do." She turned to wash the potatoes, then let out a frustrated sigh. "What about dessert? I hadn't even thought about that. I could make an apple pie, but the weather's too nice to be eating a warm dessert."

"We can have ice cream," Seren suggested. "Everyone will be happy with ice cream."

"Can you check if there's some in the freezer?"

Seren found half a tub of chocolate chip, but there was no way that would be enough. "I'll run into town and buy some," she told Mirren. "Do you need anything else?"

"I don't think so. Although I'm not sure my brain is functioning properly today. I'll probably think of something later."

"Are you okay?" Seren asked, draping her arm around Mirren's shoulders.

Briefly, Mirren leaned her head on Seren's shoulder. "I think so, love."

"I'll be back soon. Call me if you think of anything else you need."

As well as getting the shopping, Seren nipped home for a shower, then picked up a bunch of flowers for Mirren on the way back to the house.

"I see I've been outdone," Seren said, noticing a huge bouquet of flowers on the table when she handed over her own bunch.

"They just arrived. Jago sent them."

"That's nice of him."

"Yes. He called me earlier too. It was good to speak to him."

"How is he?"

"Busy, as always, but he seems happy."

Seren went to the freezer to unload her shopping bag. "I couldn't decide which flavours to get, so I bought three different ones."

Mirren sat at the table, her lips pulling to a frown. "I should have baked a cake, shouldn't I? Did I bake a cake for his birthday last year?"

"I'm not sure." Actually, Seren clearly remembered there being chocolate cake last year and the year before – Terry's favourite. "It doesn't matter though. We're all together, remembering him, that's the important thing."

"I don't have time to start baking a cake now." Mirren took a deep breath and sat up straighter. "Can you do me one more favour?"

Seren nodded as she closed the freezer. "What is it?"

"Could you check on Kit?" Mirren lowered her voice. "He's in the living room. He's not coping well today, but he won't talk to me. See if you can get him to open up. It'd do him good to talk."

"I'll try," Seren said before going in search of him.

Sprawled out on the couch with his eyes closed, Kit looked

fast asleep, but she assumed he wasn't. When she perched beside his hip, he blinked his eyes open.

"You again," he said with a lazy smile.

"Me again." She felt a pang of guilt at enjoying the closeness to him, which was only happening because he was feeling so down. "Your mum's worried about you."

"I'm okay." He slung an arm behind his head and gazed up at her.

"I never asked how Lowen was when you saw him ... I'm surprised you went over there."

"I woke up feeling like crap, and I called Trystan."

"How's he doing?"

"He sounded okay, but he was worried about Lowen, as usual. I said I'd go and check on him. It seemed like a good way to keep my mind occupied. Then I saw Dad's boat, and it seemed like a nice idea to take it out."

"Is Lowen okay?"

"I don't think so, no. It's hard to tell because he hardly speaks anyway, but he seemed more subdued than usual."

"I'll bet he was glad to see you."

He gave her a look as though she'd told a bad joke. "I don't think so. Especially since I ended up having a go at him."

"How come?"

"I tried to get him to come and have dinner with us. Then I got annoyed when he refused." He rubbed at his forehead. "Dad would hate how he's distanced himself from us. I told him as much and he snapped at me. Said it didn't matter what Dad would think since Dad's dead."

Seren shook her head. "I'm sure he didn't mean it."

"I don't understand him. He's the eldest, so I feel as though he should be looking out for us. But he acts more like a teenager than a forty-year-old man."

"I get annoyed with him too sometimes, but I'm not sure it's right to expect more from him because he's the eldest. He's also missing his dad."

"I guess you're right. It's difficult to have a lot of sympathy for him when he's so grumpy and self-involved. It's as though he thinks he has a monopoly on grief. Like he's the only one hurting."

"It was good that you went to see him anyway."

He shrugged and looked at her intently. "I need to ask you something," he said, sitting up.

With an inkling what his question would be, Seren's heart rate picked up but she forced her smile to stay fixed.

"On the boat earlier ..." His cheeks pinked slightly. "You kissed me."

Seren opened her mouth to speak but couldn't think how to respond. Her instinct was to apologise and brush it off as nothing, but there was a part of her that wanted to tell him the truth.

Kit squeezed his eyes shut and shook his head. "I'm sure it was nothing – you were worried about me and I guess you were just relieved to see me ..." The statement rose at the end to sound like a question.

"Yes," she said weakly.

"I thought so, but I wanted to check." His slow smile brought out the dimple in his cheek. "This is why I should never have told you how I feel. Every time you kiss me now I'm going to read too much into it."

She put a hand over her face as she laughed at his stupid sense of humour. Clearly her kissing him was an unusual occurrence, and she owed him more of an explanation. She only wished she was brave enough to tell him the truth.

"I was very relieved to see you," she said, moving her hand from her face. "That was definitely part of it. The other part is that I miss you. I hate not seeing you. I miss your face."

"It's a very nice face," he said cockily, causing her to give him a playful shove.

"Are you planning on avoiding the pub forever so you don't have to see me?"

His eyes sparkled with amusement. "I'm in there all the time when you're not working. Sometimes I even wait around the corner until you leave and then I go in."

"Kit!" She shoved him harder this time. "You better be joking!"

"Of course I'm joking, you idiot."

"I miss you teasing me," she said quietly.

"Part of my problem is that whenever I see you, it feels as though someone is stamping on my heart. I thought it would be nice to have a break from that for a while." He rubbed at his jaw. "I'm also quite embarrassed around you now."

"Don't be." She fought off tears. The last thing she wanted was for him to be embarrassed about his feelings for her.

"Easier said than done." He gave her a friendly punch on the arm. "I'll start coming into the pub again sometimes."

"When I'm working?"

He laughed. "Yes. I'll come and sit at the bar and annoy you like I used to."

"I'd like that."

"I suppose one day things will get back to normal between us."

Seren nodded, ignoring the twinge of disappointment at his words. She was fairly sure that the two of them being friends would never feel quite right again. "I heard you're seeing Holly Burton?"

"That's bad information I'm afraid. We're just friends. But since we're on the subject of dating, there are rumours flying around about you and Felix."

She rolled her eyes. "Don't you love island gossip?"

"So, it's not true."

"Definitely not true."

"I feel as though this is stating the obvious, since you know how I feel about you, but you can do way better than him."

"I happen to agree with you," she said with a smile. "We should go and cheer your mum up. She's fretting that she didn't bake a cake."

They'd just stood up when Kit took her arm. She looked up at him, surprised by his height.

"I know things are a bit weird between us at the moment," he said, looking adorably bashful. "But I'm glad you're here today."

"Me too." She melted into his chest when he hugged her, and it was an effort to pull herself away.

In the kitchen, Keira was walking in the back door with a cake in her hands and a look on her face as though something terrible had happened.

"What's wrong?" Mirren asked her.

"I might have misjudged this," she said, grimacing. "I wanted to do something nice for you, so I thought I'd bake a cake. It seemed like a good idea when I thought of it, but I just realised it might be insensitive to bring a cake today. And I also thought that maybe you'd rather it's just family this evening. I can go and take the cake with me if you want?"

Kit moved swiftly to take the cake from her. "You're not taking *that* anywhere."

"Of course we want you here," Mirren said. "You're family now."

"Are you sure?"

"Yes." Mirren's voice was thick with emotion, and tears spilled down her cheeks.

"But I've made you cry," Keira said, placing a hand on Mirren's arm.

"Only because I was annoyed with myself for not baking a cake. Now you've brought one, so that's perfect." She wiped at her cheeks. "We're all emotional wrecks today, aren't we? We could do with Trystan here to put the music on and get us dancing around the kitchen."

There was a noise at the door as Trystan dropped his bag and then wandered into the room. "That could probably be arranged."

"What are you doing here?" Mirren asked, through more tears.

"Kit called me this morning and it sounded as though he could use a hug, so I jumped on a plane." When Kit raised a sceptical eyebrow, Trystan smiled sadly. "Fine. I thought I could use a hug."

"You big softie," Mirren said as she embraced him. "I'm glad you're here."

"Me too." He hugged them all in turn. "It sounds like dancing and cake is in order."

Mirren sighed. "I'd never have mentioned dancing if I'd known you were in hearing distance."

"And we can't have cake until Noah gets here," Keira said.

"Where is he?" Trystan asked.

"Still at work," Mirren told him. "But he should be finished soon."

Trystan checked his watch. "Perfect. We can all go down there. I managed to convince Lowen to come over and meet me for a drink."

"Can't you get him to come up here?" Kit said, his voice tinged with annoyance. "Mum's cooking."

"We can eat late," Mirren said. "Going to the pub first is a good idea."

"It doesn't mean anyone gets out of dancing," Trystan announced as they bustled out of the door. "We'll dance around the pub."

"You're really embarrassing," Kit told him.

Out in the fresh air, Trystan draped an arm around Kit's shoulders and pulled Seren close to him at the other side. She put her arm around his waist and smiled in the sunshine. As usual, Trystan had managed to bring the mood up in an instant. Everyone was in better spirits as they headed for the Mermaid Inn.

CHAPTER TWENTY-SIX

Having Trystan around for the weekend felt like a breath of fresh air for Kit. Life felt normal again. From drinks in the pub on Saturday evening, to the usual rowdy dinner, then the lazy day with all of them hanging around at their mum's place on Sunday, everything was relaxed and easy. Being around Seren gave him hope that they'd be able to get back to some semblance of normal.

If nothing else, the weekend had shown him that he couldn't ignore her forever. She was a huge part of his life, and he didn't want that to change just because he wanted more than friendship. Even if she didn't love him the way he loved her, she still loved him; that much had been obvious from the way she'd come looking for him on the boat on Saturday.

His mind returned repeatedly to the moment she'd kissed him. He'd known at the time that it didn't mean anything, but he couldn't help but hope that her feelings for him had changed. It had been slightly embarrassing asking her about it later, but he'd needed to know for definite so he wouldn't go back to spending his time pondering the possibility of there being more between them. She loved him as one of her oldest friends, and that was all. He had to learn to live with that.

His phone rang shortly after he got home from work on Wednesday, and he swiped to accept the call from Holly.

"Fancy going out for a midweek drink?" she asked him.

"Sure. Where and when?"

"I was thinking of the Mermaid Inn. How soon can you get there?"

"Oh … Um …"

"Hopefully soon. I'm just leaving work and I'd rather go straight to the pub than home first."

"Why don't you come to my place? I've got beers."

"I'd rather go to the pub. I haven't eaten dinner and I'm craving their fish and chips."

"Right … I guess that's fine." He was fairly sure Seren would be working, but he'd promised to start going in the pub again. It felt a bit weird going in with Holly, but there was no reason why it should be awkward. He'd explained that he and Holly were only friends. Not that Seren would care about his relationship status. "I'll leave now," he said into the phone as he headed for the door.

He bumped into Holly on his way to the pub, standing outside of the post office on Hugh Street, chatting to the woman who worked there. She looked relieved at the excuse to extract herself from the conversation and gave his arm a grateful squeeze as they continued along the road.

"You saved me from having to eat leftovers," she said. "And saved me from Dawn's gossiping too."

"Happy to help," he said as they made their way to the pub.

Charlie was behind the bar, and Kit felt momentarily relieved at the thought that Seren wasn't working. It didn't last long though – they'd taken a seat near the window when she walked out from the back room. She paused when she caught sight of him, then came over to say hello.

"I take it you found him in the end?" Holly said, beaming up at Seren.

Seren shifted her weight and glanced around the pub. "Yes. I did."

"Found who?" Kit asked in confusion.

"You," Holly said.

"I saw Holly on Saturday when I was looking for you," Seren explained. "I asked if she'd seen you."

"Oh." He tried to catch Seren's eye, but she was looking anywhere but at him. When the door opened and a group of local fishermen walked in, she said she'd be back in a bit and went behind the bar. "Where did you bump into each other?" Kit asked Holly.

"We didn't bump into each other. Seren came into the tourist information specifically to ask if I knew where you were. She seemed pretty worried. You must have known her ages, right? Isn't she good friends with one of your brothers?"

"Seren's been best friends with Noah since they were little. They were inseparable when they were growing up, so she was at our place a lot. Still is. She's like part of the family." His words sounded hollow as he looked over at Seren. There was a flutter in his chest when she looked up and caught his eye. She looked away quickly and he forced his attention back to Holly, asking her about work.

He already knew that Seren had been looking for him on Saturday, so he wasn't sure why his mind was working overtime with the fact that she'd gone into the tourist office. Maybe it was because she clearly hadn't wanted him to know the lengths she'd gone to find him. She also didn't seem overly comfortable with him being in the pub. Which made no sense since she was the one to complain about him not coming in any more. Was it him being with Holly that was the problem?

That was exactly the kind of thinking he'd been trying to avoid, and he made a conscious effort to keep his mind on the conversation with Holly. Seren didn't linger when she brought their food out. Try as he might to stop himself, Kit couldn't help but glance behind the bar from time to time. Each time he looked, Seren was looking back at him and would either snap her gaze away or give him a quick smile.

When Holly asked if he wanted dessert or another drink, he told her he'd rather get going. They moved to the bar to pay, and Kit had just said goodbye to Seren when Rebecca wandered in with Felix.

"You're not leaving now, are you?" Rebecca asked. "Stay and have a drink with us."

"I've got some things I need to do this evening," Kit said when Holly looked questioningly at him. There was no way he was going to hang around and have a drink with Felix.

"I should get going too," Holly said. "We'll see you at the party on Friday though. I can't wait."

"Are you coming?" Rebecca aimed a playful jab at Kit's ribs. "You didn't reply to my message."

"Sorry," he said weakly. "I wasn't sure if I could make it—"

Holly interrupted him. "He's coming."

"You have to," Rebecca put in. "Seren was worried she wouldn't know many people, so you need to come."

Kit swung around to Seren. "Are you going?"

"Well … I …" She opened her mouth a few times and he got the distinct impression that she was about as keen to go as he was.

"She'll be there," Felix said, his lips curling in amusement. "Rebecca wants you there, so there's no point in arguing. The little princess always gets her way." He shot his sister a look that was full of affection. Considering Kit had only ever seen Felix sneering at people, it came as something of a shock.

"We'll see you on Friday then," Kit said, taking steps towards the door. He hung back while Holly had a brief exchange with Rebecca about what she could bring. Catching Seren's eye, he held her gaze for a moment and flashed her a small smile.

"Come on!" Holly broke his trance, taking his arm and leading him away. When he glanced back, Seren was still watching him and didn't take her eyes off him until he was out of the door.

CHAPTER TWENTY-SEVEN

Knowing that Seren was going to Rebecca's party should have been further reason for Kit to make an excuse, but it had the opposite effect and he found himself looking forward to it.

He hurried home after the gig race on Friday evening and had just got out of the shower when Holly arrived at his place. She hung around in the kitchen while he finished getting ready. They'd planned on walking over to Rebecca's place, but he had a last-minute urge to drive over there.

"I thought you'd want to have a few drinks," Holly remarked when he mentioned it to her. "It's Friday night."

"I won't drink much anyway." Kit held the door open for her and she went ahead. Outside, he took a couple of steps in the direction of the garage before she pulled on his arm.

"Let's walk. We can drink some shots and get silly."

"Trying to get me drunk?" he asked, giving up on the idea of driving.

"Maybe," she said with a grin.

"I hope you're not intending to seduce me?"

She laughed loudly. "No! I just thought it'd do you good to loosen up a bit. Any chance your crush is going to be there?"

"I'm not sure."

"You said it's someone I know, so I'm guessing it's someone we went to school with."

"I don't recall saying you knew her."

She pursed her lips. "It was implied. You wouldn't be secretive about it unless it was someone I know. And you obviously think she's going to be at the party, judging by the amount of effort you've gone to."

"This old thing," he said, looking coyly down at his favourite shirt.

"You smell good too."

"Thanks."

"If your mystery woman is at the party maybe you'll have the courage to do something about your crush after a few drinks …"

"Like tell her I'm in love with her?"

"No, idiot. Like kiss her! Or ask her on a date."

He wrinkled his nose. "Do you think that'd be more appropriate than telling her I'm in love with her?"

"Yes!" She shook her head in amusement. "You can't just tell someone you love them."

"Oops." He grimaced. "At least now I know where I went wrong."

"You told her you love her?" she asked, hooking her arm through his.

"Yeah."

"Oh my goodness. You're the sweetest. How did she not fall into your arms?"

"Maybe kissing her would have been a better tactic." He touched the edge of his lip, remembering the way she'd kissed him on the boat.

"Here's a plan," Holly said. "We'll drink shots at the party, and if the opportunity arises you can kiss her."

"That's not going to happen. I can't kiss her now that she

told me she's not interested. I'm also not getting drunk. I'm working in the morning."

"Not early though. You'll have plenty of time to get rid of a hangover."

"I can't," he said, swatting at a wasp that buzzed by his ear.

"Why not?"

"It's not really that I *can't,* I just won't. It's not worth it." He smiled at a kid who walked past with one of his balloon animals in his hand – he'd been on his last ride of the day. "When I bought the train, some of the residents were against it. There were a lot of people who either wanted me to fail or expected me to. They were looking for any possible thing they could complain about. People thought I was too young to run a business and make a go of it … I went out of my way to make sure I never put a foot wrong."

"Surely no one can comment on what you do in your spare time."

"How long have you lived on this island for?" he asked jokily.

"Okay, good point. People would definitely comment … but you could always ignore them."

"I'd rather not give them anything negative to comment on. Besides, I hate the thought of being seen stumbling out of the pub by some family on their holidays who've been on the train with me. Or turning up to work with a hangover. It's not the image I want to give out."

She squeezed his elbow. "Very sensible. I guess I'll be drinking alone this evening."

"I didn't say I won't have a beer or two."

"Have a beer or two and introduce me to your mystery woman."

He decided not to respond but smiled at how eager she was to know who it was.

"Oh, I forgot! You don't need to introduce me because I already know her. You may as well just tell me who it is."

He pointed in the vague direction of the horizon. "I reckon it's going to be a great sunset this evening."

"And I reckon you're trying to change the subject, but you're also right about the sunset."

By the time they reached the party, the sun had dipped low, streaking the sky with swathes of pinks and reds.

The living room of the spacious house felt like a school reunion, with the majority of people they'd gone to secondary school with milling around. Having lost track of Holly the moment they'd arrived, Kit sought her out after half an hour.

"I heard there's food in the kitchen," he told her, nodding in that direction.

"There are more people than I expected," Holly said. "Is your lady friend here? We could play a real-life game of Guess Who …" She scanned the crowd. "Does she have purple hair?"

He laughed. "No, it's not Georgia Hart. And she's not here, so the game is pointless."

"I see, that's why we're moving to the kitchen? To see if she's in there? Good plan."

"We're moving to the kitchen for food," he said, but he was definitely on the lookout for Seren. There was no sign of her, and he felt a pang of disappointment. Maybe he should have messaged her earlier to casually encourage her to come. But it might be a good thing that she wasn't there … it wasn't really her crowd, and while he liked to think she'd hang out with him, there was also the possibility that she'd spend the evening hanging out with Felix.

A buffet was laid out on the kitchen island and Kit helped himself to a couple of sandwiches before moving along to the selection of sweets.

"The brownies are amazing," Holly told him with her mouth full.

Rebecca appeared behind them. "They're my own recipe."

"They're delicious," Holly said, turning to Rebecca.

Kit held up the remainder of his brownie as he chewed slowly. "Have they got peanuts in?"

Rebecca's eyes widened. "They're peanut butter brownies. You're not allergic, are you?"

"No." He popped the rest in his mouth. "Seren is. Maybe we could put a note beside them in case she comes later."

"I had no idea she was allergic to peanuts." Rebecca called out to Cadan across the room, demanding to know why he hadn't volunteered that information. He was deep in conversation with Felix and only shrugged in response.

"I'll definitely put a note beside them," Rebecca said, opening a drawer and pulling out a notepad and pen. She frowned as she surveyed the food. "I think they're the only thing with peanuts."

"Would you mind if we just put them away?" Kit asked. "Sometimes Seren's throat gets scratchy just being in a room with peanuts."

"Okay." Rebecca got a container and helped Kit load the brownies into it.

"Thanks," Kit said as she stowed them in the fridge.

Holly thrust a beer at him and pulled on his arm. "Come outside with me."

"What's going on?" Kit asked, as they stepped out through the patio doors.

"Gavin's here! I had no idea he'd be invited. I think he's friends with Cadan, but it didn't occur to me that he'd be here."

"We can always leave if you want."

"No, it's fine. I'd just rather have another drink in me before I speak to him. Let's wander down to the beach and watch the sunset."

Kit glanced back inside, checking for Seren but thinking she probably wasn't going to turn up.

CHAPTER TWENTY-EIGHT

After a long day at work, going to Rebecca's party was about the last thing Seren felt like doing. She was very tempted to curl up in bed instead. It was only the thought of seeing Kit that enticed her. Then again, watching him with Holly on Wednesday evening hadn't exactly been fun. She'd hardly been able to take her eyes off them. Kit had insisted he and Holly were only friends, and there hadn't been anything in the way they interacted that suggested otherwise, but that didn't stop Seren from feeling sick with jealousy.

What if she got to the party to find Kit was too busy hanging out with Holly to even notice her? Shaking her unhelpful thoughts away, she forced herself off the couch to shower and change.

Taking the car seemed to be a sensible idea since it meant she could leave quickly if she needed to. Obviously the downside was that she wouldn't be able to drink. In the end, alcohol won out and she set off walking. As she left the town and followed the curve of the road, the steady incline got her heart pumping faster. With the warm sea breeze driving against her she felt invigorated and paused to take in the view when the road levelled off. The setting sun had turned the sky a heavenly shade of pink and tinged the listless sea as well.

Continuing on her way, Seren's stomach fluttered at the thought of seeing Kit. She quickened her pace until the house came into view.

Felix was out on the patio, chatting to a couple of guys. She tipped her chin in greeting and slipped inside before he could corner her.

"There you are," Cadan said, breaking away from a cluster of people she didn't recognise. "I was starting to think you weren't coming."

"I got held up at work." Her eyes darted towards the living room but there was no sign of Kit. Maybe he'd decided not to bother with the party. If that was the case, she wouldn't hang around for long.

"There's loads of food." Cadan tipped his chin towards the table. "Rebecca went a bit overboard if you ask me, but she's a good cook. Are you hungry?"

"I ate at the pub. A drink would be nice though." When she stole his beer, he rolled his eyes and went to get another one.

"Did you see Felix?" Cadan asked, perching on a stool at the counter. "He'll be happy you made it."

Ignoring the comment, she craned her neck to look further into the busy living room. "Is Kit here?"

"Yeah. I saw him earlier."

Felix loped up beside Seren and draped an arm around her shoulders. "The littlest Treneary?"

"Don't call him that. You know who he is."

He rolled his eyes. "He just walked down to the beach with his girlfriend."

"I presume you mean Holly," she huffed.

"I guess so. How many girlfriends has he got?"

"None." She shoved Felix's arm off her. "She's not his girlfriend."

"They looked pretty close," Felix said.

Seren took a long swig of beer, then turned on her heel and walked back out onto the patio. The group of guys moved inside as she plonked herself into a chair and stared out over the coastline. In the fading light she could just make out two figures sitting in the sand.

Telling herself she had no right to be upset didn't make her urge to cry any less overwhelming. What had she expected, that Kit would wait for her to come around to the idea of being with him? She was tempted to run down and pull him away from Holly and tell him she'd caught up, that she was terrified of messing things up but was ready to dive in regardless. She wanted to tell him she loved him too.

It was a bit late now though. Besides, if he'd really been in love with her there was no way he could move on so quickly. No one could get over someone in that amount of time. He probably hadn't been in love with her at all. It was just a crush. Angrily, she took a swig of her drink.

"What's up with you?" Felix asked, breaking her thoughts as he sat beside her.

"Nothing."

"You could have fooled me." He leaned back in the chair. "You're obviously upset. Maybe talking about it will help."

"Like I'd ever talk to you about my problems," she mumbled.

"You're never going to forgive me, are you?"

Her jaw clenched. "No, I'm probably not."

"I've changed," he said, picking at the label on his bottle. "You could give me a chance to prove it instead of constantly assuming the worst of me."

"You haven't changed," she spat. "You go out of your way to antagonise people for no reason. Why would I ever want to be friends with someone like that?"

"Who do I antagonise?" he asked, his brow wrinkling.

She let out a humourless laugh. "The other week when you

came in the pub and started having a go at Kit for absolutely no reason."

"Oh, that."

"Yes, that! What's wrong with you?"

"To be fair, I did have a reason in that instance."

She shook her head. "No, you didn't. You're just a bully who gets a kick out of talking down to people."

"Okay, sure." He stood abruptly. "Think whatever you want."

"What else am I supposed to think? What reason could you possibly have for having a go at Kit?"

His nostrils flared. "Because he's a Treneary."

"What the hell has that got to do with anything?"

"Really?" He tilted his head. "You can't imagine why I'd have a problem with the Trenearys?"

"I know you and Noah never got on, but that was because he always thought you weren't good enough for me – and it turned out he was right."

"The Trenearys overshadowed our entire relationship. You were obsessed with them. It was like your life revolved around them."

"They're my family," she said defensively. "And I think you're exaggerating slightly."

Shaking his head, he leaned against the table. "Noah was the reason we split up."

She laughed loudly. "That's strange! I always thought we split up because you slept with Cindy Taylor on my twenty-first birthday … but of course you're going to somehow blame Noah for that! God, you're pathetic."

"I didn't sleep with Cindy." His calm voice was unnerving.

"I'm fairly sure you did."

He looked away from her, his gaze settling on the horizon. "I snogged her at your party, which was a shitty thing to do, but I didn't sleep with her."

"Yes, you did," she argued weakly.

He sat beside her again. "For our entire relationship, I felt as though you were about to leave me for Noah Treneary."

"Noah was my best friend."

"Didn't I know it? Most of our dates involved you crowing about how great Noah was. I felt as though I was in constant competition for your attention. And most of the time I seemed to lose that battle."

"You knew he was just a friend."

"I thought so, but surely the rumours didn't escape you …"

"Stupid, untrue rumours." She took a swig of her beer. "Who cares what other people think?"

"Weirdly enough, I cared. Having people insinuating that my girlfriend was cheating on me was difficult to ignore. My mates all thought I was an idiot and that you were playing me for a fool."

"We discussed it at the time and you knew there was nothing going on between me and Noah."

"I know that's what you told me …"

"But you decided to believe what your mates said instead of me?"

"It might have been easier to believe if Noah hadn't been in my ear about you and him."

"Whatever Noah said was a joke. It was nothing he wouldn't say in front of me. It was always very clear that he was joking."

"You'd never believe anything bad about him, would you? There's no point in us having this conversation."

"Noah didn't do anything," she said wearily.

"At your twenty-first party, he pretty much told me that you and he were together. He said you were planning on breaking up with me."

"I'm sure he wouldn't have said that since it wasn't true. I had no plans to split up with you. Even if things weren't perfect between us, I thought we were okay." She sat up straighter. "None of that excuses what you did anyway. You humiliated me and broke my heart. If you didn't sleep with Cindy, you happily let me think you did."

He inhaled deeply. "There didn't seem to be any point in denying it. Clearly things were over between us, and I just wanted to get out without being the joke of the island. I was pretty certain you were sleeping with Noah behind my back."

"I wasn't."

"He certainly wanted me to think that."

"I don't believe you." At least she didn't *want* to believe him. Her thoughts were a mess, and she didn't know what to believe.

"It doesn't really matter what happened back then," he said, setting his bottle on the table. "But I would like you to believe that I'm sorry."

Tears filled her eyes, though she couldn't swear it was Felix who was making her emotional.

His hand landed tentatively on her knee, before searching for her hand and entwining their fingers together. "I don't blame you if you never forgive me," he said softly. "What I did was horrible. Of all the stupid things I've done in my life, that's the one that haunts me. I *am* sorry."

With no idea how to reply, Seren turned away from him. Laughter drifted on the breeze, floating up from the beach where Kit was with Holly.

The feel of Felix's thumb stroking her hand drew Seren's attention. His other hand rose to gently caress her neck as he leaned in, slowly enough for her to object if she'd wanted to. There didn't seem to be much reason to object, though. She'd missed her chance with Kit, and now he was probably kissing Holly while the sun set over the beach.

Felix wasn't so bad really.

When his lips touched hers all she felt was an odd sense of detachment. She made no move to stop him when his tongue explored her mouth, but her heart definitely wasn't in it.

Slowly, he pulled away. "I'm getting the feeling you're not really into this."

"I'm not." She gave a small shake of the head and touched a finger to her lips. "What have you been eating?"

He flopped back in his seat, chuckling. "Brownies. Why?"

"I can taste it. Maybe don't go stuffing your face the next time you intend to stick your tongue down someone's throat."

"I'll bear it in mind. Do you want another drink?"

"If you're thinking I'll be more enthusiastic about kissing you when I'm drunk, you're probably going to be disappointed."

"I wasn't trying to get you drunk. Even if I have no chance with you, I don't like seeing you upset. The least I can do is keep you company while you drown your sorrows." He flashed her a mischievous grin as he stood up. "If you want, you can even bitch about Noah and his new girlfriend to me."

"I'm not upset about Noah." She growled in frustration. "Just get me a beer."

The sensible move would be to go home before Kit reappeared with Holly, but the suggestion to drown her sorrows was tempting too.

"You look confused," Felix said, handing her a beer.

Her brow was creased in a frown as she ran her fingers over her lips, wondering at the familiar tingling sensation on them. "What did you say you'd been eating?"

He shrugged. "Brownies. Do you want some?"

"Probably not." She poked her tongue out as the tingling spread throughout her mouth. "Did they by any chance have peanuts in them?"

"Um ..." Sheepishly, he screwed his face up.

"Are you serious?" She slapped him on the arm. "You ate peanuts and then kissed me ... are you trying to kill me?"

"Obviously I wasn't thinking about what I'd recently eaten when I kissed you. But now that you mention it, they might have been peanut butter brownies."

"Felix!"

"Sorry. Are you okay?"

"I'm having an allergic reaction to your kiss," she snapped.

"You're having a reaction to *peanut butter,* not me. How are you so allergic that you have a reaction from second-hand peanut butter?"

"I really hope you're not expecting me to apologise for having an allergic reaction. You're such an idiot!" She put a hand to her neck as a tickle niggled at her throat.

Felix rubbed her shoulder. "Are you going to be okay?"

"Probably. Can you get me a glass of water? And grab my bag too. It should have my antihistamines in there." As she said it, she had a sinking feeling. The bag was new and she couldn't remember if she had her emergency supplies in there or not. Usually she always had antihistamines and her EpiPen with her.

Her mouth felt as though she'd been eating sand by the time Felix returned with Cadan behind him.

"Are you all right?" Cadan asked.

She nodded and swilled her mouth out, then spat the water onto the grass before rummaging in her bag for her meds.

"I should be fine in a bit," she said.

"Can you seriously get an allergic reaction from kissing someone who's been eating peanuts?"

"I don't see why you're confused by the concept," she said, looking at Cadan and then Felix. "I'm allergic to peanuts – it doesn't make any difference how they get into my system."

"Do you need to go to the hospital?" Cadan asked.

"No." She was certain she'd be fine if she got her antihistamines. "I just need my medicine."

"Do you have it with you?" Felix asked.

"No. I'm going to go home."

"I can drive you," Felix said.

Seren took a long steady breath. "Are you sober enough to drive?"

"Not really." He shrugged. "It'd be fine though. Or I can see if anyone else can drive you."

She shook her head. "Don't worry about it. I'll be fine. It's not as though it's far."

"I'll come with you at least." Felix moved to her side.

"Don't start trying to play the hero now," she said, rolling her eyes. "I think we've established that you and I aren't meant to be."

"I'm not trying to be a hero. I'm just worried about you. Let me walk you home."

Seren paused. The evening wasn't going her way and she just wanted to be alone to wallow in self-pity. But this perhaps wasn't the best time to be stubborn. She was about to tell him he could come when Rebecca shouted to him from the kitchen. Something about more beers.

"Stay here," Seren said. "I'm okay. I'll walk home and get my meds. It's not a big deal."

"I can come with you," Cadan offered.

"I'm fine. Honestly. I'll message you when I get home."

"Call if you have any problems," Felix said, slightly drowned out by Rebecca calling for him again.

"Are you going to come back?" Cadan asked.

"No. I'll take my meds and go to bed to sleep it off." She started walking away, not wanting to linger too long. It didn't feel as though it was going to be a strong reaction, but the sooner she got her meds the better.

As she wandered along the lane in the last of the daylight, her breathing became steadily laboured and she put all her attention into breathing evenly. She hoped the tactic might also have the benefit of keeping her from thinking about Kit and Holly on the beach. It didn't quite work, and her jealousy made it even more difficult to breathe.

She was five minutes from home when the last of her energy deserted her. Trying not to panic, she glanced down the narrow lane that was bordered by high hedges. The houses a little farther along were close enough that she should be able to shout for help. Or she could, if she were capable of shouting. Which she absolutely wasn't.

She just needed a rest, that was all. Sitting at the side of the road she told herself she just needed a minute to catch her breath … then she could make it home.

After a couple of minutes had gone by with her only getting worse, she pulled out her phone. Calling Noah would guarantee a lecture about her not having her meds or EpiPen with her, but it would also guarantee that someone came to help her.

She swore quietly when she saw she had no phone signal.

It really wasn't her lucky night.

CHAPTER TWENTY-NINE

The sun had just set when Kit walked back up from the beach with a very giggly Holly. She'd finished her beer and then helped him with his before declaring she was perfectly fine to face her ex.

Cadan and Felix were blocking the door into the kitchen but stepped aside for them.

"She's not answering," Felix said to Cadan, holding his phone to his ear.

"Maybe she got home and fell asleep," Cadan replied.

Rebecca stepped towards them, shaking her head. "If she's not answering the phone, one of you needs to go and check on her. I don't want to be responsible for anyone dying of an allergic reaction thanks to my baking."

"What are you talking about?" Kit asked, panic fluttering in his chest.

"Seren was here," Felix told him. "She had an allergic reaction and went home. She said she'd message when she got there, but I haven't heard from her."

Cadan stretched his neck. "She also said she just needed to go home and sleep it off. I guess she forgot about messaging and went straight to bed."

"You let her drive home alone while she was having an allergic reaction?" Kit asked in disbelief.

Cadan chewed the corner of his thumbnail. "She was walking. We offered to go with her, but she insisted she was fine."

"Of course she said she was fine," Kit said shaking his head in exasperation. "Why didn't anyone go with her?"

"She was adamant she was okay," Felix said. "She just needed to get to her meds."

Kit had already dialled her number and pressed his phone to his ear. "It's going to voicemail."

"Please can someone go and check on her?" Rebecca said.

Felix stepped outside. "I'm going."

"Call me when you find her," Cadan shouted after him.

"Hey!" Kit called, rushing after Felix. "I'm going to look for her. You may as well stay here."

"We can both go."

Kit grabbed Felix's arm to stop him in his tracks. "You couldn't be bothered to go with her in the first place. Don't try and make out you care now. The best thing you can do for Seren is stay the heck away from her."

He'd expected an argument, or possibly a punch in the face, but Felix's features softened and he stepped away. "Just let us know she's okay."

Kit was on the road when Holly shouted after him. He waited while she caught up.

"Should I come with you?" she asked.

"It's fine. Stay here. If I don't come back, are you okay getting home?"

"Yes. Of course." She smiled sadly. "It's Seren, isn't it?"

"What?" he said, feigning innocence.

"You're in love with Seren. Isn't she like ten years older than you?"

"Six and a half. It's not that much." He shook his head. "I need to check she's all right."

"Yes." She nodded. "Go. Give me a shout if you need any help with anything."

"Thanks." He took off at a jog, then slowed after a couple of minutes to try calling Seren again. Pretty soon it would be pitch black, and if she hadn't made it home he'd struggle to find her in the dark.

"Hi," she panted when she answered the phone.

"Where are you?" he asked, relief flooding through him. "Are you okay? I heard you had an allergic reaction. Why weren't you answering your phone? Sorry, that's loads of questions. Are you all right?"

"Yes." The wheezing suggested otherwise.

"You don't sound it. Are you at home?"

"No," she said faintly. "Almost."

"Okay. I'm on my way to find you. I left Felix's house a few minutes away. Do you have your EpiPen with you?"

"No." She breathed heavily. "Don't need a lecture."

"I wasn't going to."

"I just need to …" She paused, her breathing loud. "Get my meds. Then I'll be … okay …"

He picked up his pace again. "If it gets too dark you'll need to switch the torch on your phone so I can find you … Seren?" He looked at his phone but had lost the connection. Calling back just got him her voicemail. He cursed the dodgy phone reception before concentrating on where he was going. As he ran he called out to Seren at regular intervals but assumed she was somewhere on the road and would be easy to spot. He was approaching the edge of the town when he finally set eyes on her.

"Are you okay?" He crouched in front of her, a hand on her shoulder.

"I just …" Her chest heaved with every breath. "I needed a rest."

"Do you need to go to the hospital? I'll go and knock on a door, get someone to drive you …"

She shook her head firmly and strained against him to get to her feet. "I just need to get home."

"Can you walk?"

"Think so," she whispered, holding his arm for support.

"You don't sound good." The wheezing was intense, and he wondered whether he should be taking her to the hospital rather than home.

"I'm okay," she said, taking painfully slow steps.

"I can carry you," he suggested. "Put your arm around my neck."

"No." Her eyes flashed with amusement. "I can walk."

"I can see that, but it'll take less than five minutes if I carry you, and approximately all night at the speed you're walking. Let me carry you … that way I might make it back to the party sometime tonight."

Seren stopped walking. "Need to get back to your girlfriend?"

"Will you please put your arm around my neck?" When she did as he asked, he lifted her into his arms.

"I knew this would happen," she murmured into his neck.

"That I'd end up carrying you home after you ate peanut butter brownies?" he joked.

"No. I knew it was just a crush."

"What are you talking about?"

"You said you were in love with me … but I knew it was just a crush and you'd be over it in about five minutes."

The bitterness in her voice made him think she wasn't okay with the idea of him getting over her. He thought of the way she'd been looking at him in the pub on Wednesday, and his tragic heart was filled with hope once again.

"You're already loved up with someone else," she said. "So, I was right."

He hoisted her higher in his arms. "I already told you, Holly's not my girlfriend."

"Yeah, right."

It was difficult to read her features in the dim light, but she sounded jealous.

"We're almost home," he said, then kept quiet until they were at her door. Gently, he set her on her feet and paused to catch his breath. With the door open, they both stared at the steep staircase. "Couldn't live on the ground floor, could you?" he teased.

"I can manage," she said, taking one tentative step after the other.

"Good." He waited patiently behind her while she made her way up. "I mean I could definitely carry you … no effort at all really …"

Her laughter brought on a coughing fit halfway up the stairs, and he put a hand on her back while she calmed herself down again.

"I'll stop with the jokes." He kept a hand on her back as she continued. When they got into the flat, she clutched the edge of the kitchen work surface and heaved in a few gasping breaths before moving to the bathroom. Opening the cabinet, she took out a packet of tablets and popped one from the packaging.

"I'll be better in a sec," she murmured after washing it down with water from the tap. With a hand on the edge of the bath, she lowered herself down to sit on the floor.

He joined her on the bath mat and she leaned against him. "How did you get hold of the brownies anyway?"

"How do you mean?" she asked, nestling her face against his chest.

Raising his arm, he slipped it behind her back. "I made Rebecca put the brownies away so you wouldn't accidentally eat one."

"Did you?" Her hand rested on his leg as she curled into him, her eyelids drooping.

"I guess someone took them out again."

Her features tensed and she shifted away from him. "I guess so."

"Are you all right?" He put a hand on her arm to steady her as she struggled to her feet, looking like a drunk person.

"I want to go to bed."

He reached to open the bathroom cupboard again. "Where's your EpiPen?"

"Don't need it." She shook her head as she perched on the edge of the bath.

"I just want to know where it is … because you don't actually seem to be getting better."

She pointed to the top shelf in the cabinet. "There … I'm okay though. It takes a few … minutes. My throat's getting … better."

"If you say so." He took the EpiPen out and set it on the back of the sink to give him easy access to it. Then he turned back to Seren, lifted her into his arms and set off for her bedroom. Her breath brushed over his neck, giving him goosebumps, and he hesitated for a moment by her bed, not keen to let go of her.

"How are you doing?" he asked when he lowered her down, pulling the covers back at the same time.

"I'm okay. Just need to sleep."

After pulling her shoes off, he looked down at her heavy eyelids. "Do you want me to undress you?" He caught the twitch of Seren's lips and couldn't help but smile himself. "That sounded creepy."

"Help me with my jeans," she said, unfastening the button and struggling to get them over her hips.

Kit peeled them the rest of the way, then draped them over the chair in the corner.

"Thanks," Seren said quietly, snuggling under the covers.

"Do you need anything else?"

Her eyes were almost closed when she shook her head, but he caught the sadness in them nonetheless.

"I can stay if you want." Crouching beside her, he brushed her hair from her face.

"No," she said tearfully. He thought she was going to push

his hand away, but instead she curled her fingers around his and held tightly.

He sighed and felt his brow wrinkle. "I'm happy to stay."

"I'm exhausted." She uncurled her fingers from his and tucked them under the pillow. "I'm just going to sleep. You don't need to stay. Thank you for looking after me."

"Sleep well," he said as he stood. Her eyes completely closed and her breathing was more even when he left her and went into the living room. His eyes roamed the bookshelves before he checked his phone to find various messages and missed calls. He tapped out replies to Cadan and Holly, letting them know that Seren was okay. He told Holly he'd speak to her tomorrow and wrote that he hoped she was having a good time.

After getting himself a glass of water, he wandered back to the bedroom. The bedside lamp was on, and he was surprised to find Seren looking straight at him.

"I thought you were going back to the party," she said hoarsely.

"No." He crossed the room and sat beside her with his back against the headboard. "I only said that so you'd let me carry you. I didn't have any intention of leaving you alone. But I was expecting you to fall asleep so I wouldn't have to bother arguing with you about it."

She rolled her head to look up at him. "So you were planning on hanging around and watching me sleep?"

"That was the idea, yes." He smiled widely. "I saw you have the *Twilight* books on your shelf, so I figured you'd be fine with someone watching you sleep."

"Have you read them?" she asked with a sleepy smile.

"No. But I once heard a couple of women on my train having a heated debate about them. One of them reckoned the books romanticised stalking or something. She thought it was very creepy that the guy came in uninvited to watch the woman sleep at night." He tilted his head. "But the guy's a vampire, right? So he must've been invited in or he wouldn't be able to get in the house … or is there more to it?"

"I think she'd invited him in another time," she said wearily. "Then he just came in whenever he felt like it and watched her sleeping."

"What's your take on it?" he asked with a mischievous grin. "Creepy or romantic?"

"I think it's perfectly acceptable in fiction."

"Of course. In real life no one's going to be cool with a vampire lurking in their room at night."

"Definitely not," she said, chuckling.

"Just to be clear though – I was going to hang out here to make sure you keep breathing, not because I'd get any pleasure from watching you sleep."

She shifted her head on the pillow. "Won't your girlfriend have something to say about you staying here?"

"I imagine if I had a girlfriend she might have something to say about it."

"Everyone knows you're seeing Holly."

"You mean everyone except me? I don't think Holly knows either, so that's slightly awkward."

"Deny it. Whatever. I'm going to sleep now."

"Why do you have such an issue with me hanging out with Holly?"

"I don't," she insisted as she closed her eyes.

He watched her for a moment, then scooted down the bed a little. "I went on two dates with Holly," he told her. "I thought it would be a good way to take my mind off you. It didn't work and I felt bad for leading her on. Only it turned out she was using me as a distraction from her ex. We like hanging out together, so we kept seeing each other … as friends."

Seren's eyes slowly opened. "*Just* friends?"

"Yes."

"I thought you were seeing her."

"No." The spark of hope he'd felt earlier increased dramatically. "Would you have a problem if I was seeing her?"

"Yes. I would." She pulled her hand from the bedding and sought out his. "I'd have quite a big problem with it."

He lay on his side to look at her. "I thought there was something going on between you and Felix."

"Definitely not." She smiled lightly but looked exhausted. "Can we continue this conversation tomorrow?"

"Yes. You should sleep."

He ran a hand over her hair and their eyes locked for a moment before her eyelids slowly closed.

CHAPTER THIRTY

When Seren woke, the events of the previous evening came back to her in slow flashes. Beside her, Kit slept sitting bolt upright against the headboard. The way his head slumped on his shoulder looked anything but comfortable.

As she gave his leg a shake, she registered the Harry Potter book face down on his lap.

"You have no respect for books," she remarked when his eyes flickered open. "It ruins the spine when you leave them open like that."

Her teasing didn't go down well and he just looked confused as he set the book aside and stretched his neck. "I couldn't sleep, so I thought I'd read a few pages."

"You got through quite a lot. You must be a fast reader."

"Yeah." He swung his legs off the bed and slowly rolled his head from shoulder to shoulder.

"Are you all right?" she asked, sitting up and reaching out to touch his arm.

"Yeah. Fine." He smiled through a yawn. "How are you feeling today?"

"My throat's killing me, and I feel as though I could sleep for the entire day. But otherwise I'm fine. Much better than last night."

"Good." He checked his watch and swore. "I need to get to work."

"I think I'll ask Charlie if he can get someone to cover for me today."

"Do you know if Noah's working?"

"Yeah, I was supposed to be on the day shift with him." She reached for her phone to message her uncle.

"Shame," Kit said. "I'd have asked him to drive the train this morning so I could go back to bed."

"Sorry," she said, registering how pale he was. "Can you ask Keira?"

"She's doing a first aid course all day. I organised it. Thought it would be good, with her working on the train."

"Is there someone else you can ask?"

"Not really, but I'll manage. Are you going to be okay?"

"Yes. I'm fine." She shifted the pillow behind her to get comfy. "Thank you for looking after me last night."

"You're welcome." He put a hand in front of his mouth as he yawned again. "I really have to go."

She thought of their conversation the previous evening and the relief she'd felt at hearing that Holly wasn't his girlfriend after all. It would be better if he didn't have to rush off so they could talk properly, but that obviously wasn't an option.

"Can we get together later? I think we need to chat everything through properly."

He met her gaze and smiled. "Yeah. I'll pick up some dinner after work and bring it here."

"Have a good day," she called as he left.

Not bothering to get dressed, other than pulling on a pair of pyjama bottoms, she relocated to the couch, taking the bedding with her. From there she sent a message to her dad, knowing he'd be furious if he found out about her allergic reaction from somebody else. He called her immediately, asking how she was and if she needed anything. Naomi was in the background, asking if there was anything she could do.

Once Seren had convinced them she was fine and didn't need anything, she reached for the TV remote and began searching for something mindless to watch. Half an hour into a cooking show, a message came through from Noah, checking she was okay. They exchanged a few messages before she put the phone aside and settled down again.

The next interruption came from someone at the door.

"How are you feeling?" Mirren asked as she bustled inside. "I heard you had a rough night. I've brought soup and a tub of ice cream to soothe your throat."

"Thank you." They trudged up the stairs. "Did Noah call you?"

"No, Kit did. He was worried about you and asked if I had time to call in."

"Did he tell you how he looked after me yesterday?" Seren asked, taking the soup and ice cream from Mirren.

"He said he brought you home from the party and stayed here to make sure you were okay."

Seren felt a rush of anxiety as she thought of what could have happened if Kit hadn't come looking for her. She liked to think she could have made it home alone, but she might have underestimated the situation.

"It's not too early for ice cream, is it?" She looked longingly at the tub of chocolate goodness.

"I don't think it's ever too early for ice cream."

"Do you want some? We could watch baking shows and pig out."

"I reckon I've got time for one episode before I get back to the cleaning."

"Have you got guests arriving?"

Mirren nodded. "A woman and her daughter are arriving later to stay in Trystan's place for a week. I hope the weather picks up for them. It's very grey out today."

"Is Trystan coming back next weekend?"

"Yes." Mirren took a bowl of ice cream and headed for the couch.

Seren struggled to concentrate on the TV. Her mind kept drifting to the previous evening and how she'd left things with Kit. Tonight they'd have a proper talk, but she wasn't quite sure what she was going to say. Before she'd drifted off the previous evening, she'd been certain she should stop putting up barriers and give the two of them a chance. In the cold light of day, things didn't feel quite so simple. Especially not when she was hanging out with Mirren. It was another reminder of what she might lose if things didn't work out between them.

"Hey!" Mirren broke her thoughts by giving her leg a playful shake. "Are you awake?"

"Sorry. What did you say?"

"I said I should go before I get involved in the next episode."

"I was miles away." Seren reached for the remote to stop it from rolling straight into the next episode.

"You'll be worn out after your reaction last night. Why don't you go back to bed?"

Seren pushed her bottom lip out, feeling suddenly emotional. "Did Kit tell you that he carried me home?"

"No." Mirren chuckled. "He didn't mention that."

"I thought I'd be fine going home alone. I told Cadan and Felix I was okay and set off walking, but my breathing got bad and my phone signal kept cutting out. When Kit heard what happened he came looking for me. By the time he found me I could barely walk." She paused as a lump formed in her throat. "He picked me up and carried me home and refused to leave me alone."

"That sounds like Kit," Mirren said, with more than a hint of pride.

Tears threatened and Seren blinked them away. "Do you remember when I told you that there was a guy who I liked but I thought it was a bad idea?"

"Yes. It looks like you were right. I can't believe Felix didn't even walk you home yesterday."

Seren cocked her head to one side. "I wasn't talking about Felix."

"Oh. Sorry, I just assumed."

"It was Kit."

"What was Kit?"

"The guy I like. I was talking about Kit."

Mirren's eyes widened and she stayed quiet for a moment. "I was sure you were talking about Felix. I'd have given you different advice if I'd known you were talking about Kit."

"Would you?" Seren asked, her stomach churning with nerves.

"Yes. But I don't understand. You said it felt wrong …"

"Because it's *Kit*," Seren said, pulling the blanket up to her chin. "He's so young … and I've known him forever."

"He's very mature for his age." She gave Seren a sympathetic smile. "I don't know why it's a bad thing that you've known him for so long."

"It feels weird." Seren took a deep breath. "A few weeks ago he told me he's in love with me."

"That doesn't surprise me. He's been looking at you as though you're some kind of goddess for years."

"I gave him the brush-off," Seren said. "Told him I don't feel the same."

"But that wasn't true?"

"No. But the thought of being with Kit …"

Mirren wrinkled her brow. "Feels wrong?"

"No. It doesn't feel wrong. But I guess lots of people will think it's wrong. He's so much younger than me."

"So you're not going to be with him because of what other people might think? And for the record, I don't think anyone would care."

Seren grimaced. "What about you?"

"Why would I care?"

"Won't it make things weird?"

"I don't see why."

"But what if I got together with Kit and things didn't work out? What would happen then?"

"That's a very pessimistic attitude," Mirren said lightly.

"I'm trying to be realistic. I don't want to end up as an outsider like Lowen."

Mirren shook her head. "What on earth are you talking about?"

"Things are so strained between you and him," Seren said cautiously. "I can't stand the thought of things not working out between me and Kit and you being upset with me."

"Unless you really tried, you're not going to upset me." Mirren shuffled along and put her arms around Seren, giving her a big kiss on the cheek. "I promise."

"You'd really be fine if me and Kit got together? What if I hurt him?"

"Try not to hurt him," Mirren said with a look of mock consternation. "But I don't see any reason why you shouldn't give it a go. I might still think of Kit as my little boy, but he's a grown man. If the two of you want to be together, don't use me as an excuse not to."

"I'm scared," Seren admitted. "I'm pretty good at messing up relationships. I hate the thought of messing things up with Kit."

"I don't think you mess up relationships. You've just haven't picked your boyfriends very well in the past."

Seren thought about her conversation with Felix the previous evening. "I don't think me having bad taste in men was the only problem."

"The relationship wasn't right then. It doesn't matter, you can't give up on relationships just because they haven't worked out in the past." She tilted her head and smiled. "I just thought of something ... do you remember a few years back you came over to the house and Kit was hiding around the corner and soaked you with the hose?"

"It rings a vague bell."

"The next time you came over you got him back. He was about to go and meet his friends and he was annoyed at you for messing his hair up."

Seren beamed at the memory. "He chased me around the garden and we both ended up soaked."

"Terry came home from work to find you two fighting like a pair of kids, and he made some comment to me about how long it would be before your play fighting would turn into something else entirely."

Seren's chin twitched. "Did he?"

"I couldn't see it," Mirren said, her eyes shining. "I thought you'd end up with Noah, but Terry always rolled his eyes when I said that."

"Kit's coming over for dinner tonight," Seren said, with a burst of hope that things might just turn out after all. "We're going to talk everything through properly."

"Well …" Mirren gave her leg a playful tap. "Don't talk too much. It's overrated."

Seren cracked up laughing at the teasing in Mirren's eyes. "I can't believe you just said that!"

Chuckling, she stood up. "Love you, sweetheart."

"Love you too. Thanks for coming over."

Left alone, Seren couldn't stop smiling.

The evening couldn't come soon enough.

CHAPTER THIRTY-ONE

K it's morning train tour felt endless. Once it was over and he'd modelled balloon animals for all the children who wanted one, he set off for home to grab a quick nap. Hopefully that would revive him enough to make it through the afternoon. Then he'd pick up a takeaway and head over to Seren's place. The thought brought a smile to his face as he made his way through town.

He hadn't made it far when he caught sight of Cadan wandering along the other side of the road. Seeing Kit, he raised a hand in greeting and crossed over to him.

"I was going to go and see Seren," Cadan said. "But I called her and she said she was about to have a nap. She sounded okay though. Reckons she's feeling better today."

Kit never had a lot of patience when he was tired, and he was hit by a surge of anger that Cadan had let Seren leave the party alone. "She wasn't in a good way when I found her last night," he said through gritted teeth.

"So she said. Reckoned it was a good thing you got to her when you did." Cadan looked completely unremorseful and it irritated Kit. "She seemed okay when she left the party. And I honestly didn't think it would be that bad since she hadn't actually eaten any peanuts."

Kit narrowed his eyes. He needed more sleep to engage in conversation with Cadan. "You realise peanut butter is made from peanuts?"

"Yes." He laughed. "But since she didn't actually eat any herself, I thought it would have less of an effect. It never occurred to me that she could get a reaction that way. I guess she takes her life in her hands every time she kisses anyone."

Kit's smile tightened. He had questions, but he didn't want Cadan to know that he had no idea what he was talking about. "I've got to get on," he said, moving around Cadan and striding away. Instead of continuing home, he detoured to the tourist office, thankful to find it devoid of customers.

"Hey!" Holly said brightly. "How are you? You look a mess, no offence."

"I didn't sleep much." He leaned on the high desk, deciding to get straight to the point. "Did anyone say anything about Seren after I left the party last night? About her allergic reaction?"

"Yeah. Everyone was talking about it." Her sympathetic smile was a good indicator that he wasn't going to like whatever had been said.

"What were they saying?"

She raised her eyebrows. "Don't you know?"

"I've got a good idea. But I'd like to hear it from you." Even better would have been to hear it from Seren.

"Apparently she was kissing Felix after he'd eaten the peanut butter brownies." She winced. "Sorry."

"It's okay." His stomach twisted to a knot and he felt vaguely nauseous.

"Didn't Seren tell you?"

"No. She didn't mention it." Not only had she neglected to mention it, but she'd also lied to his face. On two occasions. Once when he'd asked how she'd come to eat the brownies, and once when she'd told him there was nothing between her and Felix.

"How is she?" Holly asked.

"I sat up all night to make sure she was breathing," he said sadly. "She seemed to be fine this morning."

"That's good. You're so sweet to look after her like that. It's her loss if she doesn't realise what a catch you are."

"Yeah." He turned and made for the door.

Holly moved around the desk and intercepted him. "I'm sorry," she said, a hand on his arm. "Have I upset you?"

"No, it's not you. I'm just having a bad day."

"Can I do anything?"

"No." He gave her a quick hug and was all set to leave when he realised how self-involved he was being. "How was it with Gavin, by the way?"

"Fine. We said hello, then politely ignored each other. It was easier than I expected."

"That's good." He pulled the door open. "Sorry to dash off. Let's hang out soon and chat properly."

She gave him a big kiss on the cheek and he walked out into the bright sunlight. At home, he collapsed on his bed for an hour but couldn't get his brain to switch off, so sleep was elusive.

His afternoon was fuelled by coffee and fake smiles. He gave the train tours on autopilot, barely even recalling what he'd said when he came to the end. It wasn't his preferred way to work, and he hoped not to repeat it anytime soon.

Checking his phone after his final tour, he read a message from Seren asking what time he'd be over. She also commented that she was looking forward to seeing him, which annoyed him immensely. He tapped out a reply, telling her he wasn't going to make it. The message was abrupt; he didn't even bother with an excuse.

He was driving the train home when his phone rang. Muting the call from Seren felt petty, but he didn't have the energy to speak to her.

Seren had been full of excitement when she'd typed out a message to Kit, but his curt reply immediately put a dampener on her mood. That morning he'd seemed keen to have dinner with her, so she couldn't fathom his message. A feeling of dread swept through her when he didn't answer her call, but she told herself he was probably in the middle of something. Half an hour later, she tried again, pacing the living room to the rhythm of the long beeps as it rang.

Something had happened, and she had a horrible feeling it involved Felix. Pushing her feet into a pair of trainers she rushed down the stairs and out onto the street. Taking her car to Kit's place was unnecessary, but even the five-minute walk felt like too much thinking time.

After ringing the bell, she shifted from foot to foot until Kit's voice came on the intercom.

"It's me," she said, leaning close to the speaker. "You didn't answer your phone."

"I'm just going to bed."

"Can you buzz me in? I need to talk to you."

"I don't want to talk now."

"Kit." Tears pricked her eyes. "What's going on?"

"I feel like crap and I need to sleep. Let's talk another time."

"I need to talk to you *now*," she said firmly. "Buzz me in."

The silence that ensued was excruciating, and she was about to press the bell again when the door finally clicked open. Rushing up the stairs, she found him standing at his door in only a pair of jogging bottoms.

"What's going on?" she snapped.

"I don't want to do this now."

"Fine, but I'm going to need you to come up with a better excuse than needing to go to bed … it's seven o'clock."

"I realise that." Reluctantly, he stepped aside as she barged inside. "But after I carried you home last night, I sat up all night to make sure you kept breathing. Then I had to work all day, so now I really want to sleep."

She whipped around to him. "You stayed up all night?"

"Yeah," he said bitterly.

"I'm sorry."

"I think if you're going to be sorry for anything, it should be for lying to me rather than disrupting my sleep."

Her heart felt as though it stopped dead. "What are you talking about?"

"You told me there was nothing going on between you and Felix."

"There isn't."

He exhaled loudly and dropped onto the edge of the bed. "Remind me again how you came to have an allergic reaction?"

"I'm guessing you already know that," she said quietly.

"Surely you knew I'd find out. I imagine that's going to be island gossip for a good while." He dropped his head to his hands and dragged his fingers through his hair. "It doesn't even matter. It's none of my business who you kiss."

"Don't be like that."

"Like what? You made it very clear that you're not interested in me, so you don't need to feel guilty for kissing someone else."

"Felix kissed *me*," she said desperately. "But there's nothing going on between us."

"That might be easier to believe if you hadn't outright lied to me yesterday."

"I should have told you the truth." She took a step towards him, swallowing hard. "I wasn't thinking straight, and I didn't particularly want you to know. But I swear it was one-sided." She paused, waiting for a response, but he kept quiet. "If I'm honest, I didn't bother to stop him kissing me because I knew you were at the beach with Holly and I was jealous."

He rolled his eyes. "I see – you don't want to be with me but you don't want me to be with anyone else?"

"No." She looked him right in the eyes. "That's not how it is."

"It's kind of suspicious though – that you weren't remotely interested in me until you thought I was seeing someone else." He shook his head. "If we got together you'd be bored of me in a week."

Tears filled her eyes and spilled down her cheeks. "That's not fair."

"Really? Because it seems to me that you prefer guys who treat you like crap. Guys who can't even be bothered to make sure you get home okay when you're having an allergic reaction."

She shook her head. "Why are you so angry about Felix not walking me home? It's starting to sound as though you might not have bothered coming to find me if you knew it was kissing Felix that had brought on my attack."

"Are you serious?" His head shot up and his features were a mixture of sadness and disbelief. She wanted to take it back immediately. "You think I'd have left you?"

"I shouldn't have said that. Of course I don't think that. I just need you to believe that I don't want to be with Felix. I want to be with you. And it's got nothing to do with me being jealous. I wanted to be with you since before you told me how you felt. I was just too scared to admit it."

"I'm struggling to believe anything you say." He hung his head. "Can you please leave?"

"I'm really sorry," she whispered.

"Just go."

She stared at him for a moment before deciding there was nothing left for her to say.

Rain was falling heavily when she stepped outside. In her car, she listened to it drumming on the roof while tears fell freely down her cheeks.

CHAPTER THIRTY-TWO

S eren spent a while composing a message to Kit on Sunday morning, apologising again and asking if they could talk. She hoped that the tension the previous evening had partly been borne from Kit's lack of sleep and high emotions. Hopefully after a full night's sleep, he'd feel differently. He hadn't replied by the time she started her shift, and as the afternoon went on she began to resign herself to the fact that he didn't want to speak to her.

Part of her was annoyed with him for not even bothering to reply to her message. Mostly, she felt utterly devastated. Rain came down constantly all day, apparently putting people off from venturing out to the pub. The place was almost empty when Noah arrived for his shift late in the afternoon.

"How are you feeling now?" he asked her.

Giving her feet a break, she perched on a stool at the end of the bar. "Fine." She glared at him. "Did you make Felix believe there was something going on between the two of us?"

"The two of *us?*" he repeated, waving a finger between them.

"Yes. You and me. When I was with Felix, did you say anything to make him believe I was cheating on him with you?"

He shrugged. "I don't think so. I always enjoyed winding him up, but it wasn't serious."

"So on my birthday you didn't imply that I was sleeping with you?"

"I might have made a joke about you sleeping at my place more often than his." He rolled his eyes and leaned onto the bar. "What's with all the questions?"

"Did you tell him I was planning on splitting up with him?"

He straightened up, eyes flicking to the window. "Not that I remember."

"I can tell when you're lying, Noah."

"Fine. He was pissing me off and I might have said something along those lines. It's not a big deal, is it?"

"Kind of, yes." She raised her voice, then lowered it when she realised there were customers at the other side of the room. "I wasn't planning on breaking up with him."

"Things definitely weren't good between you. You were always complaining about him being possessive and jealous. It was pathetic how he had such an issue with you spending time with me."

"Was it? Or did he have a point? Maybe I should have been more considerate of his feelings. He was jealous of me spending time with you, and I told him he was being ridiculous."

"It *was* ridiculous."

"I think you might have double standards."

"What's that supposed to mean?"

"It means that when you got a girlfriend, you dropped me."

"No, I didn't."

"We don't hang out any more," she pointed out.

"You could always call me if you want to hang out."

"It's fine with me that we don't hang out any more, because I'm respectful of your relationship with Keira. But you didn't pay me the same courtesy."

"Are we seriously having this conversation? It's not as though it was my fault that Felix broke up with you."

"I think it was actually. At least partly."

He threw his hands up. "The guy slept with someone else on your birthday. I don't care what I said to him, it doesn't excuse what he did."

"I don't think he slept with her," she said sulkily.

"Are you defending the guy? I heard he wouldn't even walk you home on Friday when it was his fault you had an allergic reaction."

She slipped off the chair as her emotions threatened to overwhelm her. If she wasn't careful she was going to say something she'd regret.

"Hey!" Noah followed her to the door, snatching at her elbow to stop her. "Are you really annoyed with me about something that happened seven years ago?"

"Yeah." She shrugged him off. "You make out that Felix is the worst person in the world, but you're just as bad as he is."

His grip on her arm loosened until he released her. "If that's what you think it's a good job we don't hang out any more."

"I agree." She held his gaze, hiding her emotions. Somehow, she managed to keep her chin up as she sauntered out of the pub. Outside, she put a hand to her mouth to stifle a sob.

Setting off into town, she checked her phone. Her emotions heightened even further at the lack of contact from Kit. Instinctively, she walked straight through the narrow streets of Hugh Town and then kept going, picking up her pace as she approached Old Town Bay.

Rushing into Mirren's kitchen, she burst into tears.

"What's going on?" Mirren asked, appearing from the living room.

"I messed everything up," she sobbed in Mirren's embrace. "Kit won't speak to me and I've fallen out with Noah too."

"Calm down." Mirren rubbed her back. "It's probably not as bad as you think."

"It is." She wiped at her eyes as Mirren led her into the living room. "I was so scared of getting together with Kit in case things didn't work out, but I managed to ruin things without even being in a relationship with him. He won't speak to me."

"What happened?" Mirren asked, her eyes shining with affection.

"Felix kissed me on Friday night. That's how I ended up having an allergic reaction – not because of anything I ate." Seren sank back on the couch. "It was just a stupid thing – *he* kissed *me,* I didn't kiss him back. But Kit found out and he's furious that I didn't tell him, and he's convinced there's something going on with me and Felix, even though there isn't."

"Kit will come around."

"He won't even speak to me."

"That won't last long. He probably just needs some time to get his thoughts in order. It'll have hurt his pride finding out you kissed Felix."

"*He* kissed *me,*" she said again.

"Give Kit time to calm down and you'll figure things out."

"I'm not so sure."

Mirren tilted her head. "He's been in love with you for years. There's no way he's going to let a stupid kiss get in the way."

"*Years?*" Seren frowned. "I don't think so."

Mirren slouched back beside Seren. "I *know* so. Yesterday, I was talking to Keira about the two of you. Apparently Kit told her he's been in love with you since Terry died. I don't think I'm supposed to know that."

"Oh god." Seren covered her face with her hands. "I had no idea."

"I have absolutely no doubt that you'll sort things out."

"I can't stand the thought of him being upset with me."

"You just need to be patient. Now, tell me what happened with Noah."

Hesitantly, Seren explained the conversation she'd had with Felix, then told Mirren about the confrontation with Noah.

"I'm sure you think I'm deluded and that Felix is lying," she said when she'd filled Mirren in. "But I honestly think he was telling the truth."

Mirren rolled her eyes. "I might be a bit soft when it comes to my sons, but I'm under no illusion that any of them are saints. It wouldn't surprise me at all if Noah had interfered with your relationship with Felix. He hated having competition for your time. No one could mention Felix's name without Noah making some derogatory comment."

"If I wasn't so upset about the situation with Kit I probably wouldn't have been so hard on Noah, but I'm also really angry with him."

"You're allowed to be," Mirren said. "But you're also going to have to sort things out with him."

"We've never properly fallen out before."

Mirren choked on a laugh. "When you were kids you fell out just about every other week."

"Only about stupid stuff."

"Yes. And in a few weeks this business with Felix will be filed away under the category of stupid stuff too."

Seren sighed heavily. "I hope you're right."

CHAPTER THIRTY-THREE

The wet weather continued into Monday, along with grey skies and low hanging fog. The dreariness of it perfectly reflected Seren's mood.

With the weather so bad, Kit wouldn't be taking the train out, which meant she had no chance of bumping into him on her way to work. After speaking to Mirren she'd decided to give him some space. Not too much though; her nerves couldn't take it. She'd go over to his place after she'd finished her shift and hope he was willing to talk.

A few tourists braved the elements at lunchtime, propping their umbrellas by the door and leaving wet footprints all over the floor. Things quietened down again after lunch, and she sighed when Felix walked through the door.

"I've been trying to call you," he said, standing at the end of the bar. He didn't bother to take his rain-soaked jacket off, so she was hopeful that he wasn't planning on hanging around.

"I've been ignoring you," she said bluntly.

"I only wanted to check you were okay after Friday night."

"I'm fine."

"Glad to hear it." He straightened up, fingering his car keys in his hand. "Kit Treneary was pretty upset when he heard what had happened."

"Was he?" she said without inflection.

"Yeah. He was." After taking a couple of steps towards the door, he turned back. "I got the wrong brother, didn't I?"

Seren's heart rate picked up and she shifted her weight. "How do you mean?"

"I thought you were upset about Noah having a girlfriend, but it was Kit."

"I have no idea what you're talking about."

"Sure you don't." His lips twitched to a smirk. "First I had Noah Treneary as competition, then Kit."

"He's not competition. I just don't want to be with you."

"I sort of figured that out. So are you and him together?"

"Not that it's any of your business but no, we're not."

"Has that got anything to do with his curly-haired friend?"

"No, I don't think it has."

"Does it have anything to do with me kissing you on Friday night?"

She shook her head. "It doesn't matter why we're not together. We're just not."

"If it's because of me, I'm sorry."

"He thinks I still have feelings for you," she admitted. "I'm not sure how to convince him otherwise."

"I hope you figure things out." He was almost at the door when she called him back.

"I'm sorry if I hurt you when we were together."

He shrugged. "It wasn't meant to be."

"If it makes you feel any better, I had it out with Noah. He admitted what he'd said to you on my birthday and we're no longer speaking."

His gaze was intense when their eyes locked. "If you think I'd get any joy from you falling out with your friend, you're mistaken."

Her emotions were all over the place as she watched him walk out of the door.

~

Two days of torrential rain suited Kit down to the ground. Having to be cheerful for train passengers would have been a strain. Lying around his flat watching films and playing video games was exactly the therapy he needed. When his mum called him on Monday he was tempted not to answer, but it was near impossible for him to ignore phone calls from his mum.

"Do you want to come over for lunch?" she asked while he stared at his paused video game on the screen in front of him.

"No, thanks. I don't fancy going out in the rain." Wind drove the persistent precipitation at the window pane, confirming his decision.

"I can drive down and pick you up."

"Why are you so desperate for me to come for lunch?" he asked suspiciously.

"I may need a small favour … there's a dripping tap in Trystan's cottage. I think the woman staying there is already being driven around the bend by the fact that she's stuck inside with an energetic five-year-old. A dripping tap might send her over the edge."

"I don't have the foggiest idea about plumbing issues."

She clicked her tongue. "Just Google it. You'll no doubt find a video online that shows you exactly how to fix it." She paused and he opened his mouth to protest but wasn't quick enough. "I'll pick you up in ten minutes."

After she hung up Kit stared at the phone for a moment, then opened a search engine to research leaky taps.

Ten minutes later he dashed through pouring rain to his mum's car. He ran his fingers through his damp hair, causing drips to fly around him.

"I can probably fix the tap, but apparently dripping taps usually need a new washer."

"That's no problem. We had the same problem in Noah's cottage a while back and we ordered a pack of washers. Noah said it was easy to fix."

Kit frowned. "Wouldn't it make more sense to get Noah to fix it then?"

"I didn't want to disturb him on his day off. Put your seatbelt on."

He did as he was told. "I was quite enjoying *my* day off," he pointed out.

"I'm always asking Noah to do things."

Kit raised his eyebrows. "Apart from when he lived in Bristol for a year and you had me and Seren running around for you." The mention of Seren caught him off guard, and he directed his attention out of the fogged-up window.

"I just thought you could fix the tap and then we could have lunch together."

"Yeah, okay." From her tone, he suspected there was more to it than that.

The garage door stood open and they drove straight in. A toolkit was waiting, with the new washers sitting on top of it.

"I'll get started on lunch," his mum said, leaving him to it.

In the fifty metres to the cottage, Kit struggled against the wind and lashing rain. He leaned close to the door when he rang the bell, holding his hood in place. He practically fell inside when the woman opened the door.

"Sorry," he said. "I'm here to fix the tap."

"That was fast." She closed the door behind him. "There was no rush. I only mentioned it because I didn't want it to get worse and cause a flood or something."

Pushing his hood down, he smiled at the middle-aged woman. A blonde bob framed her face and her eyes were warm and welcoming. Motion in the living room drew his attention to the little girl who was bouncing up and down on the couch.

"Hello!" She beamed. "I'm five."

"That's an unusual name." He wiped his shoes on the mat. "I haven't met anyone called Five before. I think I like it though."

She stopped bouncing, her smile widening even further. "It's not my name!" she shrieked. "It's how old I am."

"Oh!" He grinned at her. "In that case, I'm twenty-two. And my name's Kit." He turned back to the woman and smiled.

"I'm Beth," she said. "And the one with too much energy is Ellie."

"Mummy, he thought my name was Five!" She howled with delight and hopped down from the couch to follow Kit to the kitchen. "Fixing drippy taps is a funny job."

"It's not really my job," he told her. "It's just what my mum told me to do today." He flashed Beth a smile and set the toolbox beside the sink where the tap dripped into the stainless-steel basin.

"You're Mirren's son?" Beth asked and he nodded in reply.

"Mirren drove us from the airport," Ellie told him, twirling on pointed toes beside his legs. "She's a very nice lady."

"She is," he agreed. "She can also be a bit of a bossy boots."

Ellie laughed and did another twirl. "What's your real job?"

"That's a lot of questions," Beth said, resting her hip against the counter. "Maybe we should get out of Kit's way and let him work."

Ellie stopped her twirling. "I only wanted to know what his job is."

"I drive a train," Kit told her. His eyes landed on the selection of flyers on the kitchen island and he reached for the one advertising his train. "Here, that's my train."

"That's you!" Ellie said, pointing at the image of him standing beside the train.

"It is. When the rain stops, you can come for a ride with me."

"Can we, Mummy?"

"Yes." She shot Kit a weary look. "If you could arrange for the rain to stop very soon, I'd appreciate it."

"You've been pretty unlucky so far. This weather's unusual for the time of year."

"I honestly expected bright sunshine. I hear there's a stunning view and a lovely beach outside the door, but I'm not sure I believe it."

"The fog's crazy," he agreed. "But it's not usually like this and it never lasts for more than a couple of days, so it'll probably clear up tomorrow or the next day."

"Have you seen the weather forecast for the week?"

"Yeah." He winced. The bad weather was expected to continue. "But I choose not to believe it. No way it can rain for your entire holiday."

"It's not even the kind of rain we can go out and jump in puddles in. It's painful to be outside." She sighed. "Sorry. You didn't come to listen to me complaining. The lack of adult interaction might be getting to me."

"Don't worry about it." He looked down at Ellie, who had her hands clasped behind her back as she swung her hips. "So, Five ... sorry, I mean *Ellie.* How much do you know about fixing taps?"

"Nothing," she said with bright eyes.

"That makes two of us." He flashed Beth a look of mock panic. "That was a joke. I've actually watched a full three-minute YouTube video so I can't imagine there's anything I can't handle."

"Do you want a coffee?" she asked, amused.

"Yes, please."

"Can I help you fix the tap?" Ellie asked.

"I was hoping you would." He picked her up and set her on the counter. "Could you please take the tap apart ..."

She let out a high-pitched giggle. "I don't know how!"

"Well, have a look at it. Can you see any screws or anything?"

"There's a screw." She pointed to the base of the tap.

"Good. I need to turn the water off, then we can try unscrewing it and see what happens." He picked up the washers. "We're looking for something that looks like this," he told Ellie. "Hopefully it will be worn out and broken, so we'll just need to put a new one in and everything should be fixed."

Beth smiled at him. "If she starts to bother you at any point, feel free to shoo her away."

"She's fine." In fact, as much as he'd begrudged being forced to leave the comfort of his flat and the self-pity he'd been wallowing in, he'd managed to go a full ten minutes without thinking about Seren. It felt like a win.

The tap turned out to be an easy fix, which both Beth and Ellie seemed slightly disappointed by. He lingered for a while, since they seemed to be enjoying the company, then he braced against the elements to return the tools to the garage and dash up to his mum's house.

"They're nice," he said, shrugging his coat off in the kitchen.

"The little girl's adorable. I feel so sorry for them getting such terrible weather. It looks as though it's going to stay like this for the week."

"So long as it doesn't go on for longer than that. I don't mind taking a week off, but I don't like the loss of business to go on for too long."

"It won't." His mum set a plate of toasted sandwiches on the table and two bowls of soup. "What else is going on with you?"

"Not much." He dunked his sandwich in the soup before taking a bite.

"Have you seen Seren since you saved her life?"

He rolled his eyes. "I don't think I saved her life."

"I think you were very heroic."

"Thanks."

Silence fell and he took a few spoonfuls of soup before realising his mum was glaring at him.

"Kitto Treneary!" she growled.

He flinched slightly at the use of his full name. It usually preceded a lecture where his mum was concerned. "What?"

"Tell me what's going on, please."

"How do you mean?"

"Don't act innocent with me! I had Seren here last night in floods of tears."

Kit kept his attention on the food in front of him, but the thought of Seren being upset affected him more than he'd like.

"She's fallen out with Noah and she said you're not speaking to her."

"Why has she fallen out with Noah?"

"Long story involving Felix."

"I might have guessed. The guy seems to enjoy causing trouble."

"So, what about you and Seren?" his mum asked impatiently.

"What about us?"

"You love her, don't you?"

He held her gaze for a moment, then continued with his soup. "This is why you wanted me to come over for lunch then?"

"Yes. Stop being stubborn."

"She kissed Felix," he told her.

"I know."

His eyebrows rose. "She told you that?"

"Yes. Actually she said he kissed her. Though I don't think it matters much."

"Her kissing another guy doesn't matter? I should be fine with that?"

"If it makes her realise she's kissing the wrong guy, then yes you should be fine with it. She doesn't want to be with Felix. She wants to be with you."

He took another bite of his sandwich, refusing to let the conversation ruin his lunch. "She lied to me."

"And she feels terrible. Get over it."

"You could be on my side, you know." Though if he was honest, he was kind of glad she was taking Seren's side.

"There are too many men in our family. Us girls have to stick together." Mirren pursed her lips. "Besides, you're being an idiot."

"Thanks!"

"You'll sort things out with her, won't you?"

He exhaled loudly. "It's *Seren*. It's not like I'm never going to speak to her again. We'll sort things out one way or another. I just need time to get my thoughts in order." With his mum seemingly placated, he ate a few mouthfuls of soup. "Do you have any of our old toys in the attic?" he asked when he reached the bottom of the bowl.

"Probably. There's all sorts of junk up there. Why?"

"I thought I'd see if I can find anything for the girl in Trystan's cottage. She's bored out of her mind."

"That's a good idea. Go up and have a look. I reckon there's a big box of Lego somewhere. That might keep her entertained for a while."

After a bit of digging around, Kit found a box of Lego and dropped it off with two very grateful guests before setting off home. As he made a dash from his mum's car to his building, he registered the figure on the doorstep, dressed in black with a hood up.

"Can I help you?" he asked automatically as he put his key in the door.

"I was looking for you, actually."

Kit tensed as he registered it was Felix. "What do you want?"

"Mind if I come in? It might be easier to chat out of this rain."

After holding the door for him, Kit didn't move further than the entranceway.

Drips flew around as Felix pushed his hood down. "I saw Seren this morning," he said.

"Nice of you to come and tell me." Kit's hands clenched to fists and he forced himself to keep calm.

"I just wanted to tell you there's nothing going on between me and Seren."

"What?" Kit blinked rapidly.

"She said you didn't believe her that there was nothing going on between us. I don't know if it makes any difference, but I wanted you to hear from me that it was me who kissed her. And I stopped pretty quick when it was clear she wasn't interested." He reached for the door handle. "That's all."

"Wait." Kit shook his head. "That's what you came to tell me?"

"Yeah."

"That's *all* you came to tell me?"

Felix shifted his weight, his hand still on the door. "It was difficult enough for me to come here and say that much. Don't make me drag this out ..." His eyes rose heavenwards. "Just don't let your pride get in the way of something great ... trust me when I say it's not worth it." He was out of the door before Kit could say anything.

All he could do was stare after Felix as he disappeared into the misty rain.

He checked his watch and felt a pang of annoyance that Seren would still be at work.

CHAPTER THIRTY-FOUR

Seren left work half an hour early to avoid seeing Noah when he arrived for his shift. It was petty, but she just couldn't face him. She was also hyped up on adrenaline at the thought of paying Kit a visit. He'd had enough time to calm down, and she was determined for them to smooth things over.

Instead of going straight over to his place she made a stop at home to pick up a peace offering. She'd take all the help she could get.

Opening her front door to face the elements again, she almost collided with Kit. She backed up quickly and they huddled inside.

"Were you going somewhere important?" he asked, rain dripping from his hair despite his hood.

"No." She shook her head. "I mean, yes. I was going to see you. Come up," she said, setting off up the stairs.

"How are you doing?" he asked, hanging his dripping coat inside the door.

"Fine." Anger came unexpectedly and she glared at him. "I'm a bit pissed off, if I'm honest."

"With me?" He swallowed hard, which only fuelled her outburst.

"Yes, with you! I don't care how annoyed you are, it's rude of you to ignore my messages and calls."

"Is that what you were coming to tell me?"

"No." She sighed and shoved her gift bag at him. "Here."

He peered in at the Harry Potter books. The ones he hadn't read yet. "Are there bookmarks in here as well?"

Her lips drew to a smile. "I thought you could use the ticket from Warner Brothers Studio."

"I don't want to ruin my keepsake."

"But you're fine with ruining books? What's wrong with you?" She caught the teasing in his eyes and suppressed a laugh.

"I promise to use a bookmark," he said with a cheeky grin. "Were you coming over just to bring me books?"

She moved around the coffee table and took a seat on the couch. "I also wanted to tell you again that there's nothing going on between me and Felix."

"I know," he said softly.

"That's good." She was slightly taken aback. "I was hoping we could sort things out ... but I'm not actually sure how."

Kit set the bag on the table and sat beside her, his body angled to face her. "I've spent so long hoping that there might be something between us one day, but I never really believed it until Friday. So when I heard that you'd kissed Felix, I felt like such an idiot for thinking you'd ever want to be with me."

"I do want to be with you," she whispered, reaching for his hand. "I should have told you the truth about Felix from the start."

He interlaced his fingers with hers. "Do you remember the time I came over and told you I was in love with you?"

She couldn't help but smile. "I have guys coming over all the time to tell me they're in love with me ... but yeah I think I recall it."

"Someone pointed out that it might have been a better approach to ask you on a date." He quirked an eyebrow. "Or maybe just kiss you ..."

She felt heat flash in her cheeks. "That might have been a good idea …" When he leaned slowly towards her, she put a hand in the middle of his chest.

"What's wrong?" he asked.

"At the risk of killing the romance … could I ask what you've recently eaten?"

He cracked up laughing. "Not peanuts."

"Okay, good. Carry on then." She pressed on his chest again. "No, wait."

"What now?"

She flopped back and grimaced. "I don't know. It just felt kind of weird that you were going to kiss me."

"That's not a compliment!"

"Sorry." She pulled him beside her and snuggled into his arm. "I'm freaking out a bit."

"How about we switch to the date option instead?"

She wrinkled her nose. "When?"

"Now."

"I'm not keen to leave my flat in this weather."

"Who said anything about leaving the flat?"

"We're going to have a date here? Now?"

"Yeah. We can do whatever you want … cook dinner, watch a film, anything. There's one rule though."

"What is it?"

He sat up straight. "No kissing."

"What?"

"You're not allowed to kiss me." He walked to the kitchen and she followed him.

"Are you serious?"

"Yeah. It shouldn't be difficult, since you find the idea of kissing me weird."

"That's a stupid rule." She folded her arms across her chest as he opened the fridge and peered inside.

"I think it's a good rule."

"It's terrible."

Taking his arm, she pulled him around to face her. In the moment when their eyes locked, she realised the no kissing thing was a ruse to get her to kiss him. The stubborn part of her wanted to call him out on it. But that would mean ruining the moment, and she wasn't quite stubborn enough to do that. Not when he was gazing at her as though he could see right into her soul.

Her legs trembled slightly when she lifted onto her toes. As her lips pressed softly against his, her breath caught in her throat. The sound of the rain on the window seemed to stop abruptly. Bringing her hands to the sides of his neck, she closed her eyes and angled her face to lean deeper into the kiss. Feeling light-headed, she was thankful when Kit's arms tightened around her waist, pulling her firmly against him.

He took a couple of steps until her back collided with the kitchen counter. As her heart rate went through the roof, she pushed her fingers into his hair, needing something to grip onto as her lips moved in a perfect rhythm against his.

When they broke apart he remained pressed against her, their noses touching and their uneven breaths merging between them.

"You're so easy to manipulate," he said, eyes sparkling with amusement.

She laughed. "I knew you just made the no kissing rule to get me to kiss you."

"You're like a teenager." He drew back slightly. "Tell you not to do something and you suddenly want to do it."

"It's not that I didn't want to kiss you. Things just feel a bit awkward … we know each other so well, but now we have to get to know each other all over again. In a different way."

"I think that's a good thing."

"So do I, but it's also a bit scary."

He smiled lightly. "Was kissing me weird?"

"No." She gave him another lingering kiss. "I like the idea of date night … but *with* kissing."

He shook his head. "I think we should stick with the no kissing rule. You definitely shouldn't kiss me."

After swatting at him playfully, she pulled him close again and swept her lips over his. Her stomach flipped when he tightened his arms around her back and kissed her deeply.

Finally, they moved apart and set to work making dinner, then gravitated back to the couch and spent the evening alternating between chatting, kissing and watching TV. Kissing Kit quickly felt like the most natural thing in the world.

"Are you okay?" he asked her, catching her staring into the bowl of popcorn while the over-the-top American baking show played in the background.

"Yeah. I'm fine."

"You looked miles away." He gazed at her intently. "This will sound odd, but were you thinking about my brother?"

"Yes." She smiled at how well he knew her.

"Mum said you'd had an argument with him. She didn't really tell me what it was about."

Hesitantly, she filled Kit in on the situation with Felix. "I know you'll think I'm completely naive," she said when she'd explained everything. "But I believe what Felix said. I'm not saying he was blameless in our break-up, and I certainly don't think his behaviour was acceptable, but I don't think he's a terrible person. He cares about me in his own way." She waited for Kit to tell her she was an idiot, or at least to roll his eyes. He didn't though.

"I reckon you're probably right."

She blinked a few times in quick succession. "Excuse me? Did I just hear you right?"

"Yes." His shoulders hitched. "I think he's probably not so bad. And he definitely cares about you." When she glowered at him, he smiled back at her. "He came to see me this afternoon. Told me there's nothing going on between you two."

"See." She snuggled into Kit's chest. "He's quite sweet really."

"Let's not go too far." He ran a hand over her hair. "What are you going to do about Noah?"

"Avoid him."

"That's mature!"

"Well, he's too stubborn to admit he did anything wrong."

"You're both stubborn. And you're both going to be miserable until you sort things out. Just call him."

"No," she said firmly. "I don't want to. I just want to hide away with you and forget about the outside world until the rain stops."

"When are you working next?" he asked.

"Not until Wednesday afternoon."

"If the weather forecast is right, I've got the whole week off. I really hope it doesn't end up being longer than that." Brushing her hair from her forehead, he tilted her face up to his and kissed her – softly at first and then with more passion. As things heated up, they shifted to lying on the couch. Their heavy breathing was partially muffled by the sound of the rain hitting the windows. Seren's heart felt as though it was going to beat out of her chest as the weight of Kit's body pressed down on her. His hand slipped under her T-shirt while his lips trailed over her jaw, then nuzzled her earlobe and her neck.

"Kit," she said breathlessly.

He groaned in response and continued kissing her.

"Kit," she said again, with more control. Her body tensed involuntarily.

"What's wrong?" He shifted to look down at her.

"Nothing." She swallowed hard. "It's just that technically it's our first date."

"Yeah." He looked slightly puzzled before realisation flashed in his eyes. "Sorry," he said, pulling himself off her. "I got carried away."

"It's fine." Sitting beside him, she ran a hand through his hair.

"I don't suppose it's going to help if I tell you that you're not allowed to have sex with me?"

She laughed into his neck. "I'm afraid not."

He kissed her forehead, then turned his wrist to check the time. "It's really late. I should probably go home."

"I don't want you to go." With her face nestled against his neck she inhaled the scent of him. "I like you being here."

Snuggling down again, Seren pulled the blanket over them and they lay tangled on the couch, chatting in the low light while the wind pelted rain against the window panes. As her eyelids grew heavier, Seren murmured about moving to her bed, but Kit was already sleeping soundly. Not wanting to wake him or leave him, she settled her head on his bicep and drifted off with her lips set in a gentle smile.

The following day was spent as lazily as the previous evening. In the middle of the afternoon, Seren looked longingly out of the window.

"I'd quite like the rain to stop now. It'd be nice to go for a walk or hang out on the beach for the afternoon."

"Except if it wasn't raining I'd be at work," Kit pointed out, standing behind her and slipping his arms around her waist.

She leaned back against his chest. "Is having Keira working for you going well?"

"Yeah, it is actually. Which means I'll be able to start taking more time off."

"Next time we have a day off together and the weather's nice, we should find a quiet beach and take a picnic and chill out for the day."

He snuggled his cheek against her ear. "We should take Dad's boat out and sail around the islands, stopping off at beaches along the way."

"I like the sound of that." Watching raindrops trickle down the window, she thought about how she and Noah used to spend whole days out on the boat. She felt a tightness grip her stomach. When Kit had said she'd be miserable until she sorted things out with Noah he'd been right. Or if not quite miserable, it certainly played on her mind and left her with a vague feeling of discomfort.

"What are you thinking about?" Kit asked. "You've gone all tense."

"Nothing." Pasting on a smile, she turned in his arms. "What are we going to have for dinner? I have a craving for crab cakes from the Tanglewood Kitchen. I haven't had them for ages." Again, the thought of crab cakes made her think of Noah and all the times they'd eaten them together. She pushed the thought aside. "Do you think they'll deliver?"

Kit bit down on his lip, looking thoughtful. "I guess I could go and pick some up."

"I knew you'd come in useful." She flashed him a mischievous smile and gave him a quick peck before heading to the bathroom. When she came out again, Kit was standing in the kitchen, resting his forearms on the counter. He straightened up quickly when she approached him.

"What are you looking so guilty about?" she asked.

"I'm not." He gave a subtle shake of the head, then planted his lips on hers in what she would've sworn was a deliberate distraction tactic. It worked well and she forgot all about the guilt in his features as he pressed his body against hers while the kisses grew in intensity. Slipping her hands under his T-shirt, she ran her fingers over his smooth back.

Her hesitation the previous evening had only been fear and not any lack of desire. In her head, sleeping with Kit felt like crossing a line that she couldn't come back from. Now it occurred to her that she didn't *want* to come back from it. She wanted everything with Kit; no hesitation, no half measures, *everything.*

"I was thinking I might pop home for a bit," Kit said, pulling back.

Her heart sank. "How come?"

"I could do with a shower."

"You could always shower here," she suggested.

"I need fresh clothes."

She pursed her lips and coyly ran her hands over the front of his T-shirt. "Clothes are overrated, don't you think?"

"Well …" He swallowed hard and took a step back. "I've never really thought about it. I'm just going to run home and then I'll pick up food on the way back here. Okay?"

Grabbing at his hand, she stopped him from moving any further. "I'm not really that hungry."

"I'll take my time. By the time I get back you'll be hungry."

That wasn't her point, but he seemed suddenly keen to get away. Maybe *she* was coming on too strong now.

"I'll see you later," he said, planting a kiss on her cheek and rushing off. She was about to call after him to see if he wanted a lift home, but the front door banged behind him before she could get a word out.

The way he'd pulled away from her so abruptly left her with a knot of anxiety in her stomach. She told herself she was being paranoid. He'd be back soon and everything would be fine.

When the doorbell rang an hour later, she skipped down the stairs on a rush of anticipation.

"I missed you," she said as the door swung open.

Noah stood on the doorstep with boxes of crab cakes in his hand. He looked momentarily surprised. "I missed you too," he said, stepping inside and giving her an awkward hug while balancing the takeaway boxes behind her back.

"What are you doing here?" She backed away and scowled at him.

"Bringing crab cakes like you told me to. What do you think I'm doing here?"

"I didn't tell you to bring crab cakes."

"Yes, you did."

"I think I'd remember that. I told Kit to bring crab cakes."

"You might have thought you were messaging Kit, but you actually messaged me." Huffily, he reached into his pocket for his phone.

"I didn't message anyone."

He held the phone out. "What's this then?"

Squinting, she read the message, which appeared to have been sent from her phone. *Come over and hang out after work. Bring crab cakes and I might forgive you for being such an arse.*

"That's exactly what I would have written," she said, feeling a touch emotional.

"What's going on?" Noah asked.

"Kit sent the message from my phone. I suppose he noticed it was bothering me that we'd fallen out."

"Well, my brother's an idiot. If you didn't invite me, I really don't need to be here."

She growled as he stepped outside again. "If you leave with those crab cakes, I swear to god I will never speak to you again."

He stopped but didn't turn back. "Is that a threat or a promise?"

"Come in," she said, her lips twitching to a smile as she held the door for him.

"I'm sorry," he said as they walked into the flat. "I should never have got involved in your relationship with Felix. In my defence, I didn't think he was good enough for you. I had the best of intentions, but I should have trusted your judgement."

"Did you come to this conclusion yourself?" She took the takeaway boxes from him and went to the kitchen. "Or did Keira tell you you're an idiot?"

"When I explained the situation, she might have taken your side. Which was kind of annoying."

"I'm sure it was."

"It was only my stupid macho way of looking out for you."

"I know." She flashed him a small smile. "It *was* stupid though."

"Sorry." He wrapped her in a hug and she relaxed into him.

"I have a question for you," she said, moving away from him. "Do you think Kit's good enough for me, or are you going to interfere and cause issues between us too?"

He tilted his head to one side. "Please tell me that means you two got together?"

"Yes. We did."

"Wow! I knew there was something weird going on with you when you were making up excuses why you couldn't be with him instead of just saying you didn't like him." His smile lit up his face. "I'm really happy for you. And I'm surprised I haven't heard about it from Kit. He must be pretty chuffed with himself."

"He came over yesterday evening and we talked everything through. Then we've just been hibernating here." Annoying as the rain was, spending so much time with Kit away from prying eyes and gossiping tongues was good. It gave Seren time to get used to the relationship before going public with it.

"I'm happy for you." Noah gave her a lazy smile. "I'm not saying Kit's good enough for you … but I reckon I'd have a tough time scaring him off."

Seren chuckled. "I imagine you suggesting to your brother that you've been sleeping with his girlfriend wouldn't go down too well – regardless of whether or not it was a joke."

"That's very true." He winced. "You said you'd forgive me for being an arse, but you're not going to let me *forget it,* are you?"

"I didn't say anything about forgiving you. That was Kit, remember? Which reminds me, I should have a word with him about going into my phone without permission."

"You forgive me though, right?"

"Yes. The crab cakes swung it for you."

"Speaking of which, I'm starving."

Seren got a couple of plates out, then paused. "Would you mind if we hang out another time instead?"

"How come?"

"I was expecting to have dinner with Kit." Her mouth watered when she looked down at the crab cakes. "I was *looking forward* to having dinner with Kit. And I was freaking out slightly because he was acting all sketchy and then left in a hurry. Obviously, he wanted to be out of the way when you got here … I'm really glad everything is cool between us, but …"

"But you're going to ditch me in favour of your boyfriend?"

Seren smiled at the thought of Kit being her boyfriend. "Yeah. That's exactly what I'd like to do."

She grabbed her toothbrush and a change of clothes before walking outside with Noah. "Do you want a lift home?" she asked, feeling it was the least she could do since she'd taken dinner from him.

"I've got Mum's car," he said as they stepped out into the rain which had settled to a steady drizzle. "I guess I need to stop and pick up more crab cakes too."

"I guess so."

"Can we hang out soon?" he asked.

"I'd like that." She gave him a hug and thanked him for dinner, then got into her car for the short drive to Kit's place.

He sounded vaguely confused on the intercom when she rang the bell, then looked concerned when she stepped inside his flat.

"Am I in trouble?" he asked.

"No." She set her bag down and draped her arms around his shoulders. "I love you, Kitto Treneary."

The smile crept slowly over his face. "Good. Did you sort things out with Noah?"

"Kit!" She gave him a playful shove. "I told you I love you. You're supposed to say it back."

"Oh, that's how it works, is it? I'm fairly sure I said it to you about five times and you didn't say it back."

Smiling at the teasing in his eyes, she touched her forehead to his. "I love you, I love you, I love you."

"I love you too," he said, then kissed her with an intensity that made her heart flutter. It took a while for them to break apart, and Seren was left slightly breathless.

"I assumed you'd hang out with Noah for the evening," Kit said, his face still close to hers.

"It was a bit sneaky of you to message him from my phone."

"I know. But I knew you wouldn't feel right until you guys sorted things out. And I knew you'd sort things out quickly if you'd just see each other."

"You were right. We sorted everything out." She broke away from him and lifted the takeaway boxes from her bag. "I decided I'd rather have dinner with you."

"You took the crab cakes and ran? Nice move."

She took them to the kitchen and popped them in the microwave, then went and perched on Kit's knee when he sat at the kitchen table. "I also brought a change of clothes and my toothbrush. I hope that wasn't too presumptuous."

"Not at all," he said, circling his arms around her waist.

"Really? Because I panicked that you'd gone cold on me earlier."

"No." He smiled broadly. "When you made the comment about clothes being overrated, I was tempted to sneak into your phone and tell Noah you never wanted to speak to him again."

She chuckled. "Thanks for pushing me to smooth things over with him."

"You're welcome." He touched their noses together. "I love that we tricked my brother into buying us dinner."

"He made me promise that I'd hang out with him soon, so we might be able to do it again."

Amusement flashed in Kit's eyes but faded quickly. Seren's stomach filled with butterflies as he brought his hands to cup her face. His lips met hers so tenderly that her heart seemed to swell in her chest.

They ignored the microwave when it pinged.

Dinner could wait.

ALSO BY HANNAH ELLIS

The Isles of Scilly Series

The Weekend Getaway (Book 1)

A Change of Heart (Book 2)

The Summer Escape (Book 3)

The Hope Cove Series

The Cottage at Hope Cove (Book 1)

Escape to Oakbrook Farm (Book 2)

Summer at the Old Boathouse (Book 3)

Whispers at the Bluebell Inn (Book 4)

The House on Lavender Lane (Book 5)

The Bookshop of Hopes and Dreams (Book 6)

Winter Wishes in Hope Cove (Book 7)

There's Something about Scarlett (Book 8)

The Loch Lannick Series

Coming Home to the Loch (Book 1)

The Castle by the Loch (Book 2)

Fireworks over the Loch (Book 3)

The Cafe at the Loch (Book 4)

Secrets at the Loch (Book 5)

Surprises at the Loch (Book 6)

Finding Hope at the Loch (Book 7)

Fragile Hearts by the Loch (Book 8)

New Arrivals at the Loch (Book 9)

Always With You (Standalone novel)

The Friends Like These Series
Friends Like These (Book 1)
Christmas with Friends (Book 2)
My Kind of Perfect (Book 3)
A Friend in Need (Book 4)

The Lucy Mitchell Series
Beyond the Lens (Book 1)
Beneath These Stars (Book 2)

ABOUT THE AUTHOR

When she's not writing, Hannah enjoys spending time with her husband and kids. She loves to read and also enjoys yoga and jogging. And tea … she really loves a good cup of tea!

Hannah can be found online at the following places:

Facebook: @authorhannahellis

Instagram: @authorhannahellis

Twitter: @BooksEllis

Website: www.authorhannahellis.com

Feel free to contact Hannah at any of the above or email her at this address:

authorhannahellis@gmail.com

If you'd like to be kept up to date with news about Hannah's books you can sign up to her receive emails from her through her website:

www.authorhannahellis.com/newsletter

Printed in Great Britain
by Amazon

57083814R00162